Revenge is Not Enough

REVENGE IS NOT ENOUGH

A DAVID HARRIS & EMMA JACKSON
MYSTERY: BOOK TWO

ANGELA VAN BREEMEN

Iconic Scribes Press Inc.

ISBN

978-1-7383130-3-7 (Paperback)

978-1-7383130-5-1 (eBook)

1.FICTION, Mystery & Detective / General

2.FICTION, Mystery & Detective / Amateur Sleuth 3. FICTION, Occult &Supernatural

Distributed to the trade by The Ingram Spark Company All rights reserved.

ANGELA VAN BREEMEN

In Praise of Revenge is Not Enough

Revenge Is Not Enough is a thoroughly satisfying follow-up to Angela van Breemen's Past Life's Revenge. Emma Jackson and David Harris have now launched their own private investigation firm, and are working with the New Elgan Police Service investigating cold cases. The story opens with Emma's disturbing vision of the rape of a teenage girl, and the suspense builds from there. Using her psychic abilities, Emma identifies the victim as 16-year-old Maggie Stacey. David and their two partners follow up with solid detective work, and learn that Maggie was one of several Ontario girls who went missing two decades earlier. The investigation takes the team to British Columbia, and to the mountains of Nicaragua for the action-packed climax. The Emma Jackson and David Harris paranormal mysteries have got off to a great start and have a promising future. I was delighted to read that the third mystery will be released in the fall of 2026.

ROSEMARY MCCRACKEN, AUTHOR OF THE PAT TIERNEY MYSTERY SERIES

What if? What if your line of work was researching cold cases? Imagine you had started looking into the disappearance of attractive young women whose whereabouts were, many years later, still unknown to the police. What skills would you need for this work? And what if you discovered an international gang had abducted and used these women to produce babies for sale? Until the child bearers were no longer useful and gang members could dispose of their bodies? What skills would you need to bring those criminals to justice? And what if the biological siblings these women had produced started meeting one another? Or if a spirit in the underworld had started taking unexpected and uninvited possession of your mind and body. Author Angela van Breemen answers these and other questions in Revenge is Not Enough, the second book in her David Harris and Emma Jackson series of mysteries. I won't spoil your enjoyment by telling you the answers to these questions. But as a hint, why not try to imagine a 21st century Thin Man series in which protagonist Nora Charles has the gift of psychic powers. In short, I urge you to read Angela van Breemen's new book and enjoy!

LORNE TEPPERMAN AUTHOR OF THE RACHEL TILE MYSTERY SERIES DEADLY DONATION (2024) DOWN COUNTRY (2025)

Action packed from the start, van Breemen wastes no time taking readers on an epic adventure both across Canada, and around the world to aid young women kidnapped into slavery.

DIANE BATOR, AUTHOR OF WRITTEN IN STONE

Right from the start, this novel was incredibly compelling and rich with world-building that readers will instantly become pleasantly lost in. The realism of the investigative aspect of cold cases was perfectly balanced by the paranormal/supernatural elements of Emma's psychic abilities and the spirits that come forth to seek justice. The visceral nature of the crimes themselves and the haunting coldness of the criminals will chill readers to the bone as they dive deeper and deeper into this novel's lore.

AUTHOR ANTHONY AVINA

The Silver Sphere

Time flows through my fingertips
Like water
Elusive and impossible to hold
Each droplet a silver sphere
Encapsulating a memory
Iridescent in the sunlight
As each drop cascades
To the surface
The water ripples
Welcoming each precious bead
As its own
Into the deep pools of the subconscious
Merging all memories
No longer only mine
But also yours and theirs
Ours
The universe all knowing
For all Time

ANGELA VAN BREEMEN

Acknowledgements

I am grateful to the extraordinary people who have helped make this book a reality. Thank you so much to alpha reader and author Peter Thomas Pontsa, and beta reader Teri-Lyn Smethurst. The editorial suggestions made by author and editor Diane Bator were invaluable, as is her friendship and support. Thank you.

I would like to make special mention and thanks to Mona Findlay, a fellow volunteer at Procyon Wildlife, who at the Second Annual Procyon Wildlife Fundraising Gala (2024) won the final bid at the Silent Auction to have her name appear in the book as one of my fictional characters. Her generosity and dedication to wildlife in need are truly appreciated.

My sincere thanks and appreciation also go to award winning poet, Mike Madill for editing the final manuscript.

Finally, any errors or inconsistencies are my own, keep in mind that this book is a work of fiction and meant to entertain.

I hope you will enjoy Revenge is Not Enough: Book 2 in the David Harris and Emma Jackson Mystery Series!

With humble thanks,

Angela van Breemen

This book is dedicated to my wonderful husband Peter Thomas Pontsa. The writing journey upon which we each have embarked wouldn't be possible without each other's love and support. It's been a glorious journey thus far. Partners for life.

Contents

One

The Vision

SQUEALS OF LAUGHTER echoed through the dense forest. The girl turned her head around to look at her pursuer and tucked a stray tendril of light-colored hair behind her right ear. "Catch me if you can," she taunted.

The boy stopped in his tracks, transfixed by her beauty in the soft light of dusk filtering through the trees. Thin, new subtle curves hinted at the fuller shape she would soon possess.

"Come on," she said. "We're almost there." She turned on her heels and started running, strong and supple, as she wove through the tangled vines interlacing the pathway which led to the old gristmill.

The boy picked up his pace and raced after her, unwilling to be left behind in the growing dim. "Wait up," he shouted, breathless from the exertion.

"Last one there is a dirty rotten egg," she teased.

That final goad did it, and the boy's long legs closed the distance. When he was within an arm's length of her, he reached out and grabbed a long strand of her golden hair, stopping her from running.

"Hey," she screamed. "That hurt!"

He roughly whipped her around and grabbed her around her slight waist with one hand and still clenching a fist full of her hair, mashed his lips against hers and forced his tongue down her throat, causing her to gag.

"Yuk!" The girl jerked her face away from his and coughed. She tried to wriggle free, but he wound her hair even tighter around his fist, making it impossible for her to move her head. "You're hurting me." Her voice was thick with fear and terror.

"Stay still." He could feel the panicked hammering of her heart against his chest which made him feel strong and superior. The more pain he caused, the more intense was this new-found pleasure coursing through his body.

He kicked her feet from under her and pushed her to the ground. The flailing of legs and arms against his body aroused him even more. He released her hair, and, in a fluid motion, grabbed both her wrists and pinned them to the ground. He rammed his mouth against hers again and this time bit her lower lip hard. He savored the iron taste, as the warm blood gushed into his mouth. He moaned with excitement and whispered, "Maggie."

***

Emma Jackson groaned and shifted in bed, then kicked David Harris hard in the shin. He switched on the nightlight and watched her squirming in her sleep, her breathing erratic. Worried, he placed his hand on her shoulder, to calm her, but she continued to thrash, her eyes open, clearly seeing something other than their cozy bedroom.

He shook her shoulders gently. "Emma, honey. Wake up." He was relieved when his wife's breathing returned to normal and the haze of fear in her emerald-green eyes dissipated. He helped her sit up and adjusted the pillows behind her, then pushed the unruly curls of auburn hair away from her face. He took a corner of the bedsheet and carefully wiped away the tears from her cheeks.

"Bad dream or a vision?" he asked in a gentle voice.

"Vision." Her voice cracked with emotion. "David, it was awful." She buried her face in his chest, hot tears staining his dark-blue silk pajama top. When her sobs had subsided, she pulled away and said, "I'm sorry."

"It's okay, honey." He filled a glass from the crystal pitcher of water resting on the nightstand. "Here, drink this."

Her hands shook as she took a few sips. "Maggie," she whispered and handed the glass back to David. He gently placed the glass on the nightstand and waited for her to continue. "Her name was Maggie."

He handed her a notepad and pen and said, "Here, write everything down."

She nodded, leaned forward, and with trembling fingers took the pen and began to write. When she finished, she leaned back against the pillows and said, "That's all I can remember." She closed her eyes, dark circles around them punctuating the depth of her exhaustion.

"Let's try and get some rest." David took the pen and notepad and slid them into the drawer of the nightstand. He shut off the light and adjusted his body until he formed a protective spoon around her slender form. He looped his top arm around her protectively, kissed the nape of her neck and waited till he heard the soft rhythm of her breath.

As usual, sleep was never an easy companion for him, and his thoughts were preoccupied with Emma's burgeoning psychic ability. He worried he wouldn't be able to protect her. *Was it really last year that they had first met and fallen in love?* It seemed like a lifetime ago. Together, they had pursued Enrico Bianchi, the man who had murdered him in his past life. Sometimes, he wondered if his quest for revenge had been worth it. They had both lost loved ones in their pursuit of bringing Enrico to justice and not one day went by that he and Emma didn't miss Anna, his Uncle Liam and Sarah.

He questioned their decision to work cold cases together. Perhaps this idea of working on decades-old cases of missing people and murders using the help of spirit guides, such as Spirit Anna, was flirting with a danger best left alone.

He checked the time on his phone: 3:00 a.m. Even if sleep might elude him, at least he could keep watch over Emma and comfort her if her vision recurred. In the morning, he'd call Laura and Bryan Grant, his in-laws and his and Emma's business partners from their newly formed company, Jackson, Grant & Harris Investigations. Was it time to reconsider this venture? *Wasn't Emma's safety and her sanity worth more than trying to solve cold cases the police had abandoned years ago?*

Frustrated and conflicted by these thoughts, David brushed away a lock of wavy brown hair from his dark eyes. He was roughly six feet tall with a slim and athletic build and kept fit by rowing, lifting weights and practicing yoga. Although powerful and strong, he worried if he had what it took to keep his young wife safe.

Two

The Decision

―――――――――――――――

EMMA WIPED SALTY tears from her eyes and looked back and forth at David, her mother Laura and her stepdad, Bryan Grant. "You really want to quit before we've even got started?" She tucked her feet under her legs and leaned against David, who was seated beside her on the couch. They had agreed to meet at Laura's house in the country since David's former law office, Foster and Harris, was undergoing renovations to accommodate their new company.

"Your health and well-being come first," said Bryan. "David and I can work on cold cases on our own. The New Elgan Police Service will appreciate our assistance on any level."

Bryan, a newly retired police inspector, was referring to the contract he and David had made with the police to work on decades-old unsolved crimes. Bryan was of medium height with gray eyes that were as solemn as those of a funeral director. He was sixty-four years of age, still strong, with an agile and perceptive mind.

David rubbed the back of his neck, signaling he was uneasy. "Last year, we lived apart for too many months. But I always knew there'd be a day when we'd be together again, once Enrico was apprehended." He gave a heavy sigh. "The thought of losing you again, perhaps for good, is unbearable."

"Those days were grim." Emma reached out and gently stroked his hand with her slender fingers.

"Emma, I—"

"I doubt I'd be able to stop, even if I wanted to." She gave him a weary but determined smile. "These visions, they're not going to go away, so we may as well move forward."

"I have my own concerns," said Emma's mom. Laura Jackson-Grant was an older version of her daughter with dark auburn hair, gathered in a loose chignon. Unruly wisps of hair had escaped the hairpins, framing her pretty face. She was delicate and graceful, with the vivaciousness of a free spirit. Her green eyes were as lovely as her daughter's, and both women shared the same expressive eyebrows, smile and quick wit.

Emma gave her mom a hurt look. "I thought you, of all people, would be more supportive."

"Your psychic abilities have grown, especially with the help from Spirit Anna. However, these skills are still new to you," she said, her voice uneasy. "Anna lost her life last year because of her abilities. And they were formidable." Laura was referring to how her best friend, Anna Tungsten, a psychic and Emma's instructor, had been tortured and murdered by Enrico Bianchi in order to retrieve damning video evidence linking him to the murders of David's former self, Samuel Larson, and real estate businessman, Chris Beacon. From the spirit world, Anna had helped Emma, David and Bryan solve the case, and at her request, was referred to affectionately as Spirit Anna. "I don't want that to happen to you. We lost too many loved ones last year."

"Look, let's make a pact. If we believe it becomes dangerous, or if the three of you think I'm in over my head, then we'll stop." Emma picked up the steaming cup of fragrant herbal tea her mother had poured and took a sip. "In the meantime, we owe it to the victims and their families. These restless souls and their loved ones deserve closure."

Emma peered at all three faces and said, "Nothing's going to happen to me." She turned back toward her mother. "I promise, Mom."

Laura wiped moisture from the corners of her eyes, cleared her throat and said, "So, tell us more about the vision you had."

Emma pulled out her journal and opened it to the page holding its latest entry.

"It's a pleasant summer evening, and a young woman is running in the forest with a young man in pursuit. The girl is playful and teasing." The space between Emma's eyebrows creased and her expression became frightened. "The boy suddenly got really rough and oh God, he raped her, then I think he killed her—"

"What does she look like?" asked Bryan, attempting to diffuse Emma's mounting tension with a new question.

"She's got long hair; it's light in color and she's wearing it loose around her shoulders. I can't see her clearly though because the shadows from the trees and her hair are hiding her face."

"Can you tell how old she might be?" prompted Laura.

"She's slender, early to mid-teens, I'd say," replied Emma. "Fifteen, I think." She closed her eyes, "No, she was closer to sixteen."

"Any more details?" asked Bryan. "Like clothing? Is it modern?"

"Yeah, modern enough. She's wearing faded blue jeans and a white blouse that stops midriff."

"That attire could cover a number of decades," said Laura, who had been a high-end clothing designer. She'd retired recently, as she had found the detailed work had begun to strain her eyes.

"What about language? Is it English?" asked Bryan.

"Definitely English. I can't really remember much more than that." Emma exhaled a sharp breath, her frustration evident.

"Probably not enough information to check the cold case archives," said Bryan, disappointed. "But I'll give it a try, anyway."

"Sorry…" Emma began.

"Don't be. It's early days," said Bryan.

"Be patient," said Laura, as she placed a reassuring hand on her daughter's.

Emma turned her head slightly to the side, as if listening. She nodded and said, "Spirit Anna agrees. She recommends a séance."

"When do you suggest holding one?" asked Bryan.

Emma tilted her head once more and said, "Tomorrow evening okay?"

David scrolled through the calendar app on his iPhone and said, "I'm free. No clients scheduled."

"Anything on for us tomorrow night, hun?" asked Bryan, turning toward Laura.

"No, we're free, too," said Laura.

"Great. In the meanwhile, let's look at these other cold case files."

Three

Anna's Room

AFTER ANNA'S DEATH last year, Laura, who had been named Anna's executor, had maintained the lovely Victorian home until it was time to sell it.

Laura was mildly surprised when David and Emma expressed interest in purchasing the home. Although close to downtown New Elgan, the home was situated in a quiet and mature neighborhood. The one-acre lot was filled with beautiful perennial gardens and surrounded by giant maple and spruce trees, enough to satisfy Emma's need for green space. David, a city dweller at heart, didn't mind selling his condo, if it meant he could remain in the city and keep Emma happy, which for her meant dirty fingernails and knees as she worked in the gardens.

The real estate law office which David had run together with his uncle, Liam Foster, was currently being renovated to house Jackson, Grant & Harris Investigations. Although he still planned on maintaining his law license and retaining some of the firm's long-term real estate clients, his focus was to investigate unsolved cases.

Last year, he sat the Ministry of the Solicitor General's provincial exam and was now a private investigator. The license enabled him to investigate the character or actions of individuals, their businesses or occupations and their location or that of their property. Along with Bryan's formidable investigative skills as a former police officer, Emma's psychic abilities and Laura's administrative skills, they planned to work cold cases.

When Laura had expressed surprise that David would be downsizing his practice, he had fixed his earnest eyes on her and said, "I want to provide some resolution for the families whose loved ones have gone missing or were murdered." He had massaged the back of his neck and continued, "I know too well, from my own personal experience, that uncertainty is far worse than knowing what happened to a cherished family member."

"Even if it means discovering they died?" asked Laura.

"Especially then."

Laura had smiled when she saw her daughter Emma reach for David's hand and said, "That's why I love you so: your sense of justice." She turned toward her mom, "Besides, David found someone to help with the workload."

"That's right. Trevor McAllister, a young lawyer, is joining the firm. He was called to the Bar of Ontario this past January," David had added.

"I know the family. Trev's a nice kid," Bryan had said. "His father, Mark, used to work on the force with me."

***

Emma hummed softly as she prepared the room for the séance to be held later that evening. She and David had named the space *Anna's Room*, to honor the woman who had done so much for them both. Emma had left the room pretty much the way it was when Anna was alive, the minor addition to the room being a silver-framed picture of Anna.

Through hypnotherapy, Anna had helped David regain his life. During those sessions, he had learned that the debilitating nightmares he'd had his entire life were not from undiscovered childhood trauma, but real memories from his most recent past life, when he had been murdered by Enrico Bianchi. Last year, Emma, David and Bryan Grant, now a former

New Elgan police inspector, had traveled to the Maldives to apprehend Enrico and his son. Now that the Bianchis were both in jail, Emma and David had moved forward with their lives and purchased Anna's Victorian house.

Living in Anna's former home was a way to keep her memory alive, not that Emma couldn't "tune in" whenever she needed to talk with Spirit Anna. But for her, physical space was as important as the etheric, and she found it comforting to live in the same place where her mentor had also resided.

Emma touched the igniter to the blue and violet candles – blue for communication and violet to enhance psychic abilities – then lit the cinnamon incense, used to attract spirits. She drew the drapes closed and as she passed by the centre table, where they would soon be seated for the séance, she ran her fingers over Anna's favorite Damask linen tablecloth, which she had washed and pressed earlier that day. Anna had taught her that a high-level of cleanliness purged any influence or "shadow" of previous spirit communications and provided a fresh slate for the next session. She turned to the framed photo on the nearby ornamental table, kissed her fingertips, then gently placed them against Anna's smiling image.

'I miss you.'

'I am here, child,' Anna spoke in Emma's mind.

'I know. But it's not the—'

'—same,' said Anna, completing Emma's thought.

***

Laura was an empath, whereas her daughter, Emma, was a psychic. Laura's paranormal abilities came more to her as impressions and feelings, and right now she had a sense of apprehension which she couldn't quite articulate, a trepidation that this séance would be different from the ones that they had held before.

Emma's psychic capabilities, on the other hand, came through as thoughts and visions, enabling her to connect with people from the spirit world. Laura had broached her concerns with Emma earlier in the day and after conferring with Spirit Anna, Emma told her mom she was confident about their upcoming séance.

Now ready to begin, Laura gazed with affection at the three people she loved most in the world, seated around the table. As was their customary seating configuration, David was seated to Laura's left, Bryan to her right, while she sat opposite Emma.

Emma closed her eyes momentarily, preparing herself for the session ahead, opened them, and then said, "I'm ready. Everyone, please join hands."

As one, she and her team began to inhale and exhale slowly, savoring each breath, conscious now of their breathing, and of being in the moment.

The laws of time seemed to bend. It could have been five minutes or fifty minutes later, before Emma spoke next. "Spirit Anna, welcome to our circle. I give you, and you alone, permission to speak through me."

Emma's body shook slightly, as her features transformed to those of Anna's when she had been in corporal form.

"Hello, there. It's great to be with you all again." Her voice was warm and throaty, like the great American jazz and swing singer, Billie Holiday.

"Spirit Anna, old friend, so glad you can join us," said Laura, taking the lead as had been previously instructed to her by Emma.

"Likewise. It's good to see you, Laura." Spirit Anna turned her head slightly first towards Bryan and then David. "Hello, you two." Shadows played with the contours of the spirit's face. "Let's dispense with any more pleasantries. How can I help?"

"Still to the point, as ever," said Laura smiling. "Spirit Anna, Emma had an extraordinary dream about a young girl, named Maggie, fleeing from danger. Is Maggie still alive?"

"No, she's not," said Spirit Anna. An expression of anguish flitted across the visage, the voice cracking with pain. "Sorry, too powerful. Can't hold on. Tell Emma I'm sorry—"

"Spirit Anna?" asked Laura, her throat constricting with fear.

Emma's face was transforming once again, now showing the features of a much younger woman. The candlelight in her hair made it appear lighter as if Emma was now blonde. Her emerald-green eyes were now shaded with a blueish tint.

"You're not Spirit Anna, are you?" asked Laura, trying to control the fear constricting her chest. "Who are you?"

"No. I am Maggie. And I want justice."

When David gasped and began to instinctively withdraw his hand from Laura's, she increased the grip she had on both David and Bryan's hands. She looked firmly at each man and mouthed, "Not yet. Wait."

"Maggie, you have taken over this person's body against her will."

The spirit's image faltered, then grew stronger. "I'm sorry. No, I'm not! I want justice. And you must help me."

"We'd be more inclined to help if you let your message be conveyed using Spirit Anna," said Laura.

"No!" Maggie's voice was filled with anguish. "I will relinquish Emma's body to her, but you must first hear me." Maggie's sobs were like banshees in the wind, intensifying in their fury. "You must find the babies. I cannot move on to the spirit world until I know they are safe." The wails fell silent, the soft candlelight revealing Maggie's anguished and tortured eyes.

"We will consider helping you," Laura paused, grateful that the sobbing had subsided. "But you need to answer some questions."

Maggie, fully in control of Emma's body, leaned forward slightly. "What do you want to know?"

"What is your full name?"

"Maggie Stacey."

"Maggie, where did you live?"

"Here."

"In New Elgan?"

"Yes."

"When were you born?"

"1988."

"What year did you die?"

"2014."

Laura raised her eyebrows in surprise. "Not 2004?"

"No."

"What babies do you mean?"

"Find them—"

The voice became even more feeble. Like film noir, fading to its final scene, the pronounced features of the face dissipated, revealing Emma's own. Maggie was gone.

Four

Maggie

EMMA'S EYES FLEW OPEN. "What happened?" she asked. She winced as she sat up. "My head hurts."

Laura placed a gentle hand on Emma's forehead and said, "You know that premonition I had?"

"Yeah?" asked Emma. "Is something wrong?"

"You could say that," said Bryan. His expression was grim.

"What happened?"

"Here, Em, drink this." David handed her two Tylenol and a glass of water.

"Why are you all looking so worried?"

"The séance did not go as planned," said Laura.

"Oh, no," said Emma. "The last thing I remember is inviting Spirit Anna and the rest is blank." She massaged the space between her eyes. "No wait, I've got this sense of having been invaded."

"You were," said Laura.

David's voice was strained and raw. "I'm glad you're all right." He got up and started pacing. "I don't know if we should be doing this anymore."

"Doing what?" asked Emma, registering the shock and concern on David's face. "For the third time, would someone please tell me what happened?"

"Things started off normally with Spirit Anna communicating with us and then suddenly, she withdrew, and another entity took over your body," said David.

"What?" Emma's green eyes reflected her confusion, then firmed in realization. "It was Maggie, wasn't it?" She took a sharp breath. "The girl from my vision."

"Yes," said Laura.

"And?" prompted Emma.

"According to this spirit, who claims she was Maggie, she lived here in New Elgan," said Bryan. He leveled worried grey eyes at his stepdaughter. "We also know when she was born and her full name."

"This is great news," said Emma. "We've made progress."

"Yes, but we plan to corroborate this," said Bryan. His tone was guarded and cautious. "We wanted to make sure you were fine first."

"I'm fine! Why are you guys fussing so much?" She set the glass of water back on the table, stood up, her body swaying from the abrupt motion, overwhelmed by sudden vertigo.

David grabbed her by the elbow before she collapsed, pulled the chair back, and guided her away from the table. "Come on, Em, you'll be more comfortable here." David got her settled on the settee and covered her with a crocheted blanket. He pulled an armchair closer and sat down, his expression grave and concerned.

"Emma, you have no idea what transpired. While your body was being occupied, we were worried sick," said Bryan. "Look, I'm not saying it wasn't a worthwhile session. I'm just very concerned with how we got this information."

"Someone took over your body without your permission. It's outrageous," said Laura. "We are dealing with a very troubled soul."

"I agree, it's dangerous to try this again," said Bryan. "From what we understand, and we need to verify this, it appears that Maggie has been dead for the last ten years. Not twenty."

"How can this be?" Emma's expression was clouded. "She disappeared in 2004. That's twenty years ago."

"True," replied Laura. "But her soul has not transitioned over to the spirit world. She's in limbo because she's so troubled by how she died."

"But there's more to it, isn't there?" asked Emma.

"Yes, she talked about babies. That we need to find them and keep them safe," said Laura.

"Could she have been kept captive somewhere?" asked David. "Like in a cult?"

"Perhaps," said Bryan.

"So, she can't move on, can she? Because of her babies?" asked Emma.

"Exactly. The link to this plane of existence is strong for her because she wants to be assured that her babies will be safe," said Laura.

Bryan pulled out his tablet. "Let's check Canada Cold Cases. In the morning, I'll stop by the police department and request a more in-depth background."

Bryan selected the search function on the website and keyed in Maggie's full name and read what he found to the group.

Canada Cold Cases: Maggie Stacey
Updated March 13, 2024.

At ten in the evening on Friday, June 11th, 2004, Margaret Stacey, a sixteen-year-old high school student, was reported missing by her parents, Edmund and Virginia Stacey. She was out with friends and did not come home for her curfew of nine in the evening.

In the twenty years since her disappearance, there have been no suspects, and this case remains unsolved.

Edmund Stacey was quoted as saying, "Maggie's disappearance destroyed our family. My wife, Virginia, died of cancer five years ago. Our youngest daughter, Megan, four years old at the time of Maggie's disappearance, grew up without a big sister. We can't move on, not knowing what happened to our Maggie."

If you have any information relating to this case, please contact Senior Police Constable Carlo Carducci of the New Elgan Police Service.

"Oh, my God," said Emma, her face ashen.

"What is it, Em?" asked David.

"Bryan, did you say Edmund and Virginia Stacey?"

Bryan nodded, then said, "Sure did."

"Those are Megan's parents," said Emma.

"Megan from Café Mokka?" asked David, his eyes widening in surprise.

"Yes." Emma wiped tears from her eyes, and whispered, "We've been friends for years. I never even knew Megan had an older sister."

Five

The Team

BRYAN BROKE THE SILENCE and said, "Let's review what we have learned thus far."

He nodded toward Emma and said, "You go first."

"In my vision, I saw a teenage girl running away, and her attacker called her Maggie," said Emma.

"And we have her full name now that she's revealed herself to us," added Laura.

"And according to Canada Cold Cases, she disappeared twenty years ago," said David.

Emma's brow furrowed in concentration. "Except she's talking about her babies, which means—"

"She didn't die right away," said David, completing Emma's thought.

"Right. So, where was she the ten years prior to her death?" asked Laura.

"Hard to say," said Bryan. "David, your idea of a cult has merit."

"We could try another séance and see if we can learn more from Maggie," suggested Emma.

"I think it's too soon," said Laura, her eyes meeting Bryan's. "What do you think, Bryan?"

"Why don't we see what kind of facts we can get first? We have enough details now to interview Maggie's family," said Bryan.

"Good idea. Megan was a good friend throughout high school. We could stop by Café Mokka and have a chat with them," said Emma. "I still can't believe they had an older sister."

"Yes, but if you think about it, Maggie was a lot older than Megan. It says in the article that Megan was very little when her older sister disappeared. She likely grew up as an only child," said Laura.

"Mom, you mean, *their* and *they*," said Emma, reminding her that Megan's gender identification was non-binary.

"Yeah, right. Sorry. I forget sometimes, said Laura. "But the age difference does explain why Megan never mentioned Maggie to you."

"Yeah, I guess that makes sense," said Emma. "Still, I am surprised they never said anything."

Bryan cleared his throat. "Let's note these initial questions to start our investigation."

"Sure thing," said Laura. She stood in front of the whiteboard, her pen raised midway to enter the questions.

"What was she like?" asked Emma. "Was there a photograph of her on the website?"

"Yeah, but it's grainy," said David.

"Hopefully, we can get a better picture from her father, Edmund Stacey," said Bryan. "I can ask my contacts at the New Elgan Police Services to run the image through their age estimation software."

"Actually, there are some cool online resources," said David, scrolling through his tablet. "Here's one: it's called AI Age Filter." He pressed the image with his index finger and saved it to the photo gallery. He opened the app, uploaded the image, then turned his tablet around for everyone to see.

"Wow," said Laura, her face pale. "That looks like the spirit who visited us."

"May I take a closer look?" asked Emma. After a few moments of studying the image, she said, "I see some similarities to Megan."

"Not a bad resource for a free online app," said Bryan. "Let's try and get a pic with a better resolution as soon as we can."

Bryan looked expectantly at Laura, David and Emma. "What else can we think of, in the way of questions?"

"Where did she live?" asked David.

"Where did she go to school?" asked Laura.

"Did she have a boyfriend?" asked Bryan. "And if so, was he under suspicion when she disappeared?"

"Who were her other friends?" asked Emma. "Where do they live now? Still in New Elgan?"

"Or have they moved away?" added Laura, as she scribbled out the questions on the whiteboard.

"Could Maggie still be alive? asked Bryan. "I'm not comfortable with making any assumptions."

"I understand," said Emma. "She did reach us through the spirit world, but it's unclear as to when she passed away."

"True, although her spirit said she passed in 2014. We'll still need to verify that with concrete facts," said Laura. "After all, she disappeared in 2004."

David focused his gaze on Bryan. "Do you know the investigating officer, Carlo Carducci, who was mentioned in the article?"

"Yep, sure do. Carlo entered the force about twenty years after I did, but we did work a few cases together."

"So, would he still be with the department?" asked Laura.

"Last I heard he was. I'll head to the police department first thing tomorrow morning and contact Carlo about Maggie's disappearance twenty years ago. See what he recalls about the case," said Bryan. "With any luck, he's kept his notes."

"So, what do we do next?" asked David.

"David, and Emma, if you're up to it, I'd like you to visit Maggie's father, Edmund Stacey," said Bryan.

"I'll be fine," said Emma, a hint of irritation had crept into her voice. "Stop fussing."

David placed his hand on hers. "Calm down, Em. We're watching out for you."

"I know. Sorry." Emma gave her stepdad a weary smile and said, "This session did take a lot out of me, but I am totally committed. I'll be fine after a good night's rest. No offense was meant."

"None taken," said Bryan, his expression soft. "You know you're like a daughter to me. Can't help but feel overprotective."

"I know," said Emma. "I'm fond of you, too."

"What would you like me to work on?" asked Laura.

"Can you comb through any online databases like Canada Cold Cases? See if other kids of Maggie's age and description disappeared around that same time. Make your search wide at first, maybe a few years before and after 2004."

"Got it," said Laura. "And I'll look for patterns."

"Great." Bryan massaged his temples with the tips of his fingers and continued, "I'll see what I can learn from the formal police report. Maybe the department has other disappearances like Maggie's on file."

Laura stifled a yawn and said, "It's been a productive night. I don't know about the rest of you, but I am bushed."

Bryan smiled at his wife and said, "Ready to head home, hun?" He rose and kissed Emma on the forehead. "Get some rest."

"Fine, I will, Dad." Emma rolled her eyes, in mock irritation. "Besides, I've got David to take care of me."

Bryan broke into a big grin, looked at Laura and said, "She called me Dad."

Six

Edmund Stacey

EMMA AND DAVID took their seats in chairs positioned on opposite sides of the sofa. The sixty-inch television mounted on the wall was overwhelming, making the room claustrophobic. The matching pink-and-beige floral pattern of the upholstery had been popular in the late 1980s; an attempt at replicating the look of elegant furniture from a century earlier. At one time, it would have been Megan's mother's pride and joy, but now the furniture was stained and thread-worn with its stitching undone in places, the stuffing poking out like an amorphous organism seeking freedom.

The center cushion of the sofa sagged in the middle, clearly where Edmund Stacey, Megan and Maggie's father, spent his evenings parked in front of the mind-numbing screen.

Edmund called from the kitchen. "David, you sure you don't wanna beer?"

"No thanks," said David. "A coffee will be great."

Edmund's arthritic hands shook as he entered the living room, carrying a tray laden with a Bud Light and two coffee mugs. The beer bottle bounced up and down, in danger of teetering over, and the sides of the coffee mugs showed dark rivulets where the coffee had sloshed over their edges.

David jumped out of his chair and took the tray from the older man and placed it on the battered coffee table.

"Thanks," said Edmund, trying to hide his embarrassment.

Now in his mid-sixties, Edmund was gaunt and grey, a shadow of the robust man he once had been, with thin arms and legs, a substantial gut spilling over his pants, much the same way the couch was spilling its contents.

"Don't keep cream or milk in the house. Got sugar, if you need it."

"Sugar will be great," said Emma, reaching for the mug closest to her, wincing at the coffee-stained sugar encrusted spoon sticking upright in the sugar bowl.

"So, what's this all about?" asked Edmund.

"I don't know if you remember me, but I am Megan's friend from high school."

"Sure, I do. You're little Emma, all grown up now."

"Well, David and I started a private investigation firm along with Bryan Grant, a retired cop from the New Elgan Police Service."

"I know Bryan. He's a good man. Seen 'im at the Lion's Club the other night with your mom," said Edmund. "Was playing darts with my buddies. I didn't get a chance to say hello. Tell them hi for me."

"Will do."

"So, what can I do you for?" asked Edmund.

"We've been hired by the police department to look into cold cases." David took a sip of the coffee, winced and placed the mug back on the table. "One of the case files concerns the disappearance of your daughter, Maggie."

"That's an awful long time ago," said Edmund. His voice was rough; the years of sorrow having etched his vocal cords with pain. "What do you think you guys can find out now? So much time has passed." He gave a bitter laugh.

"Not sure if we can," said David. "But we want to give it a try."

"What can you tell us about the day that Maggie disappeared?" asked Emma.

"She was a free spirit, my Maggie was." The lines in his face softened and his eyes took on a faraway look, as he remembered his daughter. "It was Friday, June 11th. Said she was going to hang out with friends after school but promised to be home before dark.

"My wife, Virginia, got worried when Maggie was still not home by ten that night." He looked away, took a swig of beer and continued, "I said to Ginny, don't fret so much, Maggie's a good girl. She'll be home soon." The grief in his eyes returned. "She told me to go look for her, but I waited." He rubbed at the edges of his reddened eyes. "I knew the kids hung out at the old gristmill. God, why did I wait?"

Emma placed her palm on top of his calloused hand. "You couldn't have known anything bad had happened."

"No, but I shoulda. Grief is what killed Ginny. Died of ovarian cancer five years ago but she was never the same after Maggie disappeared. Stopped taking care of herself and stopped working."

"That must have been so hard on her." Emma paused, creating a psychic barrier to protect herself from the waves of grief and guilt emanating from the bereaved man. "Hard on you, too," she added.

"Workin' made me forget. Ginny, well, she stopped coming to work with me. Stayed at home. Was in Maggie's room all day, sortin' the closet and drawers every day, changin' the sheets." He shook his head at the memory. "In the beginning I didn't say nothin'. Thinking she'd sort herself out. Later, I'd say, 'Ginny, honey, we need to move on.' She'd stare at me as if I were nuts and start takin' the sheets off and washin' 'em again."

"Everyone deals with grief differently," said Emma, surprised at the switching back and forth of Edmund's language from rough to more educated.

"I guess. I was bloody lucky my landscaping company paid enough that I could afford to hire an office manager and bookkeeper."

"Tough times for all of you," said David.

"The day Maggie disappeared, everything changed. I lost my wife, first to grief, then to death, and little Megan lost a mother." He made a bitter smile, "Probably why my little girl can't decide if she's a girl or a boy. What is it with this 'they/them' thing?"

Emma prickled with annoyance at his insensitive remark concerning Megan's choice to identify as non-binary, but held her tongue. *No wonder Megan's estranged from their dad*, she thought.

David deftly steered the conversation back. "Did Maggie have a boyfriend?"

"Yeah, kid's name was Jason Briggs. Local jock. But good in school, too." Edmund struggled to his feet, wincing in pain. "Damn arthritis." He walked over to the shelving at the back wall and returned with a framed photograph of two teenagers, dressed in formal wear, smiles bright and their arms intertwined. "Jason was a year ahead. He took Maggie to the prom."

Emma took out her cell, "May I take a photo of this?"

"Sure, go ahead." Edmund roughly brushed tears away from his eyes. "It's been hell not knowing what happened to my little girl."

Seven

Time for Coffee

ON THE DRIVE BACK to the office, David was surprised by Emma's outburst. "He never tried to understand Megan!"

"Maybe, but think how hard it must have been for them both: no wife for him, no mother for Megan, and no clue what happened to Maggie."

"Yeah, you're right. But still," Emma sighed with frustration. "He was the adult. He should have tried harder."

"It's difficult to know how any of us will behave when faced with a tragedy like that," said David, unused to seeing Emma so angry and frustrated. "Kids aren't supposed to die before their parents. Imagine if we had a kid and—"

"You're right." Emma's voice softened. "We're not ready for parenthood yet, but that kind of pain would be unimaginable."

"I get that you feel protective about Megan, but Edmund is coping as best he can. It's hard for the older generations to understand, let alone embrace the concept of gender choices."

"I guess so." Emma's face softened. "I have always thought that people who identify with both genders are more in tune with the male and female aspects of their souls. If someone was a woman in a previous life and was reincarnated as a man, I believe their soul remembers what it was like to be a woman."

"After last year, and what I learned about my previous life, nothing would surprise me anymore. There's some logic to your theory."

"Did you know that the Zapotec cultures of Oaxaca in southern Mexico recognize a third gender?"

"No, I didn't," said David, surprised. He lifted his eyes from the road momentarily and met Emma's gaze.

"They are called muxes. The person is male at birth but dresses and behaves in ways otherwise associated with women. People who have a muxe in their family consider this good luck and muxes are honored and revered in their culture. Even by the Catholic Church within their community."

"That's amazing."

"In fact, throughout history, cultures have recognized this third gender. It's sad Western civilization has trouble accepting this, when for centuries it was considered normal."

"I had no idea. So, the concept of being non-binary has a long history and isn't a new concept at all."

"Not new at all. Besides the Muxes, there are five more cultures around the world that believe in additional genders. The Hijras, from Hindu society, take on a spiritual role. In Indonesia, they recognize three more genders: the Calalai, females who identify as males; the Calabai, males who identify as females and the Bissu, who transcend all genders and are believed to be a bridge between the material world and the divine." Emma took a breath, and continued, "Then there's the Bugis ethnic group in Indonesia; the Sekrata from the Sakalava people, indigenous to Madagascar; the Bakla from the Philippines; and from our Indigenous North Americans, Two-Spirit."

"Emma, how did you come to know all this?"

"Megan and I were close in high school, and as they began to question their sexual identity, they shared what they learned with me."

"This is very enlightening. I had no idea. You never cease to amaze me."

"Well, I care about Megan, and it bugs me when people are so narrow-minded."

The two fell quiet and for a while all that could be heard was the hum of the tires on the pavement. As David entered the busy streets of New Elgan, he glanced over at Emma. Her face was pale and she was shivering, even though there were beads of perspiration forming on her forehead.

Her body suddenly stiffened.

"Emma, what's wrong?" David said with alarm. "What's going on?"

"Can you pull over, please?" Her voice was distant. "Spirit Anna is here."

David drove for another few minutes until he found a safe place to pull over, out of the way of the afternoon traffic. He put the vehicle in park, and noticing Emma's pale face, he placed his hand on her brow. "Your forehead feels warm." He rolled down the windows and let the cool spring air filter through the car.

He sat quietly and waited as Emma's eyes withdrew into themselves, seeing beyond this plane of existence. After a few minutes, she exhaled, the color in her cheeks returned and she looked over at David.

"You, okay?" he asked, his voice soft.

"Yeah, I'm fine."

"What did you see?"

"I saw Maggie with a young man."

"Could it have been Jason Briggs?"

"No, I—" Emma's fingers shook. "I can't tell." She rubbed the corners of her eyes with the tips of her fingers.

"How about we stop at Café Mokka for coffee? We could interview Megan," said David. "See what they remember about their sister."

"Good idea. After the stuff Edmund served, I could use a real coffee," said David chuckling. "Hard to believe two members of the same family can serve such different cups of java."

David checked his rearview mirror, then slid the new Kia EVS he'd recently purchased into the parking space a few steps from the entrance to Café Mokka.

"You know you could have let it self-park," teased Emma.

"Yeah, but I don't want to lose my driving skills."

"As if. That's what the MGB is for."

David glanced at Emma's mischievous emerald eyes, crinkling at the corners. "I love you," he said.

"I love you, too." She leaned toward him and gave him a gentle kiss on the lips.

"Before we go in, let's give Bryan a call. Give him an update."

"Good thinking."

David keyed in Bryan's name, selected the call icon and waited for Bryan to answer.

"Bryan speaking."

"Hey, Bryan, it's David. Emma and I wanted to give you an update on our meeting with Edmund Stacey."

"Great. What did you learn?"

"The details Edmund remembers are pretty much what we read on the Canada Cold Cases website."

"Not surprising. So much time has passed."

"One good piece of info, though. We got the name of the boyfriend. Jason Briggs."

"Interesting. Did Edmund know where we can find Jason?"

"Hey, Bryan," said Emma. "I found Jason Briggs online. Looks like he has an investment firm right here in New Elgan, at 55 Ashwood Lane."

31

"Can you text me the address?"

"Sure, already sent," said Emma.

"I'm going to head there now."

"Before you leave, how did things go at the department?" asked David. "Were you able to get in touch with Constable Carlo Carducci?"

"He's a staff inspector now. He wasn't in. On vacation in Prince Edward County. The police reports are in storage, but the chief of police is going to get them pulled for us."

"That's great news," said David.

"What are you two up to now?" asked Bryan.

"On the drive back, Emma had another vision."

"Emma, are you all right?" Bryan's voice was laced with concern.

"Yes, but a little unnerved. Not much to tell you, but this case has got me really rattled."

"What did you see?"

"A young man with Maggie but his face was hidden."

"No sense as to who it might be?"

"None." Emma sighed with frustration. "We took a photo of a prom picture of both Megan and Jason. Texting that to you now."

"Thanks," said Bryan. "Anything else?"

"No, we are parked outside Café Mokka. About to go in. Hopefully, Megan is working today, and we can talk with them. See what they know."

"Sounds good. Let's touch base a little later today."

Eight

Jason Briggs

JASON BRIGGS EYED Bryan with curiosity and gestured to him to have a seat in his home office. "So, how can I help you?" His fingers played nervously with the business card that Bryan had given him. "I guess you're not here for investment advice."

"Maybe some other time. I am here to ask you a few questions about Margaret Stacey."

Jason's lips tightened into a straight and severe line. "That was a lifetime ago." He paused and said, "I'm curious. Why now?"

"Some new information has come to light concerning her disappearance and we are interviewing everyone who knew her."

"May I ask what that new info might be?" Jason's voice was now eager.

"We're not at liberty to say," said Bryan.

"We?"

"My team and I are working with the New Elgan Police Services on cold cases like Maggie's. I understand you were her boyfriend."

"Yeah, for a while, but it got rocky between us before she disappeared."

Bryan's cop instincts came on full alert. He straightened in his chair, and asked, "Rocky in what way?"

"I don't know. She changed. Dressed differently. Started hanging out with other kids."

"Kids from school?"

"Nah, I didn't know who they were. But they were kinda weird."

"How so?"

"They used to meet up at the gristmill on the outskirts of town. Smoke up. I wasn't into that kind of thing. I wanted to get ahead. Go to university."

"And Maggie's goals were different?"

"She was a year younger than I was and a bit immature. I don't think she had any goals, yet." Jason looked off to the right, indicating to Bryan's trained eye that he was remembering a real event. "My family didn't have a lot of money, so I focused on my studies. I put everything into sports and got a soccer scholarship stateside. Maggie got jealous; said I was too intense. That I neglected her. But hey, I was seventeen. I wanted to get out of New Elgan." Regret flashed behind his eyes. "Maybe she'd still be alive if we had hung out more often."

"So, how do you know she's dead?" asked Bryan sharply.

"Well, she's been gone so long—" Jason frowned. "Say, I don't like what you are implying. I would never hurt Maggie. She was my first love. I was crazy about her."

Bryan changed the direction of the interview. "Did you ever make it as a soccer player professionally?"

"No, my last year of college I blew out my knee. Got an ACL injury. Can't complain; I got a great education. I worked at a large brokerage firm in Toronto. Finances. Mainly hedge funds."

"Why did you come back to New Elgan?"

"I got tired of the rat race in Toronto. Set up my shingle as an investment advisor," he said. "Also, my dad's become quite frail. He's got COPD. Didn't quit smoking soon enough. I can keep an eye on him better now that I'm back in town. Make sure he eats on time."

"Ever stay in touch with Maggie's folks?"

"Not really." Jason glanced down at his phone, and said, "Say, I don't mean to be rude. I've got a Zoom meeting with a client in five minutes. If there's nothing else ..."

"No, that's it for now." Bryan stood and shook Jason's hand. "Thanks for your time."

Nine

Megan Stacey

MEGAN SMILED WHEN they saw David and Emma enter Cafe Mokka.

"It's great to see you!" they said, smiling. Megan called out to the kitchen staff, "Gonna get these two to try our new spiced latte and then take my break."

"Sure thing," replied Carl, Megan's boss. "Take fifteen."

"Thanks, Carl."

Megan expertly carried three mugs to the blue and white checker-covered table and placed one mug in front of Emma and the second before David. They pulled up a chair, sat down and cradled their own mug in their long delicate hands. Each finger, including the thumbs, bore rings.

Megan's white-blonde hair was pulled up in a messy ponytail, with tendrils escaping the bright pink scrunchie, which was patterned with blue peace symbols.

"Haven't seen you guys in ages!" Megan paused to take a sip. "What do you think of the new latte?"

"It's delish," smiled Emma. "I like the raspberry leaves: it gives the latte a subtle flavor." She took another sip. "Spicy, too. Cayenne pepper?"

"Yep. Never could fool your taste buds," said Megan, grinning. "What do you think?" they asked, turning towards David.

"It's good, but I prefer my coffee plain," he replied, trying not to offend Emma's eccentric friend.

"How's the new business going?" asked Megan.

"Great. We're actually here on business," said Emma.

"Oh?" Megan said, question marks in their eyes.

"It's about your sister Maggie."

"Maggie? How do you know about Maggie?" Megan blinked, startled.

"What do you remember about your sister's disappearance?"

"Not very much. I don't remember her all that well." Megan averted their eyes and took another sip of their latte. "I was four when she disappeared."

"Oh."

"Yeah, Maggie was sixteen."

"Wow. Twelve years difference. That's quite a big age gap," commented Emma.

"Well, I was a surprise. Unplanned." A flash of sorrow crossed their face. "I was never sure I was the youngest, or an only child."

Emma nodded sympathetically.

"After Maggie disappeared, my mom would barely look at me. My parents had terrible fights. My dad would say you still have a young child that needs you." Megan choked back a sob. "Then when Mom died ... my dad became overprotective." Megan's voice was solemn "What I do know about Maggie is what he told me. I don't remember much about either Maggie or my mom."

Emma said, "Megan, we've been friends for how long?"

"Since the third grade."

"How come I never knew this about you?"

"No one did. Outside our home, our family didn't talk about it."

Emma reached out and touched Megan's hand and stiffened as a kaleidoscope of images pulsed through her mind. Her eyes began to flutter back and forth.

"What is it?" asked David, his voice thick with concern.

Emma gasped but didn't reply.

"What's going on?" Megan exchanged a worried look with David and instinctively moved her hand out from Emma's own.

Emma swallowed and opened her eyes. "Your sister—"

"What about her?"

"I don't think she—"

"—are you saying she's alive?"

"No, Megan, I'm not saying that—"

"Then what?"

"She's trying to show me something. To tell you. No, warn you..."

"What do you mean? Like a message?"

"I don't know, that's all I can see for now." Emma picked up her mug, saw it was empty and stared at it, her shoulders slumped. "It's not clear."

"Wait a second," said Megan, gently prying the mug from Emma's hands. "Let me get you a refill."

Ten

Missing

LAURA DIDN'T MUCH CARE for the journey into New Elgan and preferred to work remotely from home. She hadn't needed to commute when she had her clothing design business and had ventured into town to see clients as little as possible.

She certainly wouldn't be commuting all that often when the office in downtown New Elgan was finally renovated.

So much had happened this last year. Emma and David had gotten married, and she had met and married Bryan. The corners of her mouth lifted at the memory of the double wedding on the beach in Costa Rica: she and her daughter, both brides, getting married at the same time. Now that she had Bryan, the sting of being an empty-nester had lessened when Emma moved out. After having lost her first husband, Emma's father, Laura never imagined she'd find love again, believing that part of her life was over. Until she met Bryan, she didn't realize how lonely she had become, how she'd shut that part of her life off. *Well, look at me now*, she thought. *Happy. Actually happy.*

She glanced at her watch. Bryan had left much earlier to visit the New Elgan Police Service to get the files on the disappearance of Margaret Stacey. After straightening up the aftermath of their rushed breakfast, she prepared herself a steaming cup of one of Emma's blends of herbal tea and carried it to her office, ready to begin her research.

Laura pulled up the Canada Cold Cases database and reviewed the article about Maggie's disappearance. *Sixteen years old.* Laura mused. *Whatever became of her?*

She decided to start her search first with Ontario disappearances, choosing the option to search from the oldest to the most recent, with the parameters of five years before and ten years after Maggie's disappearance in 2004. She scrolled down the depressing list of missing young people. It was difficult to remain focused with all the innocent faces on the screen staring at her: all different races and ages. A pang of guilt stabbed at her when she scrolled past the pictures of the younger ones. *Poor lost little children. Perhaps in one of our next cases ...*

Reminding herself to remain focused, she concentrated on missing girls between the ages of fourteen and eighteen, looking for similarities in physical traits and the circumstances of their disappearance.

A yowl from the ginger cat, announcing he was hungry, interrupted Laura's research. She was surprised to see several hours had passed. She leaned back into her chair and noted with surprise that the late afternoon sun was filtering through the maple trees and was shining directly on her computer screen, making it difficult to see the text on the monitor.

"Come on, Snuggles, you're right. It's way past your feeding time. Sorry, I got carried away." She stroked the soft patch of fur between the cat's ears. He gave her a soft lick on her hand, nudged her hand away, headed toward the kitchen and turned his head around, telegraphing: *Coming?*

The rumble in her stomach reminded her she needed lunch, too. Sighing, she picked up her empty mug from the desk and padded over to the kitchen to prepare something to eat for the cat and herself. Munching on a kaiser bun stuffed with slices of tomato, onion and left-over roast chicken from the night before, she made a mental review of what she'd learned so far.

She'd first scoured the Canada Cold Cases database for missing teenagers of similar age and description to Maggie and found three young women who had disappeared in the early to mid-2000s. The disappearances were roughly one year apart, with obvious similarities.

In 2001, at age seventeen, Samantha Courtright from North Bay was last seen at four in the afternoon, when the school bus driver had dropped her off at the end of her laneway. At six in the evening, when her parents arrived home from their veterinary clinic, they were alarmed to discover Samantha was not at her usual place at the kitchen table, working on her homework.

Amanda Martin from Hamilton, aged sixteen, went missing during her morning walk to school in 2002. When the worried principal contacted her mother, it was already too late. Amanda was gone.

Finally, in 2003, Victoria D'angelo from Peterborough, at age fifteen, disappeared while attending a Saturday matinee with girlfriends. She'd gone to the washroom and not returned to her seat at the cinema.

And, of course, Maggie, at age sixteen, disappeared in 2004.

The common traits between the four young girls were unmistakable: fair-skinned, blue-eyed, tall and athletic, and above average intelligence. The most chilling commonality was how completely they had disappeared without a trace, their bodies never found.

Next, Laura poured over the missing person bulletins, noting the girls' next of kin: their parents, siblings, aunts, uncles, grandparents. The reports of loved ones' desperate appeals for information about the girls' disappearances were gut-churning and drained Laura emotionally.

Her mobile phone chirped. It was Bryan.

<Running behind. Expect to be home in a couple of hours. Feel like Chinese tonight?

<<That sounds great.

<Perfect. See you soon.

<<Love you.

<I love you, too.

His cheery text lifted her mood. Noting the time, almost five in the afternoon, and reluctant to continue her research, she recognized the need for some distraction from the depressing details she'd uncovered. She changed into her gardening clothes and thought, *time to work in the garden ... I could use the solace of working the soil with my hands.*

***

Over dinner, Bryan described to Laura the meeting Emma and David had with Edmund Stacey, and their plans to meet with Megan later that day. He then described the interview he'd conducted with Jason Briggs.

"Poor Edmund. And Jason sounds like he genuinely cared about Maggie," said Laura.

"Yeah, even after all these years, he's still torn up about her." Bryan pushed away his dinner plate. "That was delicious. I can't eat another bite."

"I'm full, too," agreed Laura.

"What was your day like, honey? Did you learn anything?"

A shadow passed over Laura's face. "Yes, I did. There were at least three teenage girls around Maggie's age that went missing in the early to mid-two-thousands. It was upsetting."

Laura stacked their dinner plates and said, "Let me put the leftovers away and do the dishes. Then, I'll review my findings with you."

Bryan grabbed the dishes and the takeout containers and said, "Laura, I'll take care of the dishes."

"Thanks," she said, her smile lighting up her emerald-green eyes. "I'll be back in a minute. I've printed a list for you."

Once they'd settled back at the dinner table Bryan had cleared, Laura handed him her list.

Bryan scanned the information Laura had prepared and said, "And this is just for Ontario?"

"Yes. There may be more, but in the span of four years, four young women disappeared."

"This confirms what I feared."

"I know," said Laura. "This really drained me today. It was so depressing. I can't imagine what the parents went through – are still going through. If Emma ever disappeared…"

Bryan placed his fingers against her lips, "No point thinking about things like that. It will immobilize you."

"You're right, of course." Laura took a deep breath. "You can read what I prepared later. For now, here's a summary of what I learned."

Bryan listened intently to Laura, grimaced and said, "These are solid leads that may help in our investigation, but how tragic for the families."

Eleven

The Dark Hands of Anubis

EMMA AWOKE, SCREAMING the words: *Dark Hands of Anubis! And blood, so much blood!* David turned on the night light and drew her trembling body into his arms. "Emma, honey, wake up." He kissed the top of her head and waited for her to fully awake. "There, there, don't worry, you're with me, you're safe."

After a few more minutes, Emma's eyes fluttered open like a butterfly emerging from its chrysalis.

"David, it must be true. Maggie didn't die. At least, not right away."

"Tell me what you saw," he said, his words gentle.

"A hospital ward full of babies! Row after row." Emma gave David a grateful smile as she took a sip of water from the glass he had handed her. "Like an assembly line." She gave an involuntary shudder.

"You were shouting 'Dark Hands of Anubis' and then something about blood."

Emma's normally vibrant green eyes dulled, like unpolished jade. "She died in childbirth—her fifth pregnancy. The baby's name was Simone." She sat up straighter in bed. "Oh my God... she hemorrhaged." Tears welled as she absorbed young Maggie's grief, making it her own. "They sold her babies."

"Let the emotions go, honey. You need to be objective."

Emma gave him a perturbed look. "My head knows that's true, but my heart says otherwise." She wiped tears from the corners of her eyes with her fingertips.

"Anubis. I didn't expect to hear that name again," said David, his eyebrows furrowed together. David was referring to the criminal syndicate which had kidnapped teenager Jasmijn Bakker from her school in Holland and had trained her to become a skilled assassin. Although Enrico Bianchi and his son Alessandro were responsible for the deaths of Emma's mentor, Anna Tungsten, it was Jasmijn who had been hired by Enrico to murder David's uncle, Liam, and his uncle's girlfriend, Sarah Moody.

Jasmijn had kidnapped Emma and delivered her into the Bianchis' hands: father and son psychopaths. A chill coursed through his body while he relived the memory of Emma tied to a chair in the centre of that bizarre Minoan maze on a remote island in the Maldives. There, Jazzie had had a change of heart. She had turned on Enrico, causing him to drop the knife he'd held at Emma's throat. Her actions had undoubtedly saved Emma's life. Seconds later, she had paid the final sacrifice when Enrico's son, Alessandro, had buried that same knife up to the hilt into Jazzie's back.

Emma interrupted his thoughts. "It's an abduction ring. Instead of abducting babies, they steal young women and force them to have kids against their will." More tears welled up in her eyes.

"A human baby mill," said David, his tone grim.

"And beyond a few girls who have dropped out of sight, no one is going to report babies having been stolen from the cradle if there's no record they were even born," said Emma, choking back tears.

David pulled out the pen and journal from the drawer, handed it to Emma and said, "Write down everything you remember from your vision."

Her fingers trembled as she wrote the content of the dream into the journal.

When she finished writing, she tilted her head to the side and said, "I don't know how this can be, but the Dark Hands of Anubis are behind this." She swallowed the lump in her throat.

"Emma, what does Spirit Anna say?"

"That's the thing: lately, she seems distant. Distracted, even."

"What do you mean?"

"I'm getting impressions, visions, but she's not there to help interpret." Her face was haggard. "It's like I have lost something. My connection to her seems weak." Her cheeks flamed red with frustration.

"Does she have any message for you at all?"

"She says to be careful, that we could risk losing everything—including ourselves."

"Careful in what way?" asked David.

"I'm not sure," she said, frowning. "All I see is darkness."

"Em, I think you should stop your paranormal work. At least for now. I am so worried about you."

"I can handle it." Emma thrust out her chin in annoyance.

"But what if you can't?"

"Don't you have any faith in me?" Her voice was tinged with anger. She threw off the blankets and strode to the washroom, slamming the door shut.

She sat on the edge of the bathtub and cried softly. She was unwilling to let her team know her internal struggle and doubts. Mixed with that was guilt: the last thing she wanted to do was have her family, especially David, worry about her.

David was shocked to hear the lock thrown. He tapped lightly on the door. "Hey, Em, open up."

"Go away."

"Please, Em. I'm sorry." He waited, hoping for an answer, relief flowing through him like a river breaking through its dam when he heard the lock disengaged and she opened the door.

"Oh, David, I'm so sorry. I've been horrid," she said, tears streaming down her face.

He pulled her in close, and said, "Honey, I'm sorry, too."

Her tears dampened his pajama top. "The stress is really getting to me. I don't want to let Maggie and Megan down."

Twelve

David

DAVID LEANED BACK in his office chair, tilting it at a precarious angle before easing forward again. "Emma's got me worried." He leveled his concerned brown eyes at Bryan. "Her visions are getting stronger and she's having a tough time controlling them. She never received her full training before Anna passed away."

"Isn't Spirit Anna still helping her from the other side?" asked Bryan.

"Yes, to a certain extent, but the connection between the two seems to be weakening."

"What does Emma think?"

"She thinks Spirit Anna is withdrawing, preparing to move on."

"To reincarnate? Wouldn't that be too soon?"

David shook his head. "Emma thinks it's more likely she is moving to a higher plane of existence to help newly departed souls transition to the spirit world."

"Interesting."

David's eyebrows creased together in a frown. "I wasn't expecting to ever hear the name Dark Hands of Anubis again. I thought that chapter with Enrico Bianchi was firmly closed for us."

"Yes, that does come as a shock," said Bryan.

"Emma thinks they are involved in a baby ring. That Maggie's disappearance is linked to the Dark Hands."

"It's an interesting theory." Bryan paused. "We need more evidence. Right now, this is simply conjecture."

"Do you think it would be worthwhile interviewing Enrico Bianchi, or his son Alessandro, to see what kind of connection our current case might have with the Dark Hands?"

"It's worth a try," replied Bryan. "I will get in touch with the Collins Bay Institution in Kingston, Ontario, to arrange interviews with both men."

"I thought the Kingston Pen was closed," commented David.

Bryan shook his head. "Following the closure of the Kingston Penitentiary in September, 2013, the Collins Bay Institution became the oldest operational federal men's correctional facility in the Ontario region. They house minimum, medium and maximum security inmates."

"Interesting," said David. "I've been wondering about something else."

"What's that?"

"Remember when Jazzie was in custody, and we were working with her to track down Enrico and his son in the Maldives?" David rubbed the base of his neck. "Do you think we'd be able to examine her computer and cell phone that were confiscated?"

"I see where you're going with this. I can ask my contacts at the department if we can analyze the data."

"Jazzie claimed she was keeping tabs on the Dark Hands as an insurance policy."

"Since they are linked to our current case, it's worth a try," said Bryan. "It may take some time for us to gain access to her computer devices. This could be a good lead."

"Thanks. In the meantime, what do you think I should do about Emma?" David continued to massage the back of his neck, trying to alleviate the growing knot of pain, a sure sign a tension headache was on its way.

"Not much you can do," said Bryan. His voice was rough with emotion. "That young lady has a mind of her own."

"What about her promise to stop if things got dangerous?" asked David. "I believe it's already too risky."

"Knowing Emma, she'll need to see this through," said Bryan. "I don't think she can help herself."

"I guess you're right, but I am worried sick about her mental well-being." David paused, and looked at Bryan with heavy, sad eyes. "We had words this morning. She insists on continuing."

"The best thing you can do is be there for her," he replied. "The more facts we can uncover to support her paranormal impressions, the better."

"And the sooner we can solve this cold case." David looked at Bryan thoughtfully. "So, besides interviewing the Bianchis, and mining data from Jazzie's computer, where else should we focus our attention?" asked David.

"Yesterday, Laura found three cases of teenage girls who disappeared from the years 2001 to 2003. Including Maggie, who disappeared in 2004, there are four girls missing. All are Caucasian, and of similar height, appearance, intelligence and athletic ability." Bryan's grey eyes were heavy with sadness. "This might support the theory Emma has put forward."

"Was this nationwide?"

"No, this was for Ontario only. I've asked Laura to widen the search to include up to 2014." He swallowed at the lump forming in his throat. "And to see if there were reports of similar disappearances from other provinces."

***

David tapped his Apple watch and reviewed the ingredients he'd need for the pasta dish he was preparing.

He wasn't accustomed to cooking often, but whenever he did, it had to be perfect. He was determined to surprise Emma with a delectable meal that would please her and hopefully make up for their argument that morning. *It's been too long since Emma and I had a date night*, he thought. *Just the two of us, without talking about work.*

He was struggling with Emma's burgeoning psychic abilities. Recalling the turmoil they went through last year when they first met, he questioned the wisdom of venturing into the paranormal to solve cold cases. Emma and Anna's abilities had, without question, led to the apprehension of the killer of his past life, but at a terrible cost.

In addition, Emma had still retained some clients from her website business. "To keep my workload down, I'll keep only my favorite clients," she'd reassured him. "The ones who run charitable organizations or clubs. They're always strapped for money, and this is my way of helping. To give back."

"I really worry you're burning the candle at both ends," he'd replied.

"I'll be fine," she'd said, shrugging her shoulders as if to say, *What choice do I have?*

His thoughts were interrupted when the hot water in the pot containing the linguine began to boil over. He pulled the pot off the burner and quickly wiped the mess off the ceramic stovetop. *Pay attention,* he chided himself. To avoid a second mess, he placed the pot on low heat, then tapped out a message on his Apple watch.

<Packed it in early today. When are you coming home?

<<Leaving the office now. Maybe in about 10 minutes?

<Perfect.

<<See you soon.

Next, David heated extra virgin olive oil in the large skillet, added minced shallots and garlic and finely diced red pepper. Once he'd sautéed the mixture, he transferred half into a separate pan. He added shrimp to the first pan, and previously grilled tofu to the second pan. He drained the cooked pasta, added half to the pan with the shrimp and the second half to the pan with the tofu, which would be for Emma, who was a vegetarian.

He took a Proscecco from the built-in wine fridge, uncorked it and placed it in an ice bucket. The refreshing and slightly bitter wine would pair nicely with the delicate flavors of the linguine dish.

He had just enough time to set the table with one of Emma's favorite tablecloths, silverware, and her favorite wine glasses – the ones with the gold rim – when he heard the front door open and close.

"Something smells wonderful!" exclaimed Emma. "What's the special occasion?"

"No occasion," said David, smiling, drawing her into his arms. "Good day?" he murmured, breathing in the lavender scent of her hair.

"It was a rough start this morning. I really am sorry," she said, first looking down and then glancing up at him, her eyes moist. "But now the day is outstanding."

"I'm glad," he said, pouring the Proscecco into their wine glasses. He handed her a glass of golden liquid and took the second one. "Here's to us."

"To us," said Emma, beaming happily.

"Have a seat," David said, drawing out the chair and motioning her to sit.

"Wow, I feel so spoiled."

"I'll be back in a moment." David returned a few minutes later with two plates heaped with pasta and topped with grated Grana Padano and parsley.

"Seafood linguine for you," said Emma. "And you grilled tofu for me." Her eyes were misty. "That's why I love you so much. You're so thoughtful."

***

Emma pushed her plate away, "That was incredibly delicious. You outdid yourself."

When she started to clear the dishes, David reached out and touched her arm. "Emma, I'll do them later."

He refilled their wine glasses and said, "Let's finish our wine in the living room."

Once they settled themselves on the loveseat, Emma looked at David and said, "I can't thank you enough. You made me feel so special tonight." She searched his face. "But something's on your mind, isn't it?"

"Yes," he hesitated for a moment, then spoke. "Emma, with this intense schedule, we're not making enough time for each other." He pulled her close. "In fact, the whole time we've been together, it's always been rushed."

"That's true," she admitted.

"Some people even say our romance was rushed."

"Those were intense times. The feelings we had were strong and came from knowing each other in previous lifetimes."

"But for people looking in, some of them think we moved too fast."

"It doesn't matter what others believe," her smile was gentle. "But what *we know*. We've had many lifetimes together."

"But Emma, think about this. Although our feelings are intense for each other, this lifetime is new for us, too, and so is our marriage. It means we shouldn't neglect the relationship we have *now*."

53

"You're beginning to sound like Eckhart Tolle," she teased.

"Absolutely. It's a good message: to live in the present."

"And what do you want to do at *present*?" She gave him an impish smile.

"I think you know what I want at present."

"Ah, I see," she whispered. "Now."

He pushed her back against the cushions on the couch.

Thirteen

Young Maggie

September, 2014

MAGGIE'S SCREAMS ECHOED throughout the ward. She was hemorrhaging heavily despite the futile attempts of the male nurse to stop the crimson flow. "She's lost more than one thousand ccs of blood!"

Maggie screamed again, her body contorted in an unnatural position, her heart rate elevated and her breathing shallow.

"Maggie! Stay with me!" Evan, the nurse, shouted in desperation at the orderly standing in the doorway. "Where's Doctor Sperling?"

"Still at lunch, I think," she stammered. "You're not supposed to use their names," she said, her voice filled with a mixture of fear and accusation.

"Do you think I give a fuck! Go get him now!" he growled, ignoring the reprimand. "Tell him patient number MS-two-zero-zero-nine-zero-six is fading fast!" Evan glared at her. "The Dark Hands wouldn't want to lose such a valuable asset," he sneered.

***

Doctor Sperling looked at Maggie's gray face, picked up her thin wrist and traced the road map of white scars which intersected her pale skin with his thumb. Noting the lack of a pulse, he thought, *Looks like you got your wish, Maggie; you've finally escaped.*

He pulled the sheet over her face, picked up her chart and reviewed it. "Too bad. She was one of our best breeders. Five babies in ten years." He made a heavy sigh, and said, "There's nothing more we can do here." He checked the time on his Rolex. "I am noting the time of death at 12:15 p.m." He glanced at the male nurse. "At least the baby is healthy."

Sperling pointed at Maggie's lifeless body. "Get her to the crematorium."

"Yes, Doctor," said Evan, hiding his grief, his face a stony mask.

***

Maggie floated above her lifeless body. Although free now, her astral cord severed, she was reluctant to leave her prison of flesh and bone behind. Living her last years in the cult, which had been a thinly disguised child rearing ring run by the Dark Hands of Anubis, evoked a rage within her which knew no limits.

From 2004 to 2014, she and fifteen other girls had been kidnapped for their extraordinary beauty, athleticism and intelligence. The criminals running this baby syndicate were offering "made to order" babies, according to their clients' genetic specifications.

The girls were either inseminated artificially, implanted with an already fertilized egg or for an extra fee, were forced to have intercourse with the father-to-be. The result was each girl, before her body was depleted, contributed at least four to five babies. At roughly $165,000 US per baby, each young woman could net the organization between $500,000 to $750,000 over a five-to-ten-year period.

Surviving women, believing that the threat against their families in the outside world was real, never tried to leave the compound and worked as cleaners cooking staff or as orderlies. If they were deemed attractive and still marketable, they could also be sold off to the sex trade.

Maggie moved effortlessly from her death room to the ward holding the babies and toddlers. She hovered over her fifth child, held her featherlike fingers to her lips and then gently touched her baby's forehead. The infant's eyes opened and smiled at her. *She sees me.* Maggie's spectral light grew brighter with wonder at the child's reaction.

Moments, perhaps months or years later, since time is not measurable in the afterworld, Maggie felt a comforting presence at her side. *Mom?* She was embraced by the warm and loving light of her mother, Virginia, and sensed her intent. *It's time to go.*

I can't, answered Maggie. *This little one needs protection.*

Her guardian angel will guide her well, her mother reassured her.

Not enough.

Her mother's brilliance dimmed as if to reflect her disappointment. *As you wish.* She reached her arms toward Maggie, as a final entreaty to join her and then began to fade at the edges until she receded into the darkness.

No! Don't go! I need you here, she begged. *Help me protect this little one and help me find my other babies!* There was no answer; the darkness and desolation were complete.

Maggie drew her attention back to her sleeping baby and vowed she'd find a way to keep her child safe. Her thoughts turned toward her baby sister, *Megan*.

Although the silver cord holding her to this life had been severed, Maggie knew she could never move on until she had exacted vengeance. And even then, she told herself, *revenge is not enough*.

Fourteen

A Call for Help

MEGAN THRASHED AT THE BED SHEETS, flinging a pillow across the room. It was the ensuing crash which awakened them. They switched on the Tiffany style bed lamp and moaned in dismay when they saw the mess. "Oh, no!" Their treasured nineteenth century antique pitcher and wash basin, which they had purchased last year at their favorite antique shop, Past Glories of Toad Hollow in Orangeville, was in pieces.

Megan pulled on slippers and took careful steps around the white and blue ceramic shards, which had shattered and had no doubt lodged themselves into every crevice of the room. *At least I missed the French antique clock,* Megan thought. *Shit. Three in the morning.*

As Megan swept up the broken pieces, they reflected on their dream. In the dream, Megan saw a woman holding a baby, with four other children of various ages pulling at the hemline of her dress. The image was powerful and compelling, the woman's gaze piercing and defiant. Worthy to capture on canvas, Megan decided.

When they weren't working at Café Mokka, they spent their time at the easel. *I should go back to bed,* Megan thought, but the urge to put on canvas what they had seen was too strong and their feet led them instead to the living room, which had been converted to an art studio. Megan pulled out a freshly primed canvas, set it up on the easel and began to paint, committing to canvas what they'd seen in their dream.

For several hours, Megan painted without interruption, as if in a trance and when finished, sat back to observe their work. A nagging feeling of recognition flitted at the edge of awareness. The woman in the canvas looked familiar. *But how?*

The shock hit Megan, like an avalanche, obliterating rational thought, and common sense. *My God, the woman in the painting looks a bit like me. No, like Maggie! What does this mean? Could Maggie still be alive?*

Their body trembling, Megan reached for the cell. "Emma, it's Megan. Can I come over?"

***

Emma heard the cheery doorbell chime, her empathic abilities already alerting her that Megan was at her door. Nonetheless, she checked the monitor displaying multiple camera views and confirmed it was Megan standing at the front door, with a bulky package under her arm.

Even before they had moved in, David had insisted they install a state-of-the-art security system in their Victorian home. Emma had objected at first, saying, "David, is this really necessary? With Enrico and his son behind bars, surely, we're no longer in any danger."

"For a psychic, you can be pretty short-sighted at times," he'd said.

"What's that supposed to mean?" She had held back tears, frustrated by the perceived insult, even as she'd said the words, knowing that David had meant no disrespect.

"Emma, I'm sorry, I didn't mean it that way." David had gathered her in his arms and said, "Honey, this is what led to difficulties last year, when we lulled ourselves into a false sense of security." Emma had begun to interrupt, but he had gently placed the tips of his fingers against her lips and said, "I know your psychic abilities are burgeoning, and you can sense if danger is coming. But what if you can't get help in time?"

"Do you still think that we're in jeopardy?" Emma had frowned, unsettled by the notion of not being safe.

"With the kind of cases that we will be taking on, who knows? Why play with fate?" David had hesitated. "I can't help but worry."

Emma had begun to object, but when she'd seen the concern and compassion in his eyes, she'd nodded and said, "You're right."

Emma returned her mind to the present, opened the door, and said, "Megan, come on in." She embraced Megan, then pulled back slightly, her arms straight now, but her hands still encircling Megan's waist. She noted with mounting concern the dark circles under their eyes and the slight tremor in their body. "Let me fix you an herbal tea. I have a new blend I've created specifically to calm the nerves."

"Thanks," said Megan, their laugh brittle. "I'm always the one serving you the beverages."

"Well, this time I'm treating you." Emma said, gesturing toward one of the barstools at the granite kitchen counter. "Have a seat."

She took a clear glass teapot from the cupboard, removed a cylindrical tea strainer and placed an assortment of dried herbs inside. As she poured the steaming hot liquid over the herbs, fragrances of bergamot, chamomile and lemon balm were released. She placed the teapot, its matching glass teacups and saucers, and honey from her mother's neighbor's farm, on a tray.

"We'll let it steep for a bit." Emma picked up the tray and said, "Let's go sit in Anna's Room."

Megan grabbed the package and followed Emma to the room tastefully appointed with antiques and settled into one of the plush chairs with matching throw cushions.

"You can put the cushion aside, if it bothers you," said Emma. "Some people find it too plump."

"How pretty." Megan picked up one of the cushions and traced the intricately embroidered rose pattern with their fingers. "It's beautiful here," said Megan, taking a deep breath. "And peaceful."

"It's my favorite place," said Emma, pouring the tea into the delicate cups. "So, what's going on?"

"I've had a strange dream. About Maggie." Tears welled into Megan's eyes. "I hope you can help me make sense of it."

"I'll do my best," Emma's voice was gentle and quiet. "Tell me about it."

"I'd rather show you."

"Oh?" asked Emma, surprised.

Megan removed the canvas from the bag, set the painting on the floor and said, "Take a look."

Emma drew in her breath. "This is your sister, Maggie. The same young woman I saw in my vision, but she was running away from something. She looks older here. Your painting is remarkable."

"Thanks." Megan took a sip of the fragrant tea and asked, "Emma, is there any chance my sister is still alive?"

"Oh, sweetheart, no. Like I told you before, we don't think so."

Emma took one look at Megan's suffering face and decided to tell them what she and her team had learned so far.

After she'd finished explaining their suspicions that Maggie, along with other girls, had been kidnapped and forcefully impregnated as part of a money-making baby-selling ring, Megan said, "This is unbelievable. But what makes you think Maggie is dead?"

"I had another strong vision and saw Maggie die in childbirth. That, along with her contacting me from the spirit world, makes us very sure that she is gone. And because of her insistence she has five living babies, we are doubling our efforts to trace where these children might be."

"I see." Megan's face was bright with excitement. "You mean I might have family out there?"

"We've no proof yet, of course," sighed Emma. "Anything we learn using the paranormal must have corroborating evidence before the authorities can act on it. That's what David and Bryan are working on now."

"Do you think they'll be able to find Maggie's kids?" Megan asked. "And how come Maggie doesn't know where they are?"

"Maggie is in a very fragile state. She is in what we call, 'limbo'."

"Limbo?"

"Her soul has been unable to move into the afterlife dimension and she is likely stuck on Earth until she can find a way out. Her death during childbirth and worry over her children has tied her to this plane."

"Is there any way to help her?"

"Psychic mediums can help these souls by creating a beacon of light for them, thus allowing them to leave Earth."

"Do you think Spirit Anna could help her?"

"Maybe. It's hard to say," said Emma. "I think it's up to us to find her kids. Then Maggie will get the closure she needs to move on."

"I've never had such a vivid dream. Do you think her kids really look the way I painted them?"

"I wouldn't be surprised. The detail you captured in their faces is uncanny." Emma paused, her eyebrows creased in thought. "Could I keep this painting for a few days?"

"Sure," said Megan. They raised the teacup to their lips and took a sip. "This is good. Any chance you'd be willing to supply this blend to Café Mokka?"

"I'm flattered. We can talk about that later," Emma said. "For now, let's work on finding out what happened to your sister and her kids."

"Em?"

"Yes?"

"Thanks for this. You've given me hope."

***

Emma took close-up photos of the faces rendered in Megan's painting and sent a brief text over to Bryan.

<Have you ever used facial recognition software on images taken from a painting? E.

<<Can't say I have but this sounds intriguing. What do you have in mind?

<Megan left a painting they made based on a dream they had this morning. They look so much like Maggie and Megan themselves. It got me wondering.

<<No guarantees but send me close-up shots and I'll see what I can do.

<The kids look young in the painting. Would it be worthwhile using an age progression program?

<<Leave it with me and I'll let you know.

<Thanks Bryan.

Fifteen

Cheryl

CHERYL RAINIER STEPPED off the stage, soaking in the standing ovation and basking in the resounding applause, the way a turtle soaks up the sunshine in September before winter ensues. Her parents, Marta and William, were sitting in the front row, smiling with pride. Although she knew she should appreciate their support, at seventeen years of age she was finding their continual presence constricting. She wanted to head out to the after-party by herself, hook up with friends her own age, but her mom and dad always tagged along.

She hurried backstage and joined the rest of the performers.

"You murdered that!" said her friend, Agnes.

"You slayed it tonight," said Cal, his hooded eyes telegraphing a sexy vibe. Cheryl's face flushed red.

"Way to go, Chere," said Thomas. "You totally ate that."

"Thanks, guys," she replied. "Any likes on TikTok yet?"

Thomas thumbed through the app. "Yeah, we got a bunch already." He twirled the silver stud in his bottom lip, looking puzzled. "That's bizarre."

"What's up?" asked Cheryl.

"There's some chick named Sandra Andersen who is pretty ticked with you."

"How can that be? I don't even know her."

Thomas held his phone out for Cheryl to see. "Some e-girl into emo." He was referring to the punk-rock inspired music coming back into popularity. "She says you're impersonating her."

Cal laughed at Thomas, "Not you using the big words."

Cheryl threw an annoyed look at Cal and grabbed the phone from Thomas. "Wow, she looks like me."

"Yeah, and she sings like you, too." Thomas retrieved the phone and hit the play icon.

***

Cheryl folded her arms over her chest, eyed her parents with suspicion and asked, "Was I adopted?"

Her mother averted her eyes while her father choked on the chocolate biscuit he was eating.

"How could you even ask such a thing?" asked her mother, looking hurt.

"'Cause I've always felt different. Like I didn't belong with you." She gave her mother a hard look.

Her mother lowered her eyes, then looked at Cheryl's father and said, "It's time we told her." He gave a curt nod.

"Your father and I couldn't have children together." She nervously tucked grey-blond hair behind her ear. "After several miscarriages, I could no longer conceive." She wiped tears from her cheeks with shaky fingers. "After the last miscarriage, I had a hysterectomy."

"So?" Cheryl stifled her sobs. "You adopted me?"

"Not exactly." Her father grabbed her mother's hand in a gesture of support. "We went to a fertility clinic."

"Your dad's sperm was inseminated into a surrogate mother."

Cheryl was indignant. "And you didn't think I had a right to know?"

"Cheryl!" pleaded her mother. "Your dad is your biological father, after all. And I have loved and raised you as my own."

"Why are you so upset?" asked her dad.

"Because you couldn't be bothered to tell me. That's why." She glared at her parents and said, "And because of this." She hit the music app on her phone and skidded it across the kitchen table.

Her mother frowned, noting the punk rock clothing and spiked hair, and said, "Why are you dressed like that?"

"That's not me." Her gaze was laser focused. "Do I have a twin sister?"

"Oh, Cheryl, of course not." Her mom got up to embrace her daughter.

"Don't you dare touch me!" she snapped. "Anything to say, *Dad?*"

He shifted uncomfortably in his seat. "You do have a twin—"

"—What?" Cheryl's mother interrupted. "You never told me—"

He turned to his wife. "After the clinic's fees, we couldn't afford both girls, so—"

"You separated us?" Cheryl could barely contain her fury. "No wonder I've always felt something – someone – was missing from my life!"

"Cheryl, I didn't know—" said her mom.

"You should've." She turned to her father. "You are despicable. Both of you!"

Cheryl ran to her room, sent a hasty text message to her best friend Agnes, and began to throw her toiletries and clothing into an overnight bag.

"Honey, please don't go. Let's talk." Her mother placed a trembling hand on her daughter's shoulder. "Please stay. I love you ..."

"I can't stand liars," Cheryl sneered. "I'm outta here, *Marta*." She shoved her way past the older woman and ran out of the house.

Sixteen

Sandra

SANDRA READ THE comment on TikTok. *What's this imposter Cheryl playing at? She wants to meet me. But why?*

She expanded the screen and gazed closely at the image. Different haircut and clothing, but she couldn't deny the similarities: the same startling blue eyes, a nose that was straight with a cute little upward tip at the end, and a light dusting of freckles that danced across the bridge of the nose and cheeks. The chin was pointed and the face heart-shaped, giving the girl a pixie-like impression.

Sandra had left home the day she turned sixteen. Her adoptive parents had been verbally vicious, and she'd vowed to leave that abusive environment the first chance she had. Although a minor cannot apply for emancipation in Ontario, under the Children's Law Reform Act, anyone 16 years or older can leave home and not be forced to return.

A kind neighbour, who was a lawyer by profession, helped set her up on OW, the Ontario Works program, so that she could live in her own place. The stipulation was that she remain in school and stay in touch with her OW representative. For Sandra, music was everything and going to school meant she had access to musical instruments and instruction.

Despite her punk hairstyle, piercings and fierce independence, Sandra knew education would help her move forward in life, and for her that meant a career in music. When she could have been going to movies with friends, she stayed back and poured the money she earned from part time jobs at the local convenience store and burger place into private singing lessons.

Being a vegan made it particularly hard to flip burgers, but every day she reminded herself that it was a means to an end.

Now a year into her freedom, she had yet to see the child support she was owed by her wealthy, but miserly parents. Her former neighbor was still working on this for her, but Sandra believed the best person to rely upon was herself.

The TikTok notification flashed across the screen, reminding Sandra to respond to Cheryl's message.

<Can we meet?

"What harm could it do?" Sandra wondered out loud. *Might as well hear what the girl who looked so much like herself had to say.*

Her finger hovered over the reply button. *Here goes*, she thought, as she tapped out the message.

<<You gotta lotta nerve copying my act.

<No way was I doing that.

<<Why do you wanna meet?

<No easy way to ask this. Were you adopted?

Sandra looked at the screen in surprise. *WTF?* Curiosity piqued; she typed back her response.

<<What if I was?

<I think you're my twin sister.

<< Maybe. Where do you wanna meet up?

<I'm playing with my band on Friday night at the Songbird Club in Toronto.

<<I can hitch a ride downtown.

<Wanna meet before my first set, backstage?

<<Sure.

<Come at 6:00. Tell Ben you're here to see me, he'll let you in.
<<K. cu.

Seventeen

Twins

CHERYL AND SANDRA stared at each other. "I can't believe it. We look exactly like each other," said Cheryl.

"I know. Too weird," said Sandra.

Cheryl gave a piercing stare at Sandra. "I never knew I was adopted till a few days ago. A friend of mine saw your video clip. Thought it was me at first. Till he read your comments."

"I was ticked off ... but now ... I gotta sister."

"It's even better than that ... I think you and I are twins," replied Cheryl.

"What makes you so sure?"

"My dad ... no, I'm not gonna call him that anymore. *William* admitted I had a twin sister." She choked back a sob. "Said after the costs of the invitro fertilization he couldn't afford to raise both girls, so he chose one of us."

"Wow, how does someone even make a choice like that?"

"Dunno." Cheryl looked off in the distance, then redirected her gaze at Sandra. "Haven't you felt like something – or someone – has been missing your whole life?"

Sandra's heart raced at this last question. That one had hit home. "I guess so."

"Did you know you were adopted?"

"Yep, always did."

REVENGE IS NOT ENOUGH

"It was a shock finding out, but I'm glad I know now. I'm pissed with Marta and William."

"Marta and William? They ever abuse you?"

"God, no."

"Well, mine did. Gary and Andrea Andersen. Those two are real prizes. I left home as soon as I turned sixteen."

"What did they do?"

"It was all psychological abuse. They never let me forget that I was adopted, like I was some sort of charity case."

"That's horrible."

"My uncle, Aaron Sperling, ran some sort of adoption centre. He asked his sister and her husband to take me on. Those two never let a day go by without reminding me about their generosity."

"You're brave, leaving at sixteen. What's it been like?"

"Scary at first. But I had help from a neighbor who's a lawyer. Helped me understand my rights. I've got my own apartment through government assistance. As long as I go to school, I've got a place to stay."

"I left home a few days ago ... I've been staying with my friend Agnes." Cheryl wiped away the tears forming in the corners of her eyes. "Agnes's parents said I can stay a few more days. They want me to go home and reconcile things with Marta and William."

"Would that be such a bad thing? They obviously love you ..."

"I dunno ... I need time," said Cheryl.

"I never asked you. When's your birthday?"

"May 29th, 2007."

"Mine, too."

"Geminis," Sandra chuckled at the irony. "The astrological sign for twins." She grew quiet. "I've a little money put aside from part time jobs. What about us getting a DNA test to make sure?"

71

"Sounds good," Cheryl said.

"Did your dad say what fertilization clinic he went to?" asked Sandra.

"No, I never asked. I was so angry I stormed out."

"I know you're still upset, but why don't you ask him?"

"Good idea," said Cheryl, picking up her cell, her voice tinged with reluctance, "I'll call him now."

After a few moments, Cheryl said, "Dad?" There was a long pause before she replied, "No, I'm not ready to come home." She rolled her eyes in irritation. "I have one question for you. What invitro clinic did you go to?"

"I see." Noticing the shock on Cheryl's face, Sandra reached out and took her sister's hand in hers. "No, I already told you. Not coming home. I'm staying with Sandra. You know, the twin you didn't want." Cheryl disconnected the call and wiped more tears away from her cheeks.

"It was my uncle, wasn't it?" asked Sandra.

"Yes. Dr. A. Sperling." Cheryl stared at Sandra. "What if we talked to your uncle? Assuming we're twin sisters, and I'm sure we are, wouldn't he know who our birth mother is?"

"Uncle Aaron? No can do, he disappeared about ten years ago."

"Dead, then?"

"With the Sperling family, unless there's a cold body, don't count on anything." Sandra's face was grim.

***

Maggie watched with satisfaction as her two oldest children reunited with each other. She returned her attention to the youngest, little Simone, who would now be ten years of age. Was she happy? Was she getting the care and love she deserved? She seethed with anger, not knowing.

Simone was not the result of an artificial insemination but was a love child between herself and the male nurse, Evan. He had tried to smuggle Maggie out of the compound in the trunk of his car but had been stopped by the guards. Another girl, Samantha, who had fallen in love with Evan, had overheard their plans to escape and had alerted Dr. Sperling. She saw Evan once more, on the day of her death: the day she gave birth to Simone. *Was Evan even alive?*

Maggie had remained in the in-between world of living and the afterlife, unwilling to shed the bonds of her previous incarnation and return to Source. She vowed to remain earthbound so she could watch over her children, facilitate the apprehension of Dr. Sperling and the release of the unwilling members of his cult.

But being tied to the earth also meant she could not see all, and despite gentle entreaties from her loved ones already on the other side, she could not let go.

At least she was having some success with Megan, through her psychic friend Emma Jackson. How wonderful it would be if Megan could have little Simone in their life, and Maggie's other children, too.

Eighteen

Laura Makes a Discovery

LAURA OPENED HER BROWSER and was intrigued by the headline that popped up in her newsfeed.

Toronto Times July 14th, 2024

Identical twins separated at birth find each other online. Both budding singing sensations became aware of each other after having posted YouTube and TikTok videos of their music. Sandra Andersen and Cheryl Rainier are making an appeal to the public for information concerning Dr. Aaron Sperling, who the twins believe may lead them to finding their birth mother. Dr. Sperling ran an adoption clinic north of Toronto which was abruptly closed in October of 2014. Should you have information about the location of Dr. Sperling or the identity of their birth mother, please contact the twins through their manager, Benjamin Manning, at the Songbird Club in Toronto.

Although Laura's intuition and psychic abilities were not as strong as her daughter's, her excitement mounted as she reread the post several times. When she enlarged the image of the two girls, their arms intertwined, a shock charged through her.

They bore an uncanny resemblance to Maggie and to her younger sibling, Megan. She suspected that this could be the lead they'd been looking for. Finally, a solid clue.

Using WhatsApp, she sent out a group video call to the team. Once the images of Bryan, Emma, David and herself had popped up on the WhatsApp group video call screen, she said, "I've found something."

"What is it, Mom?" asked Emma, sensing her mother had discovered something of interest.

"I'm sending you an article that came through my newsfeed this morning." Laura's aura was radiating yellow and orange streaks of excited energy. "I believe these twins are Maggie's children!"

"Wow! They look so much like the children in Megan's painting," commented Emma.

"What's even more interesting is that we have a name," said Bryan.

"Yes," said Laura. "Dr. Aaron Sperling."

"Bryan, did you have a chance to run the images of the kids in Megan's painting through aging progression software?" asked Emma.

"Yes, I did. The results came in this morning," said Bryan. "Sharing the screen with you now."

"Oh my God," said Emma. "The resemblance to the photos and the people depicted in the painting is incredible."

"So, what's next?" asked David, who had been quiet up till now.

"David, we've received approval to visit Alessandro Bianchi at four this afternoon, at the Collins Bay Institution in Kingston."

"Not his dad, too?" asked David, disappointed.

"Well, apparently Enrico is very ill and has refused to see us."

"Too bad. Hopefully, we can get Alessandro to shed some light on the Dark Hands of Anubis."

"Maybe it's for the best," said Emma. "I do have misgivings, David, about you seeing the Bianchis again."

"Emma, you know we've got to try. If there's any connection between our current case and the Bianchis leading us to the Dark Hands, we need to find out."

"I know," said Emma, placing her hand on his to reassure him. "I worry …"

"But we also need to find Dr. Sperling," added David. "The article indicates that Sperling operated an adoption agency north of Toronto." He glanced at his Apple watch. "It's after ten. We won't have to leave for our appointment for another few hours. This morning, I'll see what I can learn about his operation."

"Excellent," said Bryan.

He directed his next question toward Laura and asked, "Have you added any more missing girls to your list?"

"Yes, I have, although some of these girls are of different races," Laura replied. "They follow the same pattern of having disappeared, however, so I have created a supplemental list. Besides Maggie, fifteen other girls between the ages of fourteen and seventeen went missing from 2001 to 2014. All were reported to be good students and athletic. The majority come from Ontario, but there are a few missing girls from Montréal and Québec City, as well." Laura gave a heavy sigh. "It's depressing work, and I have as yet to expand my research to other provinces."

"It can't be coincidence that the disappearance of more girls stopped in 2014, the same year that Dr. Sperling also vanished," said David. "Laura, when did the last girl on your list vanish?"

Laura rummaged through her notes and said, "Tamara Stuart from North York. Disappeared September 15th, 2014. Sixteen years of age. Last seen walking home from school."

"Interesting. A few weeks after the last girl disappeared the clinic closed," said David.

"This can't be a coincidence," said Bryan.

"Well, time's ticking, I'll get started on my research," said David, already entering queries into the browser's search engine.

"Emma," Bryan added, "I'd like you to approach the twins. We need your empathic and delicate approach when making first contact with them."

"I'd be glad to do that." She thumbed through her iPhone and said, "Their next show at the Songbird Club is at seven-thirty. I'll head there this afternoon and introduce myself to the twins. If they're receptive, I'll introduce them to Megan, who is no doubt their aunt."

Nineteen

The Bianchis, Again?

WHEN DAVID AND BRYAN pulled up to the Federal Corrections Centre and entered the building, the younger man gave a shiver.

"This new for you, son?" asked Bryan with sympathy.

"Yeah, having practiced real estate law, this is something I've never had to do."

"Well, since we're on official business, we'll be asked to complete Form 0541, Register for Staff/Official Visitors."

"And then?"

"Once we've been signed in, we'll go through a metal detector, possibly an ION scanner, which can detect traces of drugs."

"So, not much different than going through airport security."

"About the same, but no nice trip ahead," Bryan grinned. "Also, a staff member may conduct a non-intrusive search or frisk search. This is all routine, and all visitors may be subject to this. Even babies."

"Well, that's reassuring," said David. "Do we sign a register, too?"

"No, the staff will complete a visitor's register before we enter the visiting area, but that info's kept private. Visitors don't have to sign the register. This protects the privacy of both visitor and inmate."

"Anything else I should know?"

"Finally, the areas we can enter are limited to the visiting room, public washroom and the approved route to the visiting area."

"Got it, thanks."

David sighed with relief after they had passed through the steps that Bryan had described. Once seated across from Alessandro, he breathed in deeply, preparing himself mentally for the upcoming discussion.

"Surprised to see you two here," said Alessandro. "Come to gloat?" Although his tone was neutral, overtones of his vicious nature lingered below the thin surface of civility.

"No, not to gloat," said Bryan. "But am I happy you and your father are right where you belong? Here in jail? Of course I am."

To steer the conversation back toward the reason for their visit, David said, "You had dealings with the Dark Hands of Anubis. What can you tell us about them?"

"You serious?" The nearby guard lifted his head toward them when he heard Alessandro's raised voice. "I'm outta here!" His lips were pressed together in a cruel line. "Guard!"

As the guard advanced toward the prisoner, David said, "Please, wait. At least hear us out."

"The pretty boy's so polite," jeered Alessandro. He shook his head at the guard, who retreated to the far wall. "Alright, lay it on me. What do you want?"

"Jazzie Bakker. Your dad hired her. She worked for the Dark Hands. How do we track them down?"

"You have a death wish?" jeered Alessandro.

"Look, we know your dad's very ill. Not doing well. We can arrange better living conditions for him," said Bryan. "If—"

"—you're willing to tell us what you know about this group," interrupted David.

"My dad's got the big C. He's in the hospital ward – not doing too good. It's a matter of weeks."

David watched in amazement at the transformation from tough guy to sentimental son, worried about his father. *We need to exploit this.*

"Fine, I'll talk. But first you get my dad released into a halfway house on compassionate grounds, so he can get cancer treatments." His expression hardened. "Once I know he's getting the care he deserves, I'll talk."

"It doesn't work like that," said Bryan. "Talk now, then we'll arrange for the treatments for your father and better living conditions."

The two men stared at each other, giving David pause to wonder if their visit today was going to be a waste of time.

"This is getting us nowhere," said Bryan. "Let's go, David."

David started in surprise. Alessandro actually blinked. "No, wait, don't go." His eyes softened. "You promise to do what you can to help my dad?"

"Yes, I give you, my word. But you know there are no guarantees."

"Don't leave. I'll talk."

"What can you tell us?" pressed David.

"Dark Hands of Anubis is an international cabal like no other," Alessandro said. "They're involved in espionage, assassination, high-level wet work, the destabilization of governments, prostitution and slavery rings, and unorthodox adoptions."

"You mean baby rings?" David asked, keeping his voice neutral.

"Yeah. That's exactly what I mean."

"That's sick," David muttered.

"Maybe." Alessandro shrugged, the gesture dismissive. "But very lucrative. Even members of our family used their services."

"How so?" Bryan asked.

"Relatives of ours, Franco and Bianca Shapiro, adopted two kids through the Dark Hands of Anubis." His expression darkened. "It was a hell of a thing. One of our rival gangs torched their house. Killed the whole family. Even Tammy and Charlie. Cute kids." His jaw tightened. "My father made sure their killers didn't live long."

David leaned forward. "Tell us more about this adoption ring."

"One of their subsidiary businesses specializes in adoptions. They abduct young women and force them into having children against their will. It's worth a lot of money, and they're made to order babies. Whatever genetics, intelligence and physical characteristics the prospective parents want, Dark Hands of Anubis can provide."

"How does it work?" asked Bryan. "What steps did the Shapiros take to adopt these kids?"

"Bianca, the wife, was desperate for kids but couldn't have them. My dad got her and Franco in touch with Dr. Sperling. He's the one who ran the baby ring and adoption clinic. All Franco had to do was supply the sperm. Bragged for days about what a great lay that girl was. Better than his wife. You know that expression *Happy wife, happy life*? That was no problem for good ol' Franco." Alessandro's face twisted into a perverse smile.

David felt sick listening to this twisted justification of the rape of a young girl to keep a wife content. He inhaled deeply to calm himself.

"Any idea where Dr. Sperling is now?" asked Bryan.

"Last I heard he disappeared in 2014. There was trouble at the compound where he held the girls, and he had to leave in a hurry. Heard he went to British Columbia. Started up shop there."

"Any idea where the compounds were located?" asked David, his composure regained.

"Yep, I sure do. I'll give you a hint about the Ontario location."

"Where?" prompted Bryan, irritated.

"My dad and I got him some land north of New Elgan."

"Address? And what about the BC compound?"

"Nah, I gotta leave some of the work for you two. How about you get going on helping my dad out, first?" The sneer was back. "Come back and see me when you've kept your promise." He motioned for the guard that the interview was over. "You know where to find me."

***

Back in the car, David gripped the steering wheel tightly, his knuckles white. "You know, I'd feel better if you drove."

"Sure, son."

After the men had exchanged seats, David asked, "What are the odds we can keep the promise we made?" He gave Bryan a worried look.

"Modest, at best. There's a huge overload of older individuals in federal custody who are sick and dying. In terms of personal safety and dignity, they are not receiving the care they need. Alessandro's fear about his dad's living conditions is legitimate. The problem is that there are few community alternatives for this vulnerable segment of the prison population."

Bryan pinched his fingers on each side of the bridge of his nose. "Finding a halfway house will be easier said than done."

"Are any of us in danger, if we can't keep our promise?"

"No, I doubt it. The Bianchi organization is pretty much dismantled."

"I wasn't able to find out much about Dr. Sperling before we headed out today. I can confirm that he practiced here in Ontario but it looks like he moved to British Columbia ten years ago. Around the time of Maggie's death."

David reached for his iPad and quickly established a hotspot connection with the car's wifi system. He logged into OnLand, the Ontario Land

Registration System, an online resource for land and property ownership records.

"Looks like he still owns a farm fifty kilometers north of New Elgan," said David.

"With almost a two-hour drive ahead of us, today's shot, but how about we head there tomorrow?" suggested Bryan.

"Sounds good. Let's call Emma and Laura to give them an update and see how their day has been going," said David, making the call.

"Hi David and Bryan," said Laura. "How did things go with Alessandro Bianchi?"

"Great. We made progress today. Is Emma there, too? We'd like to fill you in."

"No, Emma already left about an hour ago," said Laura. "She's gone to the Songbird Club to meet the twins."

Twenty

Meeting the Twins

EMMA THANKED THE Uber driver and admired the façade of the Songbird Club. She'd googled the club and had learned that the theatre dated back to 1914 and was originally a vaudeville theatre. In the late 1950s, it had been converted to a cinema and later still served as a department store warehouse. A group supporting the arts wanted to bring the old building back to its glory days of musical theatre, comedy routines, opera and live band performances. Over the last ten years, it had brought back a vibrancy and sense of community to the area and had helped launch the career of many people in the performing arts.

Emma's eyes adjusted to the dimly lit room and noticed a man sitting by the front door.

"Can I help you?" he said in a deep baritone that held the hint of an Irish brogue. "The show doesn't start for another hour."

"Sorry, but I'm not here for the show." She noted the flash of disappointment on the man's face, opened her phone and showed him the post about the twins. "I was looking for Benjamin Manning?"

"And you are?" asked the man.

"Where are my manners? I'm Emma Jackson," she said, stretching out her hand to shake his. "I'm with Jackson, Grant & Harris Investigations. Here's my card. Is Mr. Manning in?" she asked again,

A grin widened across the man's face. "At your service."

"Nice to meet you," said Emma.

"So, are you here about what I posted in the Toronto Times?" asked Ben. He gave her a piercing stare. "Have you any news about Dr. Sperling?"

"No, I'm afraid not, but I do have news."

"Go on, then."

"My team and I have reason to believe that we have located Sandra and Cheryl's aunt."

Ben rubbed his chin with his thumb and index finger. "So, if you've found the aunt, what about the lasses' birth mother?"

Ben caught her sad expression and answered his own question before she could reply. "It's that way is it? The mother's gone?"

"I'm afraid so."

"Well, the girls are backstage. It's been a few days since they met but they're already inseparable. Two peas in a pod, and as cute, they are."

His face broadened into another huge grin, "Come with me, now. Let me introduce you."

Emma followed him down into the main theatre area, which was arranged with small café tables, each surrounded by three to four metal chairs, before ascending the steps to the left side of the stage. "Sandra, Cheryl, there's someone here to meet you."

Emma gasped in astonishment when she saw the two girls standing beside each other. In person, the girls were even more remarkable and closely resembled Megan.

Spirit Anna spoke in her mind, *Yes, it's them. These are Maggie's kids.* Before Emma could reply, her auditory senses were overloaded by another voice. It was Maggie. *You've found them!*

Emma staggered from the emotional backwash coming from Maggie and nearly lost her balance. A strong arm encircled her waist and guided her toward a stool.

"There, there, we have a wee fáidhbhean on our hands, do we not? I see you have the sight, lass."

Emma looked at him in bewilderment. "Fáidhb—?"

"A wisewoman. I have a bit of the sight, myself," he said. "It's time you call your friend, Megan." Quickly recovering from the dizzy spell, Emma shook her head in surprise. *She hadn't mentioned Megan's name, had she?* She pulled out her phone, then tapped out a message to Megan.

<When do you get off work today?

<<Soon.

<Care to take in a show? Starts at seven-thirty.

<<Why not?

<Great. Meet me at the Songbird Club. Sending you the address now.

<<KK. Got it.

<Come early. I have some friends I'd like you to meet.

"This here's Emma Jackson," said Ben. "She's got news for you, girls."

"Hi, I'm pleased to meet you," she said with warmth.

Emma placed her phone back in her pocket and surveyed the two young women. "Amazing. Except for your hairstyles you really are identical in every way. Which one of you is Cheryl? And which one is Sandra?"

The girl with spiked hair stepped forward. "I'm Sandra, and this is my sister Cheryl." Her expression was fierce and protective, her question to the point: "What news have you got for us?"

"I'm with Jackson, Grant & Harris Investigations. We work on cold cases, and we believe we have found your aunt. Your mother's name was Margaret Stacey, and her younger sibling is Megan Stacey."

***

Emma's phone vibrated in her pocket.

"Would you excuse me? I've got to take this," she said, heading down the stairs from the stage and walking toward the front doors.

"It's lucky I answered," Emma said. "I'm with the twins now."

David felt that familiar warmth wrapping around his heart at the sound of her voice coming through the car's hand-free calling feature.

"I've asked Megan to join me so they can meet them. You won't believe the family resemblance. It's crazy." She hesitated, "You'll be on your own for dinner tonight."

"Thanks for the heads-up. We've got lots to tell you," replied David. "I've got Laura on a conference call, so she can participate."

"Hey, Mom," said Emma.

"Hi, Emma," said Laura.

"So, stop with the suspense. How did things go with Alessandro Bianchi?" prodded Laura.

"We made progress today," said Bryan. "Enrico is dying, and in exchange for making his father's last days more comfortable, Alessandro talked."

"There is a direct connection between the Dark Hands of Anubis and Dr. Sperling," said David, unable to contain his excitement. "Dark Hands is the mastermind of many illegal operations internationally. Dr. Sperling oversaw the Ontario operation until it shut down in October, 2014."

"From there, it's believed he started a new operation in British Columbia," added Bryan.

"That makes sense," said Laura. "Starting in November, 2014, girls between the ages of fourteen and seventeen disappeared in British Columbia. Like in Ontario and Québec, all different ethnic backgrounds, but all sharing several commonalities: attractive, smart and athletic."

"I'm surprised Alessandro gave you as much information as he did," commented Laura.

"Well, yes and no. In a clumsy attempt to bargain, he didn't reveal the locations of the two compounds," said Bryan.

"But, when I checked OnLand, I learned there is a twenty-five-acre property roughly fifty kilometers north of New Elgan that's still in Dr. Sperling's name," David said. "We'd like to head out there tomorrow morning and check it out."

"If all goes well, I wanted to bring the twins to the office tomorrow morning for you to meet them," Emma said. "But I'd like to come with you and see the property, too. Can you postpone your trip there till tomorrow afternoon? Spirit Anna is adamant I join you."

"Sure, we can do that," said Bryan.

"What about the BC compound?" asked Laura.

"No luck there, but if we can provide some comfort for Enrico, not that he deserves it—"

"We can get the BC location, too," said Emma, she paused. "What was it like seeing that creep again?"

"Not good, Emma, but what choice did we have?" replied David.

"Laura, we're still about an hour away from New Elgan. Why don't you and Bryan stay over at our place tonight? Emma has some homemade lasagna in the freezer I can defrost," said David.

"We'd love to. I'll make a Caesar salad," added Laura.

"Super. See you soon," said David.

Twenty-One

The Baby Ring

THE FOLLOWING DAY Megan was still shell-shocked. Last night, their life had been completely upended. The renovations for the offices Jackson, Grant & Harris Investigations had been recently completed, and Emma had invited Megan to sit on the comfortable couch that had been placed in the corner of her office. "Might as well relax while we wait for our meeting with the twins," said Emma.

Glancing at their Apple watch, Megan said, "What time should we expect them?"

"Should be another ten minutes before the twins arrive," said Emma. "David stepped out to get some coffee and donuts, and Bryan and Laura should be here any minute."

"I'm sorry if I freaked out last night," said Megan.

"No, Megan, I'm the one who should be sorry." Emma looked at them with apologetic eyes, "I didn't know how else to tell you. I should have handled things better."

"It's okay. I'm overwhelmed. I have two nieces. They're beautiful." Their eyes misted with pride. "Did you see those two perform? It's like they were one person."

"I know. Their psychic energy is nearly identical. I've never encountered anything like it!"

"It's remarkable. They seem so in tune with each other."

"Did you ever hear of the concept of a 'twin flame?'" asked Emma.

89

"No, can't say that I have."

"It's a highly spiritual concept bordering on the paranormal. Twin flames are believed to be connected psychically. They can reach out to one another when something is wrong."

"That's interesting," said Megan. "So, you think this is what Cheryl and Sandra have?"

"Yes, I believe so."

"You two look serious," said David poking his head in. "I'll take these to the boardroom." He gestured toward the tray laden with take-out coffee he was carrying and the bag containing donuts slung over his shoulder.

Megan jumped up and said, "Let me give you a hand. I see you got takeout from Café Mokka." Their voice was warm with approval.

"Best coffee shop in town, and we know the barista personally," said David, grinning.

Megan flushed, "Come on guys, cut it out."

***

Bryan checked his watch. "When did you say Cheryl and Sandra would be here?"

"They should have arrived ten minutes ago. Let me check their ETA with them," replied Emma. A few minutes later, Emma's phone pinged. "Ben texted back. They finished parking. They'll be right up."

Trevor, the young lawyer and occasional office assistant, tapped on the boardroom door and announced, "Your appointment has arrived. Shall I show them in?"

"Thanks, Trevor. Yes, please," replied David.

Once settled in, Ben said, "Sorry for our tardiness. The twins were nervous and couldn't decide what to wear. Had me waiting downstairs for half an hour."

In unison, the twins rolled their eyes and said, "Ben!"

"Kids," said Laura, smiling and looking at her daughter. "You used to be like that when you were a teenager."

Emma turned bright red and said, "Really, Mom?"

Although bemused by the interfamilial exchanges, Bryan kept a straight face and said, "Introductions are in order. My name is Bryan Grant. I'm a recently retired police officer. Meet my partners." He gestured toward his wife, and said, "This is Laura, who handles our admin, and over there is David. He is our lawyer. You've already met Emma, who is our resident psychic."

The twins' eyes rounded with surprise and mouthed the word, "Psychic?"

"Together we run Jackson, Grant & Harris Investigations. We work on a consultant basis with the New Elgan Police Service to help solve cold cases."

"We have reason to believe that your mother was Margaret Stacey. She was kidnapped at the tender age of sixteen and held against her will in a cult-like compound with other girls her age. Their sole purpose was to breed."

"Like a baby ring?" asked Cheryl, her voice unsteady.

"Yes, something like that," said Bryan.

"This is some weird shit," retorted Sandra.

"Really, how do you know all this?" asked Cheryl.

"Now girls, let the man finish," said Ben. "There are more things in heaven and earth, Horatio, than are dreamt of in your philosophy," he added.

"Hamlet," said David.

"What I mean to say, girls, is that there are many strange things in this life. Best to keep an open mind," said Ben.

"We use a combination of messages from souls in the afterlife coupled with good old-fashioned police work to solve cases," said Bryan.

"In your mother's case, Maggie contacted me numerous times, during vivid dreams and during a séance," added Emma. "Her soul is troubled, and her main objective is to find all your siblings and reunite all of you with your Aunt Megan."

Cheryl stammered, "All our siblings?"

"Yes, we think there are five of you in total." Emma stood up, grabbed a picture that had been leaning face first to the wall and brought it back to the table. "I'm not the only one your mother Maggie has been reaching out to. In a dream, she contacted your aunt."

Emma turned the painting around. Both teenagers gasped in surprise.

"Aunt Megan, those kids look like us," said Sandra.

"Is that our mom? She's so pretty," said Cheryl. "You paint really well."

Megan smiled with delight at their niece's comment. "Thanks."

"There really are five of us," said Sandra, her voice full of awe.

"We look much younger there. How old would that baby be now?" asked Cheryl.

Emma tilted her head to one side. "Spirit Anna says your mom died in childbirth having this fifth baby. She's about ten years old now."

"Spirit Anna?" said the twins in unison.

"She's her Spirit Guide," whispered David.

The sisters' eyes grew even wider. "Oh."

"So, we're right – there are more of us," said Cheryl, turning to her twin sister. "We've gotta find them."

David cleared his throat, "You should know that two of your siblings did pass on." He pulled the painting forward and pointed at the little boy and girl pulling at Maggie's dress. "Charlie and Tammy passed away in a house fire."

"Oh," said Cheryl, her eyes welling up. "So, it's the two of us and the baby?"

"What's her name?" asked Sandra.

"Simone."

"You gotta help us!" said Cheryl. "Find our little sister!"

"That's why we're meeting," said Bryan. "To apprehend and prosecute the people responsible for kidnapping your mother and other young women her age, and to locate Maggie's children. We've found you. Now, we need to locate your baby sister."

Twenty-Two

She's Too Strong

WAVES OF SORROW emanated from Maggie to the point of almost stifling Emma.

"Oh, no," moaned Emma. "She's too strong."

"Spirit Anna, help me!" Emma's features began to change, her auburn hair turned lighter, and her normally green eyes shimmered blue.

It took a few moments before Maggie spoke. Her eyebrows were pushed together into a deep frown. "Yes, there are five."

"Are we speaking with Maggie?" asked Laura. "I thought we'd made some ground rules. You were not to take over Emma's body without her permission."

"My grief is too strong."

"Say your piece, then leave," Laura said bluntly.

"Two of my children, eighteen months apart, were adopted together. Charlie and Tammy Shapiro. Find them and the baby, my little Simone!"

"I am so sorry, Maggie, but Charlie and Tammy passed away," Laura said in a gentle tone. "We're still looking for Simone. You already know we found Cheryl and Sandra."

"You have failed me!" Maggie became increasingly agitated. "This can't be!" The boardroom table started shaking and it became very cold and windy in the room.

"Enough!" shouted Laura. "Spirit be gone!"

As if she were boneless, Emma slumped forward, before her forehead could hit the table, David gently pulled her back. He picked her up and took her to her office and placed her on the couch. He put a pillow under her head, then grabbed a blanket and covered her. He pulled the blinds down and shut the door.

When David returned to the boardroom, Ben asked, "Is she going to be okay?"

"She should be, although this is the worst episode I have ever seen," said David. "She needs to rest. I'll check in on her in a while."

Cheryl started to sob. "This is terrible. We didn't even know we had a brother and another sister. And they're dead!"

Sandra placed a protective arm around Cheryl. "How do we find Simone?" she asked, trying to be brave for her sister.

"Without a last name, that's going to be tough," replied David.

"But not impossible," said Laura, her voice gentle and reassuring. "We'll find a way."

"For now, let's concentrate on what we can do," said Bryan. "Emma told me that you had a DNA test done."

"Yes, we did," said Sandra. "We're definitely identical twins."

"By chance, did you bring the report?"

"Yes, we've got it here. Emma said you might want it." Sandra handed it over to him." He turned to Laura and asked, "Can you make a copy for us, please?"

"Of course."

"Since Maggie was never found, her DNA is not on record." Bryan turned to Megan and asked, "Megan, would you and your dad be willing to undergo a DNA test?"

"I can't speak for him, but I'd be happy to do so."

"Good. We need to establish familial DNA, and you never know, Simone might be looking for you one day ..."

"And if we're registered with an ancestry DNA database, we might find each other!" chorused the twins.

"Exactly."

Cheryl's expression grew darker, "But that could take time. If she's only ten—"

"—we could be waiting a long time," said Sandra, completing her sister's sentence.

***

Emma opened her eyes and listened to the murmur of voices coming from the boardroom. How long had she been out? She winced at the bright slices of sunshine piercing through the blinds. *What time is it?* She pulled the microfiber blanket higher so it rested above her chin and luxuriated in its softness against her cheeks. Eyes finally adjusting to the dimness, she got up and opened the blinds. She noticed David had left her Movado watch on her desk. It was a little after noon-hour. *The compound!* She thought with a start. *I hope they waited for me!*

She opened her office door and headed to the restroom, where she washed her face and combed her hair. Unlike many of her friends, Emma was a minimalist when it came to makeup. She enjoyed a clear complexion and was fortunate to have had pimples rarely as a teenager. She touched up her eyes with some makeup and applied rose-colored lipstick. *There. Done.*

She joined the others in the boardroom and said, "I see Ben and the twins have left."

"Yes, they headed out a little while ago. They're doing another show tonight," David said.

"Are you feeling better?" her mother asked.

"Yes, much better."

"Em, you must be hungry," David said.

Emma smiled at him and said, "Starving."

"We got takeout from Eggplant Paradise. We saved a veggie wrap for you." David pulled out a chair and said, "Have a seat." He put her wrap on a paper plate and placed it in front of her. "Now, eat."

"Thanks, I am starving." After a few mouthfuls, Emma became aware everyone was staring. "Guys, is there something on my face?"

"No, honey, we're worried about you," said Laura. "Maggie is far too powerful."

"I know. Spirit Anna is repeatedly pushed out—"

"Emma, we're very concerned about this," said Bryan.

"I don't intend to stop!" Emma's voice was strident. "Look at the progress we've made."

"Yes, but at what cost to you?" asked David, his face was haggard with anguish. "I can't lose you."

"Look, we agreed we'd leave this decision up to me," her inflection was cranky.

"But Em, we also said we'd tell you if we thought you were in danger and you said you'd stop if we asked you." David rubbed the back of his neck, exasperated. "You can be so stubborn."

"Both my asset and my charm. It's gotten me through life so far," Emma retorted.

"Emma, we're not asking you to stop," said Laura. "It's been months since you have gone to a spiritual meeting with me. Everyone in the group has been asking about you."

"It's been busy, Mom."

"Yes, it has. When Spirit Anna passed away suddenly, your training was interrupted. We think you should consider rejoining the group. We need to find a way for you to effectively create a wall to block Maggie from taking over your body."

"You're right," said Emma. "Her spirit is troubled, but what I don't get is why Spirit Anna isn't helping me block her." She worried away at the cuticle of her right thumb with the fingernail of her index finger. "The situation is making me quite anxious."

"Do you remember Mona from the group in Toronto?" asked Laura.

"Sure I do," said Emma.

"She recently moved to the New Elgan area and has been coming to the meetings. She's a powerful psychic."

"And you think she can help me."

"I know she can."

"But Mom, it's you that I trust. I don't know her."

"My abilities are not strong enough. You need to work with someone who can keep you safe." Laura shook her head sadly and said, "What if I can't pull you out of the next episode? What, then?"

Emma covered her hand over that of her mother's. "I hear you. I'll come to the next meeting."

Her jaw was set with a determination familiar to her family, her green eyes blazing. "Don't we have a compound to visit?"

Twenty-Three

The Ontario Compound

DAVID PULLED OVER to the side of the dirt road and asked, "Is it much further?"

"It shouldn't be, except the rural route numbers are in the 4000s now," said Emma, perplexed. "I think you need to turn around. 2319 must be to the south of us."

"Something must be wrong with the information Google has on file," said David, making a three-point turn and heading back south.

"This problem is not unheard of. The problem is with the GPS lock," said Bryan.

"GPS lock?" asked Emma.

"Whenever a GPS receiver can 'see' four or more satellites, it can calculate its position. This is known as a lock or a fix."

"So, a satellite cannot always see the terrain?" asked Emma. "I thought this was infallible."

"Most of the time it is. The receivers in our phones and GPS units need to be in a clear position to be 'seen' by satellites in order for coordinates to be triangulated successfully. There are a lot of trees here and that can 'confuse' the satellites," said Bryan. "Even heavy cloud cover can be a factor. And some GPS receivers are better than others."

"Since I'm driving, Emma and Bryan please keep your eyes peeled on the signs and hopefully we won't miss the entrance this time," said David.

"Oh no," said Emma with dismay. "The numbers are below 2319. We've gone too far south this time. David, you need to turn around again."

"Em, this is getting ridiculous."

David pulled over, parked on the graveled berm and said, "You know what? Let's walk. It's an old property and abandoned. Maybe the sign is down."

"Good thinking," said Bryan, getting out of the car. "I don't mind stretching my legs." He placed his hands at the hollow of his back and massaged, attempting to alleviate the stiffness.

"Well, we can't be too far off," said Emma, gesturing toward the left. "The sign over there says 2271."

David took the lead and said, "Let's get going. It'll be on the left." Emma and Bryan exchanged surprised looks before they followed.

"He's a bit ticked," commented Bryan.

"He'll be fine," said Emma.

"Found it!" David called out. Emma and Bryan hurried over and saw him yanking away at tall grasses and vegetation obscuring an old laneway. "Look," he said, pointing at an old metal sign that was bent at the base. He wiped his hand against the surface of the metal sign, brushing away dirt and mud until he exposed white lettering embossed on a green background. "As I suspected. 2319."

"Great work," said Bryan.

"Umm," said Emma, looking down at her new boots. "Do you think there are snakes in the tall grass? Can we drive in, do you think?"

"Nope, afraid not," said David. "There's a huge tree across the drive."

"Shall we?" asked Bryan, glancing at his watch. "We don't want to waste what daylight is left."

Approaching the massive tree, David noticed some fallen tree limbs strewn about and chose a relatively straight branch, hefted it in his hand, grinned sheepishly and said, "It's something, at least."

"I'm not sure about this," said Emma.

"This driveway must be six hundred feet long," said Bryan.

"At least," replied David.

"Remind me to wear more comfortable footwear the next time we go hiking," said Emma. "These boots still need breaking in."

David stopped abruptly, causing Emma to bump into him. She halted in her tracks. "Geez, David! Watch it!"

"Emma, would you cut it out?" asked Bryan. "You've been bickering non-stop."

"Sorry, Bryan. Lately, I've been out of sorts—"

"I know you're under a lot of stress but we're all doing our best here—"

"Em, take a look," said David, interrupting them both.

"Oh, my—?" For once Emma was speechless.

The tree lined laneway yielded to a large open area, the driveway looping around to what must have been the main building. A porte-cochere, leading to the main entrance, was still in relatively sound condition, and protected visitors from the elements. A sign on the front of the covered portico read, *Welcome to Sperling Adoption and Fertility Clinic: Reception.*

On each side of the building were twenty-foot-high chain-link fences topped with barbed wire.

Emma approached the fence and peered through to see several buildings of the former complex, in various states of disrepair. Some remained intact, but the majority were dilapidated structures with walls that had fallen into each other. Moss and vines intertwined stone foundations, telegraphing a level of decay which went beyond normal decline, and instead, bordered on a residual evil that clung to the atmosphere, like stink bugs entrenched in tight corners. A door constructed of the same chain-link fence, positioned to the right of the building, was padlocked. A sign attached with zip ties indicated, *Staff Only Beyond this Point.* Like many cult compounds, there was an area for the public to visit and private areas reserved for members of the community.

Expecting resistance, Emma yanked at the padlock and was surprised when the rusted-out lock disintegrated in her hands. Wide-eyed, she turned to Bryan and David and said, "I know we should explore the entire compound, but something is pulling me to this area first."

David nodded, "We'll follow your lead, but let's stay close."

"Agreed," said Bryan, shuddering. "Even I can feel the bad juju here."

She gave the gate a push and it creaked open with a groan. She steeled her shoulders and entered the forbidden part of the complex. As if guided by an inner compass, she walked without hesitation toward a building annexed to the main building. "In here," she said.

"Em, is it safe?" asked David, massaging the back of his neck with his left hand. "Got a damn tension headache coming on."

Emma didn't reply or look back, but continued walking toward a room filled with rusty hospital beds, some with remnants of mattresses still in place. "This was the maternity ward."

Without warning, she gasped and bent over in pain. "Oh, my God. Not again," she moaned.

David ran over and said, "Em, what is it?"

Emma's face was twisted: an internal battle raging between reason and terror. A look of resolve flitted behind her eyes and her voice became firm. "No, Maggie, you may not speak through me, but you may show me," she said, all remaining traces of fear and anguish dissipating.

Emma took a deep breath and said, "Excellent. See how much more we can accomplish when you calm down?"

She closed her eyes. "Go ahead, Maggie. I'm listening."

"Let's give Emma and Maggie some privacy." Bryan pulled at David's arm and added, "We can still keep an eye on her from here."

After what seemed an impossible amount of time, Emma reopened her eyes. "Maggie died here." She indicated a rusted-out bed in the corner of the room.

"She really did live here for ten years after her disappearance?" asked Bryan.

She traced her fingers over the deteriorating mattress and nodded.

"Why didn't she leave?" David asked.

"She was afraid. They threatened to hurt her family," Emma said.

"Ironic. The threat was enough. Her value was not in a ransom, but in how many children she bore," said Bryan. Every line in his face was etched in sadness.

"Surely, outside staff members would have objected to these deplorable conditions," said David, indignant.

"There would have been no tolerance for questions," said Emma. "All workers here were coerced by threats or greed, ensuring unquestioning loyalty to Dr. Sperling."

Emma tilted her head to the side, listening to Maggie. "Ah, I'm so sorry—but happy for you, too."

She looked at both Bryan and David and smiled with wonder. "Her last child, Simone?"

"Yes?" asked Bryan.

"Simone was a love child. Maggie fell in love with a male nurse. His name was Evan Masters."

***

"Maggie says there's more for us to see." Emma tilted her head to one side. "Follow me."

She strode by the rusted beds in the maternity ward and motioned toward an empty area. "This is where the baby ward was located."

"Nothing left here," commented Bryan.

"I sense everyone left in a hurry."

"But why?" asked David.

"I think it has something to do with Maggie's death. Not sure. I'm not getting a clear reading on that." She frowned. "I'm getting images of the new compound in BC. But nothing concrete."

She inclined her head again. "Let's go outside."

She pushed open the door, and walked briskly toward a series of dilapidated buildings, then slipped in behind the largest.

David and Bryan broke into a run to keep up with Emma's rapid pace.

"Emma, wait up!" yelled David, displeased she was no longer in his sight. David rounded the corner and was surprised to find her sitting on the ground, weeping.

"This is where you'll find Maggie's remains and some of the other girls. I think this was a crematorium."

"Maybe," said Bryan. "But it looks like there was an intense explosion here, as well."

"I think so, too. Maggie is showing me images of intense heat."

"Bryan, how can you tell?" asked David.

Bryan pointed toward the ground, and said, "Look at the melted metal. Those would have been girders."

"What happened here?" wondered David. "Can a crematorium burn to the ground on its own?"

"Highly doubtful. This would have been deliberate," replied Bryan.

"Maggie told you there were more girls that died here?" asked David.

Emma nodded. "Maggie is saying yes. The remains of Amanda and Victoria are here, too."

Bryan pulled his cell phone out of his pocket and made a call to the New Elgan Police Service. "Can you connect me with Staff Inspector Carlo Carducci?" After a short pause, he said, "Hey, Carlo. It's Bryan. We're up at the Sperling property. We've found something. You're going to need a forensic anthropologist."

"Will they be able to find any remains?" asked Emma, her forehead furrowed with worry.

"It's hard to say but they should look," replied Bryan.

"Can they actually get any DNA samples from ashes?" asked Emma.

"No, but they can, potentially, from bones and teeth," said Bryan.

"Another question for you," said David. "Would the fire department not have investigated a fire or explosion of this magnitude?"

"Maybe, maybe not," replied Bryan, "It's really remote here. You know that expression?"

David's eyes lit up. "If a tree falls in the forest and there's no one around to hear it, does it make a sound?"

"From the philosopher George Berkeley," said Bryan.

Twenty-Four

Evan Masters

2014

EVAN COULDN'T TAKE it anymore. He had been recruited by Dr. Aaron Sperling right out of nursing school. The wages were irresistible: more than he could make at any of the local hospitals in the New Elgan area. Working at the state-of-the-art clinic had seemed like a great opportunity for advancement, and he eagerly embraced the strict regimen.

One afternoon, early on in his employment at the Sperling Adoption and Fertility Clinic, Evan was invited to Dr. Sperling's office.

"Have a seat," Dr. Sperling said, offering him a cognac.

"How do you like working here?"

"Great, but what's with all the rigorous round-the-clock security?"

The doctor replied, "Our clients come from prestigious homes and we need to protect their privacy, and that of their families. We take care of their 'wayward' daughters until their pregnancies come to full term, then adopt the babies out to loving parents. We obtain a positive outcome for everyone involved."

"The girls seem alone. Never any visitors."

"All part of providing the ultimate discretion. Besides, the girls have each other to befriend."

"Still, if any of them were my sister, I'd want to see them. Make sure they were safe."

"Rest assured. It's for the best."

"But not all the young women here were in the family way when they arrived," said Evan. "Why are they here?"

"They are under contract with us." Dr. Sperling's eyes narrowed. "By offering invitro and artificial insemination services to our wealthier clients who cannot conceive their own children, we make our clients very happy ... and we make money. And so do the girls. As do you."

That was certainly true. The income was great, and even though he had his doubts, Evan refused to believe that anything untoward was going on.

The doctor refilled Evan's glass and his own, then raised it in salutation and said, "We fulfill an important service here at our facility."

***

When the same girls came in and out of pregnancy often, there were no longer any illusions. Evan understood the evil nature of the operation was to permanently enslave the girls until they were no longer of any use. By the time he was privy to the shocking reality of the operation, there was no way out. And then he met Maggie. He swallowed back the rising bile, nearly retching from the bitter taste.

My poor, beautiful Maggie.

If that jealous Samantha had not betrayed them. Now, he was a prisoner along with the rest of the young women held captive at the compound. He rezipped the body bag holding the shell of the woman he'd loved desperately, closed the lid of the container and prepared her body for 'retort', also known as the cremation chamber. The cremation process would take several hours, where the powerful furnace would raise the interior temperature to above 1400 degrees Fahrenheit. At the end, all traces of Maggie would have disappeared. Maggie would be gone, save for a few teeth and bone fragments.

Evan imagined the furnace erasing his existence, too: a white heat so intense, so all-encompassing that it would eradicate the loss, the sorrow and the desolate prospect of a life without Maggie.

Amid this misery, another white heat overcame him, reminding him that although he could not protect Maggie, he still had one other helpless life for which he was responsible. *Simone.* He would protect her ... or else die trying.

***

Evan's pager beeped.

"Is it done?" asked Dr. Sperling.

"Yes, the body should be fully cremated in another two hours." He hated to refer to Maggie as a body. *She had been my everything.* A fire burned in his belly, as hot as the one burning within the cremation chamber. *I must keep my deep hatred in check before it consumes me.*

"Excellent. Time to evac the compound."

"Evacuation, sir?" asked Evan, trying to keep his emotions under control.

"Orders from above. The BC Compound is ready, and the top brass believe we've overstayed our welcome in Ontario. Too many questions being asked about the missing girls."

"I wasn't counting on moving out of province," said Evan.

"I'd like you to oversee the evacuation of the children in the ward."

"Why me?" His heart began to beat a discordant rhythm.

"Orderlies will be there to help you load the ones not yet adopted into the van."

"What of the children already adopted?"

"Not that it's any of your concern, but I have dispatched drivers to take them to their new parents."

"And the newborn?" Fear clutched at Evan's heart that Simone would already be lost to him.

"The baby stays with us. For the time being. Hurry now. There's a private plane waiting for us. We're headed to the compound in British Columbia." Sperling's voice was icy. "Don't try anything stupid, Evan. We know the baby is yours."

Evan heaved a sigh, relieved he'd be going with the kids. That meant he could remain near Simone. He'd need to act fast when the opportunity arose to spirit his baby daughter away from all this madness.

***

Dr. Sperling turned toward the guard and said, "Keep an eye on Evan. Make sure he doesn't try to escape."

"Yes, sir."

"As long as we have control of the baby, with the threat of adoption looming, we can keep Evan in check. He's an excellent nurse, and I'd hate to train another on short notice."

"He won't leave our sight, sir."

"Have you attended to the other matter?"

"Yes, sir. The explosives have been set to detonate the crematorium in two hours."

"Very good. Then let's get going."

Twenty-Five

The Compromise

DAVID AND BRYAN arrived at the Federal Corrections Centre early the next morning, announced themselves to the guard and asked for Alessandro Bianchi.

"You won't be seeing him today," he said.

"But we have an appointment that was preapproved and when we checked this morning, we were told everything was in order."

"There's been a development since then," replied the guard, shifting uneasily.

"We weren't informed," said Bryan, trying to keep his composure.

"Mr. Bianchi was attacked. He's presently in the infirmary, being checked by the prison doctor."

"Can we see him there?" asked David.

"I doubt it. Not without the warden's approval."

David gave the man a level gaze and said, "Can you please contact the warden?"

"We are here as part of an investigation into an abduction ring," said Bryan. "We would be grateful for your help." He showed a picture of Maggie. "We have reason to believe Alessandro has information that could help us find this young girl."

The guard's face softened. "I've got a kid that age," he said. "I'll call the warden." He pointed to the utilitarian chairs lining the wall. "Take a seat. You may be here awhile."

***

The warden ushered Bryan and David into his office "I apologize for the wait," he said. He was approaching his mid-fifties and wore a conservative jacket, dress pants and a clip-on necktie. His mustache was wiry grey and thick, the facial growth compensating for his bald head.

"We understand," said Bryan. "The circumstances are unique. How is Mr. Bianchi?"

"He's fine," replied the warden. "He is suffering from a mild concussion, but beyond that he's fine, He'll be returning to his cell tonight."

"Is there any chance we can still speak with him?" asked David.

"I don't see why not. I'll have him brought to the visiting area, and I will ask one of my guards to escort you there." He became pensive. "I'm aware of the request Alessandro made on behalf of his father, in exchange for information concerning the missing girls."

"What are your thoughts on this?" asked Bryan.

"Under Section 121 of the Corrections and Conditional Release Act, inmates with a life-threatening, non-curable illness can apply for release on compassionate grounds," said the warden.

"Surely terminal cancer is one of those criteria," said Bryan.

"True. However, despite Enrico's grave illness, the Parole Board of Canada considers him a flight risk. Under supervision, we've agreed that he can undergo experimental cancer treatments, but he'll be escorted to the medical centre whenever necessary and returned to prison following the treatment." He sighed heavily. "I'm not unsympathetic. You have a case to solve, but knowing Enrico's history, granting early parole and allowing him to live in a halfway house is too risky."

"We get it. We have our own history with Enrico and his son. He is likely still a very dangerous man, even on his death bed," said Bryan.

"I hope we've given you enough leverage to bargain with Alessandro," said the warden. He rose up from his chair to shake their hands. "It was good meeting you both."

***

Alessandro stared at David and Bryan with palpable malevolence. "I told you no deal if you can't get my father more comfortable living conditions."

"We've done the best we could. That's all we ever promised you," said Bryan standing his ground. "The Parole Board considers your dad a flight risk, so no halfway house."

"Then there's nothing to discuss," said Alessandro.

"Oh, but there is. We've come up with a compromise you will want to hear," said Bryan.

"They have agreed to a revolutionary cancer treatment. Your dad would be escorted to the medical facility. At the very least, it will make his last days more hopeful," said David, hiding the revulsion he felt for Alessandro and his father.

"And if that doesn't work?" asked the inmate.

"Then you can apply on his behalf for release on compassionate grounds," said Bryan.

"And if it gets really bad for your dad, he can apply for MAiD, Medical Assistance in Dying," added David. "I'll even help you with the application." *With pleasure*, thought David.

"Enough of this talk," said Bryan. "What have you got for us? Where is the BC compound?"

"Northern British Columbia."

"Can you be more specific?" asked David, irritation creeping into his tone.

"Outside Mackenzie."

"Why there?" asked Bryan.

"Remote. Few people ... fewer questions."

Twenty-Six

The Sniffles

EMMA SNIFFLED AND BLEW into the tissue. "Wish I was coming with you and Bryan."

"Honey, you heard what the doctor said," said David, concern deepening the crease between his eyes. "Besides, with that cold they'll never let you on the plane." He pulled her toward him and held her gently to his chest. "Even though those dark years of COVID are behind us, authorities remain cautious."

"I guess you're right," said Emma, her voice muffled against the cloth of his shirt. "Oh no," she moaned and grabbed another tissue and sneezed into it, "I know it's probably silly, but I feel worried."

"We'll be fine," David reassured her.

"It's just that—"

"Yes?"

"I've got a bad feeling."

"What does Spirit Anna say?"

"That's the thing. Nothing. I can't get a reading on this." She frowned. "Anna has been silent. I have this vague apprehension. MacKenzie, Northern British Columbia. I looked at the map. It's not like you're going to Vancouver. This is really remote."

"We'll be careful."

Emma watched David pick up his overnight bag and followed him out the front door and onto the wraparound porch. She pulled her unbuttoned sweater together and held it in place by wrapping her arms around her upper body.

"Text me when you land," she called out.

"Will do," David said, over his shoulder, running down the steps to the waiting Uber. She waved at David until the vehicle was out of sight, then returned inside and locked the door.

Although it was the month of May and not that chilly outside, she shivered, unsure if it was her cold or a premonition over David and Bryan's trip to British Columbia.

***

While David and Emma had made some renovations to their one hundred-and fifty-year-old Victorian home, most of it remained true to its original form.

It was in stark contrast to the avant-garde and contemporary condo that David had owned when he met Emma. A traditionalist at heart, Emma had convinced him that Anna's old home should be respected and not be gutted, as was the case with so many century-plus homes.

"It'd be tragic to lose that history. We should apply for a heritage property designation." She'd made a sly grin. "Besides, Heritage property owners, under the Ontario Heritage Act, may be eligible for grants to help conserve their home. It's good for tourism and the economy, too."

The steeply pitched roof, the ornate and decorative wooden trim, cylindrical turrets, bay windows and wraparound porch, which they'd restored to its former glory using a grant, were impressive and eye-catching.

Regarding the interior of the house, they were allowed some latitude in upgrading the home with modern conveniences. David had insisted they renovate the kitchen and the upstairs bathroom. They'd required additional permits to do so, but Emma was the first to acknowledge that the renos had been worth it.

She padded over to the modernized kitchen with its gleaming appliances, and prepared an herbal tea and walked upstairs. Sitting on the edge of the jacuzzi tub, she let the water fall over her hands until she had obtained the perfect temperature.

Once the tub had filled, she dropped her robe and stepped into the inviting water. She closed her eyes, grateful she'd conceded to this modern convenience. *A nice bath, then bed, is what I need,* she thought, as the tension in her body eased.

Twenty-Seven

The Plane Trip

DAVID'S SIX-FOOT FRAME was crammed in the centre seat of the Boeing aircraft. Bryan sat to his right, so that he could stretch his arthritic legs toward the aisle whenever the flight attendants were not looking.

Grateful for the free high-speed internet that Westjet now provided through TELUS and Starlink, David tried to ignore the annoying woman beside him by concentrating on some additional research concerning Dr. Sperling's compound in British Columbia.

He couldn't decide what had been more annoying about the woman sitting in the window seat beside him: when she had been asleep or awake. She had slept for roughly four hours of the expected five hours and five-minute trip. From time to time, her lower jaw would fall open and she'd snore, her breath the sour smell of someone who'd slept a while and was hungry.

Other times, she'd shift her body restlessly, and twice, David had to remove her head from his shoulder when it had slipped there during her slumber.

Then she woke up, smiled at him and began to talk non-stop. "This is my thirty-fourth trip to BC. I'm off to see my grandbabies. With all my WestJet rewards, the airline treats me like a VIP."

"That's nice." David had nodded politely and returned to his iPad to continue his research on Dr. Sperling, when a mobile phone was thrust in front of his face.

"Huh?" he exclaimed in surprise at the intrusion into his personal space. "Excuse me."

"Sorry, dearie."

"Perhaps you need the washroom?"

"No, dearie. I wanted to show you pics of my grandchildren."

"Um, trying to work here."

"Oh," she'd said loudly. "Sorry to bother you."

David caught the look of hurt and said, "You know what? I'd love to see the pics." He put his tablet away, checked the time on his watch, resigned to the fact that he would be hostage to the garrulous granny for the next hour. Close proximity to the older woman made him wince at her poor breath.

He dug around in his pockets and found the package of breath mints. "Would you like one?" he'd asked.

"I'd love one," she replied. "I'm hungry and that might do the trick."

She took a mint and handed him back the package.

"Keep it," David said, smiling.

"You sure?"

Before David could react, she'd pinched his cheek and said, "You're a nice young man." Eying his wedding ring, she added, "Your wife is a lucky one."

David pulled away from her. "We're lucky to have each other."

He got up from his seat and said to Bryan. "I need the can. I'll be a while."

Bryan looked up from the latest book he was reading, *Sanctity of Freedom*, an Inspector William Fox Series, and raised his eyebrows in sympathy.

Twenty-Eight

Road Trip

———

WHEN THEY DEPLANED and were no longer in earshot of 'Granny', Bryan said, "What was that all about?"

"I've no idea. Just a lonely granny on her way to see her children and grandchildren."

"Well, it was nice of you to talk with her as long as you did." Bryan playfully punched David in the arm. "Then you abandoned me. I had to hear her life story and see pics of the grandkids, also."

"Don't laugh, one of these days you might become a granddad, too," teased David.

"And I'd be as proud."

Bryan's expression became serious. "So, did you learn anything further about Dr. Sperling during the flight? You were glued to your tablet almost the whole time, until—"

"—Granny," chuckled David. "Yes, I did. I learned that he did indeed run a similar operation to the one in Ontario."

They walked into the baggage claim area. "That was fast," said David, grabbing his bag off the carousel.

"Did you discover a specific location?"

"Yeah, Alessandro didn't mislead us." He shook his head. "Emma's worried."

"A premonition?" Bryan's brow furrowed with worry.

"No, I think it's merely separation anxiety."

"That makes sense. It was tough on both of you last year, being apart from each other."

"I don't like being away from her, either, but she was too ill to come with us."

"Oh, finally. There's my bag," said Bryan. "How come these bags get separated when they're loaded at the same time?"

"Wait a sec," said David. "Let me get it for you."

"Thanks, son."

"My pleasure," replied David, easily hoisting Bryan's bag off the baggage carousel. "Let's find that car rental kiosk."

***

By the time David and Bryan were underway, it was well past five in the afternoon, but they knew they'd have at least three hours of daylight before the May sun would set. Nonetheless, with a five-hour drive planned to reach their midway point, they were anxious to get going. To avoid unnecessary stops, they'd visited a popular grocery store not far from Vancouver International Airport and stocked up on sandwiches and bottled water.

After several hours of driving, David asked, "How much further until the motel in Williams Lake?"

Bryan scanned the remote terrain. "We lost cell service some time ago." Bryan studied the road map.

"It's good you insisted on bringing a physical map," commented David. "I didn't think people used them anymore."

"Nothing like good old-fashioned low-tech," agreed Bryan. "Thank God for the CAA." Bryan was referring to the Canadian Automobile Association.

Bryan traced his finger along the line representing British Columbia Highway 97. "Probably another two hours."

"I'm grateful we decided to split the trip into two parts," said David. "No way could we have handled a ten-and-a-half-hour drive on top of that long flight. I'm looking forward to some shut-eye."

"I can drive for a bit, give you a break," offered Bryan.

"That would be great."

After David pulled over and the two had exchanged seats, Bryan said, "It's chilly. Hovering above freezing."

"No kidding. Daytime highs in Mackenzie run in the fourteen Celsius range."

"Help an old guy out here. What's that in Fahrenheit?"

David did a rough calculation in his head and said, "Not quite sixty degrees."

"In May." The older man shuddered. "For the month of May, those temperatures should be declared illegal."

"No kidding."

To keep each other alert and prevent boredom, David asked, "How about this interesting fact?"

"Fire away."

"Did you know Highway 97 is the longest continuous highway in BC? It runs 2081 kilometers along the entire length of the province."

"Interesting."

"It connects the Canada-U.S. border in Osoyoos in the south and in the north, Watson Lake in the Yukon."

"Cool. I didn't know that."

A massive, dark shape flitted across the road, looming in the car's headlights.

"Watch it, Bryan!" shouted David.

Bryan braked in time, the car idling in the middle of the road. The creature seemed to stare at them directly, and with a disdainful look disappeared into the thick brush on the opposite side of the road.

Rattled, Bryan pulled over on the verge. "My God. Did you see how big that thing was?"

"Sure did. Hitting that moose would have been like colliding with a freight train," said David.

"Looks like it was a bull," said Bryan. "A male can weigh upwards of sixteen hundred pounds. We wouldn't have stood a chance."

"Glad you stopped in time."

"How much further?" Bryan asked, the dashboard lights accentuating his drawn features.

"It's up ahead," said David pointing to the sign. "Ten more kilometers."

Twenty-Nine

Trevor McAllister

DAVID ROLLED OVER on his side and reached for Emma, then realized that she was miles away, back at home in Ontario. Adjusting to the weak morning light filtering through the motel window, he saw the outline of his father-in-law sleeping in the twin bed beside his.

He checked his Apple watch and noted it was after five in the morning. They'd agreed to leave by six in order to arrive in Mackenzie before noon hour. Noting how deeply the older man was still sleeping, David decided not to disturb him and to give him a little more time to rest.

The previous evening, when David and Bryan had expressed disappointment that coffee and the complimentary breakfast wouldn't be ready till seven in the morning, the front desk clerk had said, "Coffee's always on, but since you're leaving so early, we can prepare a couple of takeout bags for you both that we'll leave for you here at the front desk. Muffins work for you guys?"

David and Bryan had both nodded and said, "Muffins will be great."

David slipped on his jeans, pulled his sweatshirt over his head, and grabbed the room key. On his way to the motel's small breakfast nook to pick up coffees, David thought about the day ahead of them. *Hopefully, they'll finally get answers about what really happened to Maggie's children and the other missing girls.*

He was surprised to see the same clerk at the desk.

"Your shift must be over soon," David commented, while he poured two steaming cups of coffee into the paper coffee cups.

"You bet," said the clerk, glancing at his watch. "Enough time to see the kids off to school, and then it's bedtime for me." He wiped his red-rimmed eyes. "Here, before I forget: your breakfast to go." He handed the takeout bags to David.

David opened one of the bags. "These muffins look great."

"Yep, from a local bakery my wife runs."

"Thanks, again," said David. "Get some rest."

"Will do. Safe travels," said the clerk with a tired smile. "Stop by again, anytime."

***

Balancing the coffee and takeout bags, David jiggled the key into the lock and entered the room, noting that Bryan was up and the bathroom door was shut. Moments later, Bryan appeared, clean-shaven and already dressed.

"You're up," said David. "Brought us coffee and some breakfast."

"Thanks. I'm starved," said Bryan, tucking into the muffin. "This is good."

"It sure is. It rivals Café Mokka's baked goods," said David, relishing the delicious mix of blueberries and walnuts.

"It's nearly six." Bryan grabbed the car rental keys and said, "We should get going."

"Agreed. No time to waste." David scooped up the used napkins and packaging, tossed them in the wastepaper basket, slung his duffle bag over his shoulder and followed Bryan to their vehicle.

***

Outside of Prince George, Bryan said, "I need to make a pit stop. And I need more coffee, too. Anywhere decent to stop?"

David scrolled through his phone and said, "There's a Tim Horton's about a mile up on your right."

"Good call. No matter what part of the country you're in, you can always rely on Timmy's quality." Bryan parked outside the famous franchise's door.

"We've made good time," said David. "It's eight-thirty in the morning here. We should check in with Emma and Laura. It'll be almost lunch time back home."

Bryan's stomach gurgled. "Speaking of lunch, I'm hungry. My stomach's still on Ontario time. You call the gals, and I'll get the coffees. Feel like a bagel?"

"An Everything Bagel will be great."

David watched the older man enter the coffee shop, confirmed his phone was still Bluetooth connected to the car system and called Emma.

"David! How are you?" He could hear a raspiness marring her normally warm and melodic voice.

"I'm good. But, Em, are you feeling any better?"

"Yes, it sounds way worse than it is," she snuffled. "I've been drinking lots of honey and fresh lemon tea. I won't be singing ballads anytime soon," she joked.

"I've heard you sing," he teased back. "Singing is not one of your stronger traits."

"David, I'm crushed," she laughed. "It's so good to talk with you."

"Likewise."

"So, where are you?" she asked.

"Prince George. We should be in Mackenzie by noon, BC time."

"Is it beautiful?"

"Em, I wish you were with us. You would love this scenery. This is God's country. We should come here sometime on holiday, when this case is over."

"I'd love to! We could plan a real road trip," said Emma, her voice animated and excited. "BC has everything: Canada's only desert, a lush temperate rainforest, the highest peak in the Canadian Rockies and world-famous wineries."

"Yeah, definitely we've gotta explore the Okanagan Valley," said David. "You, me, a crackling fireplace and a fine bottle of Okanagan wine."

"Big, bold and red," she reminded him.

Bryan tapped on the passenger car window, "Give me a hand?"

"Hold on a sec, Em."

David got out of the car, took the coffee from Bryan and gestured for him to take the passenger seat. He walked around the front of the vehicle, opened the driver's door and got in behind the wheel. "Sorry, Em, we're changing seats. My turn to drive."

"No worries."

"Hi Emma," said Bryan. "How are you feeling, honey?"

"On the mend. I miss you guys."

"We miss you, too."

Emma cleared her throat. "We did some digging and found a picture of Dr. Sperling from his med school graduating class. Texting it to you, David."

Seconds later, David's phone pinged. "Thanks, Em."

"Is your mom around?" asked Bryan.

"She stepped out to pick up some lunch. She should be back any time."

"Oh, that's too bad that she's out," said Bryan, disappointed. "Tell her I love her, and that we'll call again when we arrive in MacKenzie."

"I'll tell her. Be safe, you two."

David started the car and said, "MacKenzie, here we come."

***

As Emma placed her cell phone on her desk, she caught a glimpse of Trevor averting his eyes, then quickly turning away from her partially closed door. *Had he been listening in?* She wondered, *and whatever for?*

Shaking off the unsettled feeling that the young lawyer had been eavesdropping, she returned to the data she and her mother were collecting on missing young women who could be connected to their current case.

***

Trevor had indeed been listening to the conversation. Having been thwarted by the investigative team's covert behavior before, he had installed bugging devices in all the offices at Jackson, Grant & Harris Investigations.

With shaking fingers, he unlocked his bottom drawer, retrieved the encrypted phone, headed to the men's washroom, entered a cubicle and hit speed dial.

"So, what have our little friend David Harris and his father-in-law been up to?" asked the man, his voice cold and distant.

"Well, as you know, he and Bryan were nosing around the old Ontario compound."

127

"That is of no concern. They couldn't possibly have found anything of use, after all these years."

"They're headed for the BC compound."

"What? When?" The expletives were colorful.

"Um, like now."

"This is not acceptable. Why am I finding this out now?"

"Well, the team has been secretive. Recently, I installed listening devices, so now I can learn more."

"Still, how did they connect the dots to the BC compound?"

"Sir, it's going to sound strange." Trevor paused, unsure how to formulate his next words without sounding unhinged.

"Go on, I'm waiting."

"Emma is supposedly a psychic, and they seem to have found a link to BC through her abilities. Also, there's the Bianchis. I overheard that Alessandro is talking in order to get his father better living conditions for his end-of-life days."

The pause was so long, and the silence so complete, Trevor wasn't sure if the man was still on the phone. "Sir? Any instructions?" He quavered.

"Yes. Send in a team to the BC compound. Tell them to evacuate the more promising inventory of young women and children. Then have them sanitize the area of less desirable stock. The bodies are to be disposed of in the crematorium."

"Yes, sir."

"Get this done asap."

"Yes, right away."

"And Trevor—"

"Yes?"

"Don't fail me again."

"No, sir, I won't."

Trevor hung up the encrypted phone, feeling guilty. *How had his life gone so completely off the rails?* David, Emma, Laura and Bryan were good to him. But even with the decent wage that David paid him, the double-digit interest rates on his student loans were staggering.

A few short months after being called to the bar, he was already corrupt. He'd pulverized his moral compass by agreeing to spy on the investigative team, in exchange for having his student debts cleared. He thought he'd feel relieved to no longer have that financial obligation resting on his shoulders, but he'd merely exchanged that debt with a burden that would never be relieved.

It was ironic that one requirement towards obtaining his law licence was to complete the Good Character Requirement. He quelled another flash of guilt threatening to over-stimulate the acid lining of his stomach. He certainly wasn't of 'good character' now.

Trevor disconnected the call, headed back to his workstation, and logged into his TOR browser to put the sinister man's orders into action.

***

Reinhard was mildly concerned by the events unfolding in Canada, and in particular, with the loose end the doctor presented.

He was confident Trevor would keep things under control. By using Trevor as an intermediary and ordering hits through the Dark Web, he was insulated from any repercussions. People like Trevor, with weak moral constitutions, could be easily coerced and better yet, replaced, if necessary, without much effort.

Thirty

The BC Compound

———————————

AFTER UNDER THREE hours of driving, Bryan said, "We're almost there." He pointed to a sign which read: *Welcome to Mackenzie: Gateway to North America's Largest Man-Made Lake. Population 3,001.*

"Pretty small place," commented David.

"All the same, they've got a recreation centre that holds a public library, a gym, swimming pool, ice rink, and community hall. There's also an art centre, a museum, two shopping malls, and two schools," replied Bryan.

"Not bad," said David. "Nice place to live. Raise kids."

Bryan gave David an appraising look. "Raise kids? Something I should know?"

David flushed. "Nah, I was talking hypothetically."

"Right, then," said Bryan switching gears. "Let's head to the District of Mackenzie Office."

"Great place to start. Hopefully, we can find out where Dr. Sperling's compound is located."

When Bryan and David showed their identification to the clerk at the District of Mackenzie Business Office, he frowned and said, "Private investigators from Ontario. You're a long way from home."

"We're working on a missing children's case, and a lead brought us to your town," replied Bryan.

"Not sure how I can help with that," he said, his expression wary.

Noticing the clerk's name badge, David said, "Chris, we're looking for a medical centre, adoption centre or fertility clinic run by a medical doctor. The last name's Sperling. I'm having trouble locating the facility on my GPS. Would you be able to tell us where it's located?"

"Not sure I've heard of that, but I'll check," replied the clerk, repositioning his reading glasses on his nose so he could see better. "Sorry, there's no business registered to anyone by that name."

"Are you certain?" asked Bryan.

"Of course." Chris's face flushed red, indignant that his competency was being questioned by out-of-towners.

"It's a matter of urgency we find this young woman," said David, keeping his tone conciliatory and pleasant. He showed Chris an image of Maggie on his iPhone. "She went missing about ten years ago, but new information leads us to think she might be here in MacKenzie." David felt a pang of remorse at the white lie he'd told, knowing that Maggie had already passed away.

"Pretty girl. Can't say I've seen her before. I have a kid that age." His look was thoughtful. "You might try the MacKenzie Adoption Agency."

"Who runs it?"

"Dr. Terrence."

Acting on a hunch, David reopened his iPhone and scrolled through his texts until he found the image Emma had sent him of Dr. Sperling. "Is this Dr. Terrence?" he asked.

"I haven't seen him for a long time, but, yep, that's him."

"Can you tell us his address?" asked Bryan.

Still miffed with Bryan, Chris directed his answer to David. "Roughly a hundred miles north of here. 'Bout ten years ago, he bought an old logging camp and converted it into an adoption facility."

"Can you give us directions?"

"Sure. It's pretty secretive, though, with tight security. Private airfield, too. Always busy air traffic." He looked at David thoughtfully, "You might have trouble getting in without an appointment."

"Got a number?"

"Sure." Chris consulted his computer and scribbled the address and number on a sticky note. "They're funny folk. They keep to themselves and seldom come into town for supplies. Most of their stuff gets shipped in by transport or by plane."

"So, not great contributors to the local economy," commented Bryan.

"Nope, not at all," said Chris, whose tone was less cranky than before. "What are you men driving?"

"A Jeep Grand Cherokee," said David.

"You'll need it. It's rugged country up there. Like I said, most visitors come in by air."

***

Even though David had been unsuccessful in reaching anyone at the clinic with the number that Chris had supplied them, he and Bryan had decided to drive up to the facility.

Outside the large iron gates, which read MacKenzie Adoption Agency & Fertility Clinic, Bryan pulled the Jeep over to the side of the road. High security fencing stretched away from each side of the two-way gates, and was a combination of razor barbed wire and welded wire panels.

"Chris was not kidding about the high security," said Bryan. "This is unbelievable."

"Clearly designed for preventing anyone from climbing up," said David.

"This type of security fencing is most often used for airports, prisons or military installations."

"Makes you wonder who they are keeping out."

"Or keeping in," said Bryan, his eyebrows creased together with concern.

"They're still not answering the phones," said David, returning his cell to his breast pocket. "And the guardhouse appears unoccupied."

Bryan pointed to the intercom and the camera system mounted on a metal post located on the driver's side of the gate. "Shall we see if anyone's home?"

"No harm in trying," said David.

Bryan pulled up to the intercom and spoke into the microphone. The frown between his eyebrows deepened further, now wrinkling his forehead. "No reply."

David got out of the vehicle and walked toward the side gate which adjoined the guardhouse. Planning to call out in case the guard was there, he leaned his hands against the gate, causing it to swing open. He turned his head back in surprise and called out to Bryan, "It's open!"

Similarly, the door to the guardhouse swung open, revealing an empty room with an austere metal desk and chair.

The desk was clear except for a coagulated cup of coffee and a metal tray which held an assortment of keys. He touched his fingers against the coffee mug, noting it was lukewarm.

Multiple monitors lined the wall but were powered off. Thinking something was wrong, *No, very wrong*, he decided to check if there was a way to manually override the gates. A caption above a green button on the wall said OPEN, and another red button said CLOSE. David pushed the green button to open the gate, but there was no reaction. *No auxiliary power, either.*

Next, he examined the keys which were sitting in the tray, retrieved them, returned outside and walked back to the Jeep.

"Bryan, there's no one here. There's a sophisticated security system inside but the power is turned off."

"Power outage?"

"Maybe, I'm not sure."

"You'd think they'd have a backup generator."

"I think the guard left in a hurry." His gaze was thoughtful. "There's a mug of coffee that is still a bit warm. Found these keys. Wonder if we can open the gate ourselves."

"I am sure we can." Bryan got out of the vehicle and together the two men examined the gate.

"Would this be considered trespassing?"

"No, I don't think so. If we have reason to believe that people are in danger," said Bryan.

"Look over there," said David, pointing to padlocks which secured the massive hydraulic arms to the gates. "Want to bet these keys will unlock the arms?"

"I'm not a betting man. But if I were, I'd say you're right."

David inserted a key first in one arm, then the next, unlocking the mechanisms. "Give me a hand here," said David. "You take one side, and I'll take the other." Each man jointly leaned his weight against the sizeable gates, swinging them open simultaneously.

"The place feels abandoned. Let's go check out what's going on," said Bryan.

"I've got an uneasy feeling about this."

"As do I."

***

The road leading to the compound was nearly a mile in length and lined with lodgepole pine, the species of trees most often logged by forestry companies in the MacKenzie area for its pulp and lumber. The conifers were remnants from when the property had been a logging site and rose nearly one-hundred feet toward the sky. Although it was a bit past four in the afternoon and would not be dark for four or five more hours, the trees cast long shadows across the roadway, creating a somber and sinister atmosphere. The road ended abruptly, opening onto a wide area with multiple buildings forming the compound.

"Remind you of anything?" asked Bryan.

"It sure does. Looks similar to Sperling's Ontario compound, but on a bigger scale."

Bryan parked in front of the main building and said, "Shall we have a look?"

"Yeah, but first I'll get Emma on FaceTime. She wants to see the compound with us, in case she can get some psychic impressions." David waited for the call to go through and said, "Em, we're here now."

"I was wondering when I might hear from the two of you," Emma's cheery face filled the mobile's screen. Any remnants of her cold were gone, and her voice was back to its lovely cadence.

"It was a long drive in," said Bryan. "First to MacKenzie, and then another few hours to the compound. The roads are not in the best condition."

"How was the reception? Were they friendly?"

"Actually, that's the thing: no one's here," said David.

"That's weird."

"Very. We're about to go in," said Bryan.

"Is that wise? Don't you need a warrant?" asked Emma. "I'm worried."

"We are bending the rules a bit, but if there's anyone in trouble, we can justify our entry to the facilities," Bryan admitted.

"I'll try and keep the video feed steady so you can see," said David, attaching his iPhone to the Golifyne Universal lanyard. He pushed the flip camera option on the camera so that Emma could get a view of the surroundings.

David pushed the front door open with his left hand and kept the phone firmly fixed with his right.

"The layout's nearly the same as the Ontario compound," she said.

"Eerily so," agreed David.

"Let's start with the wards," said Bryan.

"Good idea."

Bryan and David stopped in their tracks at the sound of glass breaking and running footsteps.

"Guys, did you hear that?" asked Emma, concerned. "I've got a bad feeling."

Bryan instinctively reached for his gun, then remembered that since he was no longer a cop and was out of province, he was not authorized to carry a firearm. Under the Federal Firearms Act, private investigators were prohibited from carrying handguns, except for unique circumstances. Permits, in those cases, were issued by the chief firearms officer for the province or territory, only if the private investigator could prove they needed the weapon because their life was in danger. *Damn*, he thought, *I hate feeling vulnerable like this.*

A second clatter echoed through the empty ward.

David mouthed to Bryan, "Did you hear that?"

Bryan nodded and pointed to the hallway leading to the right. "Let's check it out," he whispered.

An acrid smell permeated the hall as they rushed toward where they'd heard the sounds.

"David," said Emma shakily. "Be careful, I sense heat. Fire..."

A small fire had broken out in the infirmary. Against the back wall, he saw several terrified children gathered around a wild-eyed woman in her early thirties. Seeing some blankets on the nearby cots, he shouted to Bryan, "Give me a hand." The two men threw the bedding on the flames, choking out the fire.

The young woman's eyes were manic and disoriented, "Keep away from us!" Her voice was high and reedy, strung tight like a guitar string ready to snap. She brandished a glass bottle filled with liquid. "Come any closer and I'll throw this sulfuric acid at you! Trust me, I know what it can do to a face."

David and Bryan gave involuntary gasps when she turned the left side of her face toward them.

Emma's voice filtered through the adrenaline-charged room. "Let me speak with Samantha."

The young woman's face clouded with confusion, her eyes wide with alarm. "How does she know my name?"

"Please, don't be afraid," said David, unwilling to explain his wife's psychic abilities to the frightened young woman. "I am going to hand you my phone," he said, unclipping the phone from the lanyard and holding it out to her.

"Stay where you are," she said, using her body to shield the children. "Put the phone on the counter over there and then step away."

David complied with her request, then moved to the far end of the room.

"Stay here, kids." Samantha darted across the room, snatched the phone off the counter and then retreated to the back wall.

"Who are you?" she said, her hands unsteady and shaky as she held the phone and viewed the image on the screen.

"My name is Emma Jackson. My colleagues and I are here to help."

"That's easy for you to say."

"Samantha, please listen to me very carefully," Emma said softly. "Please trust me."

"Why should I?"

"Because we are your way out from this living hell."

"How *do* you know my name?"

"You may find this hard to believe, but I am a psychic. And Samantha, your family has never stopped looking for you. We are so glad we found you."

"I don't understand."

"You will in time. Now, please listen to me carefully."

Samantha gave Emma an uncertain look.

"Samantha, you are feeling calm and peaceful. I want you to breathe slowly and be aware of each breath in and each breath out. Say with me, *I am breathing in, and I am breathing out. My body is breathing in, and my body is breathing out. I am calm and peaceful.*

"What the heck?"

"Please try it, Samantha. Repeat with me. I am breathing in ..."

"Fine," she said. As the mantra continued, Samantha's voice became more even, and her breathing more peaceful.

"You are doing great, Samantha. Now, please come forward with the kids. Mary, George and Nancy. You are safe now and can go to these men."

"Men ... they frighten me," said Samantha, picking up the youngest child and holding her tightly.

"These are good men," Emma reassured her. "David's my husband, and the older guy, Bryan, is my stepfather. They are going to take care of you and the kids. Can you hand the phone back to David, please?"

Samantha held the mobile against her chest, and asked, "Can I talk to her again, afterward?"

"Of course," said David.

She handed the phone back to him and said, "She's nice."

"I think so, too," he replied, smiling. "Em, thanks for that. You were amazing."

"Glad to help. How long do you plan on being at the compound?" asked Emma.

"Probably most of the night. While you were on the phone with Samantha, Bryan called the Mackenzie detachment. We're waiting for them to arrive. He also called Staff Inspector Carlo Carducci from the New Elgan Police Service to give them an update on what we discovered."

"We'll need to tell Samantha's parents," said Emma.

"Maybe you and your mom can handle that," suggested David.

"Definitely. In fact, I'm coming to MacKenzie."

"Honey, we could have things wrapped up by then. Besides, do you feel well enough? You were pretty sick a couple of days ago."

"I feel fine. It's important I talk with Samantha in person. Perhaps her parents will want to come with me."

***

Samantha cradled the tea in the Styrofoam cup and took a sip. She turned toward the officer from the Mackenzie detachment. "I've told you everything I know." Her voice was strained and reedy. "The guards went on high alert. Like last time."

139

"Like last time?" The officer exchanged worried glances with Bryan and David.

"Yeah. Back in Ontario. They herded the younger girls and kids into the vans and left. But while they were loading us in the van, I heard gun shots and screams."

"So, when I saw they were doing the same thing this time, I took the kids and I hid." Her voice was wobbly, and the whites of her eyes were red. "There's a crematorium at the back of the property. You might want to ..." Her body shuddered and her face grew pale.

She looked at David and said, "I'm sorry I threatened to throw acid in your face. I thought you were part of the extermination crew."

David paled and said, "God, no."

Thirty-One

The Reunion

EMMA FOUGHT TO STAY awake at the wheel as she drove the last leg of the trip from Prince George to MacKenzie. She glanced into the rearview mirror at the tired couple who had chosen to sit in the back seat of the car rental. The trip had been a long one, with little spoken between the three, beyond the usual pleasantries.

Samantha's mother and father, Nancy and Henry Courtright looked drawn and haggard. Nancy's husband had kept a protective arm around her the entire trip. When they had received the call from Emma and Laura, although emotional, both said they were anxious to see their daughter immediately. They'd packed a few things and driven through the night from North Bay to meet Emma at the airport the next morning, for their flight at ten-thirty.

Laura had made flight arrangements that would take them from Toronto Pearson International to Vancouver International Airport. Arriving in Vancouver a little after one in the afternoon, they rushed to catch their connecting flight from Vancouver to Prince George at one-thirty. Now, after a nearly six-hour trip by car, they would be arriving in MacKenzie.

"My husband, David, will be meeting us at the Alexander Mackenzie Hotel," Emma told them. "Another half hour and we'll be there."

Henry cleared his throat. "I know we haven't talked much, but my wife and I, well, we wanted to thank you for all of this."

Emma gave them a tired smile and said, "I understand and, of course, I'm happy to help. I cannot imagine how difficult this must be for you both."

After Emma pulled into the parking spot at the hotel, she turned to Nancy and Henry. "I should talk with Samantha first," she said. "I'd like to prepare her that you are here. She's been through a lot, and we need to keep her calm."

***

"You brought them here!" protested Samantha. She got up from the couch, disrupting the three children who had been nestling against her. They stared at her with huge, frightened eyes while she paced the hotel room. "They said they'd kill my parents if I ever attempted to leave." She choked back sobs. "It's why I never tried to escape. Besides ..." She traced her fingers against the scars on her face. "Who'd want a monster like me?"

Emma guided her back to the couch and said, "Samantha, that's not true. You aren't a monster. Let's talk a bit first, and then I'll bring your parents in to see you. How does that sound?"

Samantha nodded and said, "Talking with you first would be nice."

"You have gone through more than anyone should ever have to experience. Your mom and dad will understand."

"Maybe you're right. And then there's another reason I didn't try to leave..." Samantha paused, then looked away.

"Yes?" Emma said, her voice filled with compassion.

"I had these three to mind." She pulled the children close to her. The youngest, Mary, her little body rigid, kept her face hidden against Samantha's chest.

"Are they yours?" asked Emma.

"No, but they might as well be. They're the clinic's rejects. Not quite up to customer expectations and specifications." She drew the kids even closer.

"Mary is two. She was supposed to have blue eyes. They rejected her because her eyes were brown."

Samantha tousled George's wavy, brown hair, and continued, "He turned six a week ago. His biological parents left him to be raised here until he could have his IQ tested. Did you know the optimum IQ testing age is between five and eight years of age? George was considered mildly gifted, with an IQ score of one hundred and twenty. Not good enough. His elite Nobel prize-winning 'parents' rejected him." She roughly wiped hot tears from her cheeks.

"And Nancy, she's three. I was the surrogate mother for her. Her parents were killed in a car accident a month before she was born. Nancy was paid for in full, and for some reason, they let me keep her. I consider her my own. All three, I consider mine."

"Your mom's going to love that you called this little one Nancy."

She nodded, her eyes bright with tears. "It was a way to keep hold of my previous life."

"Samantha," Emma chose her words carefully. "I know you were at the Ontario compound before being brought here. Did you know a girl named Maggie?"

"Maggie?" Samantha's face paled.

"Yes, do you know what became of her?"

"It's all my fault," said Samantha. "I was jealous. Over a guy."

"I'm listening," said Emma, her tone soft and gentle.

"His name was Evan. He was a male nurse." Samantha stared into the space above Emma's head, as she recounted the story. "Maggie and Evan were in love. But I was in love with Evan, too."

"What happened?"

"Maggie got pregnant. I overheard them planning to run away and I told on them."

Emma's heart raced as the scene unfolded like a video in real time: Maggie hiding in the trunk of the car, the security guard roughly pulling her out, the threats to Evan that they would kill Maggie if they tried to escape again. Then the scene flashed forward to Maggie's death in childbirth. Evan's profound grief. Then the rapid evacuation of the Ontario compound and relocation to the new one in British Columbia.

"I didn't mean for any of that to happen," Samantha whispered, as if she were seeing the same memory replay in her mind as Emma.

"You were young and afraid," said Emma. "You couldn't have known what would happen. It was a coincidence that Maggie's death coincided with their plan to move the operation from Ontario to British Columbia."

"I don't know ... all this guilt. It's been with me so long. If I hadn't finked on Maggie and Evan, they might have escaped. Maybe Maggie would still be alive."

"Maggie could have died in childbirth anyhow. None of this was your fault."

"Maybe you're right. But to have been so jealous was wrong."

"You're a good person. A good mother. Look how you've taken care of these three children."

"I guess you're right," she said. "I'd do anything for them."

"I am curious," said Emma. "Whatever happened to Evan?"

"He was transported to BC with the rest of us."

"Oh? I wonder why?" asked Emma surprised. Seconds later the answer flooded into her consciousness. "Ah, because of the baby girl."

"Yes, because of Simone." Samantha shook her head sadly. "He wasn't going to let his little girl out of his sight. It was their way to keep him working for them by holding his daughter hostage."

"What happened to Evan and Simone?"

A look of joy transformed Samantha's ravaged face, making it easy to forget the damaged skin. "They got away."

A flash of understanding coursed through Emma. "You helped Evan and Simone escape, didn't you?"

"Yes, it's why ..." She turned her damaged face toward Emma. "This was my punishment," she said, anguished.

Emma drew Samantha into an embrace and drove off the empathic pain pulsing on the left side of her own face.

She pulled back and asked, "Ready to see your parents?"

"I'm nervous." She tugged at Emma's arm. "Will you stay with me?"

"Of course." Emma placed her hand on top of Samantha's to reassure her and said, "Don't worry, it'll be fine. Shall I let them know you're ready?"

Samantha teared up and said softly. "I'm ready."

Emma reached for her cell phone and tapped out a message to the Courtrights.

<She's ready to see you. Room 308.

Several minutes later, a soft knock on the door announced they'd arrived. Emma looked through the peephole, saw it was Nancy and Henry, unlatched the chain and before she could open the door fully, Nancy brushed past her.

"Sam, is it really you?"

"Mom?"

Samantha's

"Oh, honey," said Nancy, drawing her daughter into a tight hug. "It really is you," she said, breathing in the almond scent of Samantha's freshly shampooed hair.

"Yes, it's me." Nancy traced her fingers over Samantha's face, hesitating briefly at the acid etched scars on her left cheek.

Samantha tried to pull away from her mom's probing fingers, but her mom cupped her face firmly and held it fast. "You are my daughter, and you are beautiful."

Mary toddled over to Samantha, tugged at her pant leg and said, "Mommy?"

Samantha pulled out of her mother's embrace, picked up her youngest and said, "This is Mary." She stretched out her arms and called to the two children sitting quietly on the couch. "Come here, kids. This is your grandma." She turned toward her dad, who'd been standing inside the doorway. "And this is your granddad."

Henry rushed to his daughter and held her tight, then pulled his wife into the embrace. Tears streamed down his cheeks. "My baby girl."

He released his wife and daughter, then got down on his knees. He spoke gently to the three kids. "Do you want to see a magic trick?" He pulled a toonie, Canada's two-dollar coin, from behind George's ear, who giggled with delight. Mary pushed her way forward, "Me, too!" Once he'd performed the same trick for Mary, he turned to Nancy and said, "Your turn." The shy girl's face transformed into a huge smile. "Yes, please."

Samantha turned toward her mom and asked, "Take us home?"

Emma, pleased at the heartwarming family reunion, slipped out of the room and gently shut the door. Having been separated for over twenty-three years, there'd be a long road ahead of healing for Samantha and her parents. The children, having been born outside of conventional society, would need to have their births registered, but the childcare worker assigned to the case confirmed they would not be separated from Samantha, the only mother they'd ever known.

Although the BC compound was not technically a cult, it shared many of the properties of a cult, and the children, especially the two older kids, might also face emotional consequences, such as their sense of identity.

Even Samantha, who was not much more than a child herself when abducted, would face a long journey to adjust to a world outside the compound.

Thirty-Two
Time for a Little R & R

DAVID FELT EMMA SHIFT in their bed. "You really think we can spare the time?" she asked, rolling over from her side of the bed, and tucking her body tightly against David. She placed her left arm around him and playfully nibbled on his ear.

"Mmm ..." groaned David, still half asleep. "Stop that."

"You listening?"

"Hard to do when you keep distracting me." He pulled her on top of him, her auburn curls cascading around her tanned and toned shoulders. "God, you're beautiful." He placed his hands on each side of her face and kissed her forehead, the space between her eyes, the tip of her nose, and then her soft, full lips.

She returned the kiss, then wiggled away and said, "Stop changing the subject." Her green eyes flashed with that familiar mixture of amusement and impatience to which David had grown accustomed.

"Em, of course I was listening. And yes, we deserve some time off. In fact, Bryan insisted on it."

"Too bad mom's not here, too. The four of us could have enjoyed the Okanagan Valley."

"Bryan is anxious to keep working on the case. He's got a new lead. Besides, you know he misses your mom."

"When's he heading back to Ontario?"

"Today." David glanced at the hotel alarm clock, which showed it was eight in the morning. "He's already halfway to the Prince George airport, where he'll catch a flight to Vancouver and then on to Toronto."

A shadow passed over Emma's face and she shivered.

"What is it, Em?"

"I feel apprehensive. It's probably nothing. I'm sorry I didn't get a chance to say bon voyage to him."

"You were already asleep. That's quite the trip you made, going without any rest for more than thirty-six hours. And with the time difference, no wonder you conked out early."

"Well, I feel great, now." She stretched her arms overhead, then in a fluid motion, rolled off David, jumped off the bed, both legs hitting the floor at the same time. "Shall I make some coffee?"

"That'd be wonderful." David rested back against the pillows, savoring Emma's lithe body while she deftly prepared their coffees in the Keurig machine.

"Never really cared much for these pods, but at least they have a recycling program now." She put stevia sweetener in their cups, then handed a cup to David. "Here you go, honey."

"Thanks, Em."

"So, this lead Bryan's working on. Does it have to do with the Dark Hands of Anubis?"

"Yes. Bryan's been given authorization to go through Jazzie's computer and cell phone. First thing tomorrow morning, he'll be meeting with Staff Inspector Carlo Carducci at the New Elgan Police Service to go over the data."

"She claimed she'd kept records on them. Hopefully, he will find something concrete to pinpoint the location of their organization, or at least identify their key people."

"It would be a big break in our case, if he and Carlo were successful finding a link to the Dark Hands of Anubis."

"Yes, it sure would."

"What about Bryan's own case files? Doesn't he have them anymore?" Emma asked.

"It's in movies and books that officers keep their old case files. They are supposed to be handed in and stored in the retired archives."

"Oh, that makes sense."

"Bryan has more access than most police officers, since our company works as a consultant with the department. But Bryan still has to go through the proper channels and through security checks."

"Well, hopefully he will uncover something that will help us locate the Dark Hands of Anubis."

"Hopefully," said David, taking a sip and savoring the rich coffee.

"So, he really can spare us for a few days?" asked Emma, returning to her original question.

"Definitely." He took the coffee cup from her hand and placed it on the night table. "We need some 'us' time."

"You're right." She nuzzled against his chest and gave a soft sigh. "I hate it when we're apart."

"Me, too. It's not like we were apart for weeks," he reminded her, smiling. "We're stuck at the hip, you and I."

"I love you so much," she said. "So, where are we headed today?"

"First things first," he replied. He breathed in the lavender scent of her hair, then pressed his lips against hers. "Em—" he whispered, as their bodies intertwined.

Thirty-Three
Arrival, Pillar C

———————————————

TO KEEP HER ANXIETY at bay, Laura tapped her fingers against the steering wheel. Bryan's flight was thirty minutes late. Parked in the terminal's cell phone waiting area on Network Road, where drivers were allowed to wait for up to forty-five minutes, she would have to move on if she didn't hear from Bryan soon.

She was about to put her car in gear when Bryan messaged her.

<Just got my luggage. I'll be waiting at Pillar C.

<<K. See you in a few minutes. <3

Laura drove out of the lot and merged onto the roadway to take her to the Arrivals level of Terminal 3. As she approached Arrival's Pillar C, she saw Bryan leaning against it heavily. His face appeared pasty-white in her car's headlights. Panicked, she threw the car into park and rushed over to him.

"Bryan," she cried out. "What's wrong?"

"Not feeling so good," he replied, before he collapsed. His tall frame crumpled like a skyscraper imploding on itself from the handiwork of a demolition expert.

Laura broke his fall before his head hit the pavement. A nearby security guard noticed what happened and hurried over to help, already barking a request into his two-way radio for an emergency team to respond.

"What's going on?"

"My husband ... he collapsed."

151

"I've already called for an ambulance." He knelt beside Bryan, and said, "Help will be here any moment."

"Coming through," said one of the Emergency Medical Responders, carrying a portable med kit. Despite the chilly May night, the young woman wore a short-sleeved shirt. Her exposed arms displayed ornate tattoos of morning glory flowers with their vines trailing upwards until they disappeared under the cuffs of her shirtsleeves.

Her badge displayed the name Marla. She placed her fingers on Bryan's neck. "His pulse is erratic." Then she shone a light in his eyes. "They're dilated. Does he use?"

"No, never. He's a retired police officer." Laura's brows creased with worry and a dark suspicion began to formulate. Poisons and drugs ... the kind of assassination methods used by the Dark Hands of Anubis.

Laura's thoughts were interrupted. "He your husband?" asked the medic.

"Yes."

"Has he been out of country?" she asked, wrapping the blood pressure cuff around his arm.

"No, but he arrived from Vancouver about half an hour ago."

She frowned and spoke to her colleague. "BP is dangerously low." She turned to Laura. "We need to transport him to hospital asap."

Laura watched in shock as the EMS personnel loaded Bryan into the ambulance. "Where are you taking him?"

The medic jumped into the back of the emergency vehicle and attached a saline drip to Bryan's arm. She was looking downward, her face pointed away from Laura, her reply muffled and indistinct.

Before Laura could ask again, the woman said, "Gotta go." She slammed the vehicle's doors shut with a terrifying finality. The EMS driver put the vehicle in gear and seconds later, the taillights disappeared into the night.

"Where are they taking him?" she asked again, this time addressing the security guard. Her heart pounded and red mists of panic formed at the corners of her vision.

"Etobicoke General Hospital."

"Got it." When she grabbed Bryan's carry-on bag by the handle, she winced at the sharp pinprick in the palm of her hand. She pulled off her glove to look. The surface of her skin showed a slight welt, not deep enough to have broken the skin, since she'd gripped the handle lightly, but enough to have caught her by surprise. She threw the rest of Bryan's luggage in the trunk and settled into the driver's seat. Taking a moment to collect herself, she rested her forehead against the wheel.

The guard tapped on the driver's window. "You, okay, ma'am?" he asked, concerned.

Laura nodded. "A bit shocked, but I'm alright." God, please don't take Bryan away from me, she thought.

"You know where the hospital is?"

"Yeah, thanks. I do. Humber College Boulevard."

"That's right. You drive safe, now."

***

Emma and David sat on their private deck overlooking the lush vineyard. They were staying at the famous Burrowing Owl Estate Winery's Meritage Suite, which often accommodated newlyweds.

To Emma's delight, the twelve-hundred square foot suite boasted a gourmet kitchen, an intimate fireplace, spacious rooms and even a private elevator. A massive sun deck surrounded a twenty-five-meter outdoor pool, and an all-season hot tub tempted guests to relax in its soothing waters, no matter what the season.

"David, this is gorgeous. I wouldn't mind trying out the hot tub later." She gave a sigh of contentment. "I feel like we're on our honeymoon."

"I love you so much, I'd marry you every year so we could go on our honeymoon again and again."

Emma's face flushed pink with pleasure, the very reaction he'd expected and hoped for. He clinked his glass of the 2006 Meritage against hers. "To us."

"To us." Emma swirled the deep ruby vintage in her glass, breathed in its bouquet and took a sip. "Oh my. This is intense and complex. I taste black cherry, raspberry and hints of chocolate. Your turn." She was referring to the wine tasting challenges they enjoyed during their early days of dating.

"Of course you'd taste chocolate," he said, smiling. "I do, too. But also, something sweet and spicy. A bit like you." He picked up the bottle. "This is over fourteen and a half percent."

"Oh, that's strong. No wonder I'm feeling a bit tipsy."

"The higher the alcohol content, the longer it can be kept." He took another swallow of the luscious red wine. "I'm going to order a case to have shipped home."

"Lovely idea. Then we can remember this trip whenever we open a bottle." Emma was about to take another sip when her cell phone rang. A picture of her mom showed on the phone's display.

"Hi Mom. It's great to hear from ..." Emma's face grew pinched, and her voice became strained. "When?"

"What is it?" he whispered, noting the alarm in Emma's voice.

Emma's eyes were wide with fright. "Something's happened to Bryan. He's been taken to the hospital." The cellphone slipped from her fingers.

David caught the cell before it hit the ground and said, "Laura, we'll be on the next plane home."

Thirty-Four

Was Bryan Drugged?

AFTER A TRIP that seemed to never end, their flight from Vancouver to Toronto finally landed. Emma sighed with relief when their luggage was among the first to trundle down the carousel. They hauled their bags off the track, rushed to the exit and headed toward the limo area. The timing was lucky there, too, and soon they were speeding off to Etobicoke General Hospital.

In the back of the limo, Emma thumbed through the messages on her phone, anxious to catch up after the more than five-hour flight.

David wrapped his arm around her shoulders and asked, "Any more updates from your mom?"

Emma's eyes were bright with tears. "Bryan is in stable condition. They want to keep him for another night. He should be able to come home tomorrow morning."

"Do the doctors know what happened?"

Emma shook her head. "I've asked, but mom says she wants to discuss it in person."

She leaped out of the limo before it had come to a full stop in front of the main entrance of the hospital. She was halfway to the turnstile doors when she halted and turned around. "David, I'm sorry. I should have waited—"

"Go ahead, Emma," he said, "I'll take care of things here." He tapped his iPhone against the point-of-purchase terminal the limo driver was holding.

***

The driver got out of the limo, popped open the vehicle's trunk and hauled out the luggage. "I couldn't help but overhear," he said, his broad friendly face frowning with concern. "Is the young lady's dad sick? It's not every day I take passengers directly from the airport to the hospital."

As amicable as the driver seemed, a niggling sense of inquietude washed over David at the man's overt and inappropriate friendliness. *I must be getting paranoid. He's the limo driver. Or is he something more?*

"Hope everything's okay," said the driver.

Unwilling to divulge his personal feelings or the circumstances, David simply nodded and said, "I hope so, too."

"Here's my card, if you need a drive home, later."

"Thanks," David said, stuffing the business card in the front pocket of his jeans. He slung Emma's carry-on bag over his shoulder, each hand gripping the handles of their luggage, the wheels rattling in protest as he pulled the two bags across the cracked pavement to the front doors.

***

Laura held Bryan's hand while he slept. The doctor had been by a few minutes earlier and had reassured her that Bryan would be fine.

"His vitals have stabilized. We'll know more when the lab tests come in. We can talk further then."

Filled with relief, she rested her head on Bryan's chest, closed her eyes, and listened to the steady inhalation of his breath and the even, rhythmic beat of his heart. *The most beautiful sounds in the world*, Laura thought, grateful he had not been taken from her.

Her thoughts were interrupted by another beautiful sound: her daughter's voice. "Mom, I'm here."

"Oh, honey, I'm so glad." She clutched Emma close. She pulled back a bit, peered behind Emma and asked, "Where's David?"

"Downstairs. He'll be up any second."

Right on cue, David said, "I'm here, ladies." His pleasant baritone filled the space of the hospital room. He enfolded both Laura and Emma in his arms.

"It's so good you're both here." Laura stifled a sob, straightened her shoulders and pulled out of the group embrace. Resolved to be brave, she asked, "How was the flight?"

"Great. Exactly what you want in air travel," replied David. "Uneventful."

"Mom, have the doctors told you anything yet?" asked Emma.

Laura shook her head. "No, not yet, but..."

Emma's face drained of color. "Oh my God, Mom ... was Bryan attacked?"

"The doctor hasn't confirmed what caused Bryan's collapse. In fact, he's not said anything at all." Laura sighed in frustration, her normally bright green eyes glazed with worry. "It's something the EMS attendant said."

"You think Bryan was drugged," said Emma, reading her mother's thoughts.

"Yeah, I do. The EMS worker clearly thought Bryan was on something. She said his eyes were dilated."

"There's something more, isn't there, Mom?" asked Emma.

"Here, look at this." Laura showed Emma and David the inch-long raised welt on the inside of her hand.

"What is this?" asked David, his baritone deepening another octave.

"I was wearing gloves, but I scratched myself on the handle of Bryan's carry-on bag. It's probably nothing, but it reminded me of when I passed out last year in the garden."

Laura was referring to the attempt made on her life, a hit ordered by Enrico Bianchi and unsuccessfully executed by Jazzie Bakker, an assassin employed by the Dark Hands of Anubis. She'd been injected with a high dose of Ketamine, intended to induce an asthma attack severe enough to end her life.

"It didn't break the skin, but I wondered if—"

"Where is the bag, now?" interrupted David.

"Still in the trunk of my car."

"Depending on the test results, the police may want to examine Bryan's carry-on bag."

The doctor tapped on the door frame to alert them of his arrival and walked in. A clipboard was tucked under his left arm. His hairline receded from his forehead and wiry, caterpillar-like eyebrows speckled with grey, brown, and white punctuated the kind eyes below.

"Mrs. Grant, I see your family has joined you." He stretched out his right hand and first shook Emma's hand, then David's, and said, "I'm Doctor Grady."

"This is my wife, Emma, and I'm David Harris."

"Do you have any news for us?" asked Laura, her lips drawn in a compressed line, tight with tension.

Dr. Grady nodded and said, "Your husband was injected with a high dosage of ketamine. It put him into a coma." His gaze steady, he continued, "Was your husband taking recreational drugs?"

"No, he never has. He retired from the New Elgan Police Service last year," said Laura. "He didn't take drugs—he kept them off the street. He spearheaded educational programs about the dangers of drug consumption for our youth."

"Sounds like your husband is a fine individual," said the doctor.

David interjected. "We operate a private detective agency. We have reason to believe Bryan was attacked because of an investigation we are working on."

"In that case, I am obligated to report this incident to the local police. Based on what you've told me, it's highly likely this was an attempt on your father-in-law's life."

Laura gasped at what she knew deep down was true. To hide her tears, she turned her head away.

Emma noticed her mom's distress and gently touched Laura's shoulder. "Take a deep breath, Mom," she said. Turning to the doctor, she asked, "So, will Bryan make a full recovery?"

"Yes, he'll need to sleep this off, of course. Typically, the effects will dissipate after twenty-four hours, but we'd like to keep him until at least tomorrow morning." He cleared his throat. "Had Bryan not been attended to as quickly as he had, he may have died of cardiac arrest, and we'd be having a very different conversation."

"In the commotion of Bryan being admitted, I forgot about this." Laura showed Dr. Grady her hand. "I think Bryan was injected when he grabbed the handle of his carry-on bag. I was wearing gloves when I picked the bag up. The skin was scratched but not broken."

"Let's take a closer look," said Dr. Grady. He lifted Bryan's right hand, shone a light on Bryan's palm, and carefully examined it. "See that?" The light illuminated a small pinprick. "The police will need to see this. And that carry-on bag, too."

Thirty-Five

Nothing I Can Say Will Change That

TWENTY-FOUR HOURS LATER, Laura, Bryan, Emma and David were back at Laura and Bryan's country home. Most times, the atmosphere between the four of them was synchronous and calm, but today, it was tense with undercurrents of raw emotion trying to squirm to the surface.

Laura's tone was clipped, barely containing the anger threatening to escape. "I'd like to see this entire investigation stopped." She wiped her tired eyes with the tips of her fingers. "It's not worth the risk."

"But Mom, we've invested so much time into this case. It would be a slap in our victims' faces to give up on them now."

"I don't know about that, Emma," said David. "We have already had some wins, here." He reached for Emma's hand but she snatched it away. "Come on, Emma, be reasonable," said David. "We found Samantha and the three kids."

"He's got a point," said Bryan. He had fully recovered from the near fatal ketamine dose, although his normally robust face was haggard and reflected his recent ordeal. "But—"

"But you don't think we should stop," intuited Emma.

"No, I don't." He searched each of his family members' faces. "I agree with Emma. We need to continue."

"Let's take a vote," suggested Emma. "Raise your hand if you're against continuing the investigation."

Laura and David both raised their hands. "Sorry, Em," said David, he shrugged his shoulders in apology.

"Not as sorry as I am," muttered Emma, trying not to show her hurt.

"I see we're at a stalemate," said Laura.

"You can pull back if you want," Emma's eyes flared viridescent, the way copper sulphate burns green when sprinkled on a wood fire. "I'm not stopping. I owe it to Maggie."

"But we've had success there, too," protested David. "We've found Maggie's kids – the twins – and Megan has two nieces in their life, now."

"We still need to locate Simone – Evan and Maggie's daughter," Emma reminded the group.

"Emma, it's so dangerous. I am nervous all the time, worrying about you," said Laura.

"Mom, I made a promise to Maggie we would find all her kids," said Emma. "And I keep my promises. Besides, we know that Evan and Simone escaped the compound."

"God, you can be so stubborn!" exploded David.

Irritated, Emma turned her body away from David and folded her arms across her chest.

"Look, maybe we can still do this," said Laura hesitantly. "I'm not happy saying this because every part of me is screaming in terror that I am going to lose the three people most important to me." She gave a heavy sigh. She looked at Emma, then Bryan. "I love you for who you are ... I know if your minds are made up, nothing I can say will change that, so I won't try."

Emma turned back toward her husband and gazed at him expectantly. "David? What do you say?"

"Fine, but we are going to establish some ground rules."

"Ground rules?" repeated Emma, furious that a man, even her own man, would dare tell her about rules.

"Wait, Em," said David, noticing his wife's volatile temper was resurfacing. "That's not what I meant. The four of us need to establish rules to ensure our safety."

"I'm listening," said Emma, her expression softening.

"Yes," said Bryan. "I'm curious what you have in mind."

"It's simple. No more traveling on our own. We implement a buddy system." David massaged the back of his neck to relieve the tension headache. "Bryan, I blame myself for letting you travel ahead of us."

"Son, that was my suggestion. You and Emma needed some time off together."

"I know. Still, your life was put in jeopardy because of it."

"It was very kind of you, but from now on we'll take vacay time when cases are closed," added Emma.

"And if the three of you travel out of town again," asked Laura, frowning. "What about me?"

"My love, we'll hire Harold Kruger Security." Bryan picked up his cell. "I'll give him a call right now."

Bryan waited a few seconds for the call to ring through and heard his friend say, "Harold, speaking."

"Harold, it's Bryan."

"Bryan, it's great to hear from you. It's been a while. How's married life treating you?"

"Great. I've put you on speaker. Laura, Emma and Bryan are here, too."

"Hey guys," said Harold.

"Hi, Harold," called out Laura, while Emma and David echoed her greeting.

"Listen, Harold, I have a favor to ask."

"Sure, anything for an old friend. What can I do for you?"

"We're working on a case, and I ran into a spot of trouble."

"What happened?" Everyone could hear the concern in their friend's voice.

"Long story short, I was attacked. A hitman injected me with a large dose of ketamine."

"That's rough. But you're here to talk about it."

"Thank God for that. Laura's quick thinking saved my life."

"She's a keeper, that one."

"I know it."

"So, what favor do you need?"

"I suspect we'll be heading out of town, and I'd like to hire your firm again to keep an eye on Laura. Make sure she gets to and from work safely, with an overnight security detail at our home."

"Consider it done. Laura, put my number on speed dial. We'll be there to help anyway we can."

"Thanks, Harold," said Bryan.

"We appreciate this," added Laura.

"No probs."

"Let's get together for dinner and drinks, once this case is wrapped up," said Bryan,

"Sounds like a plan."

Bryan ended the call and said, "I'm glad that's settled."

"Thanks, Bryan. I feel relieved," said Laura. She placed her hand on Bryan's shoulder. "You still look so tired. We should turn in early."

"Good idea. I am bushed." He gave a tired smile.

He turned his attention to David. "We've been delayed as a result of my being attacked, but I've talked with Staff Inspector Carlo Carducci, and we have rescheduled our meeting for tomorrow morning, instead."

"Those files might hold the lead we finally need to track down the Dark Hands of Anubis," said Emma, her face flushing with excitement.

Thirty-Six

Our First Real Lead

BRYAN ARRIVED AT THE New Elgan Police Services a few minutes before eight in the morning and was greeted by a fresh-eyed Carlo Carducci.

In his mid-forties, Carlo was of Mediterranean descent with animated dark eyes and thick wavy brown hair interspersed with streaks of slate grey. His mother's family was from Northern Greece and emigrated to Canada in the mid-1950s, while his father was from Florence.

"It's great to see you again," said Carlo. "Feel like some coffee?"

"Sure, that'd be great," replied Bryan, heading toward the lunchroom.

"Nah, this way. Let's head to my office."

"Isn't the coffee machine that way?"

"Got something better. My own espresso machine."

Bryan followed Carlo to his office and settled down in the chair opposite the desk, while Carlo operated the espresso machine. "Sugar?"

"No, straight is fine."

"I like a bit of sugar myself to soften the bitter taste." He opened the desk drawer, removed a tin and selected a biscotti. "Would you like one?"

Bryan shook his head. "I'm trying to cut back on my sugar intake," he said, patting his belly, which had lessened in size now that he was enjoying Laura's wonderful home-cooked meals, instead of eating greasy fast food.

"Coming up through the ranks, I was in awe of you."

"Thanks," said Bryan, unaccustomed to compliments, however well-meaning.

"Do you miss it?" asked Carlo, handing one of the steaming cups of espresso to Bryan.

"Miss what? The coffee?"

"Very funny. Being on the force."

"Actually, not so much. The years were wearing me down." He took a sip of the potent and bitter beverage. "Not bad." He took another sip and set down the demitasse cup. "Working as a consultant for the police department keeps my mind active, and I know I am still doing something good for society. Less stressful."

"Less stressful?" Carlo chortled. "Like getting attacked at the airport and injected with a large ketamine dose?" Carlo gave him an incredulous look.

"Well, that's not a usual occurrence," countered Bryan.

"I'm razzing you." He bit into the biscotti, causing some of the hard biscuit to crumble. He took a napkin, fastidiously scooped up the crumbs and placed them in the waste basket.

"Good work on locating some of the missing young women," said Carlo. "How is the family settling in? The parents must be delighted to have Samantha back in their lives. And with grandkids, too."

"They have a long road ahead of them, but they'll be fine." Bryan shifted in his chair. "Thanks for getting the Jazzie Bakker files together for me."

"My pleasure. So, now that coffee is out of the way, let's get working on those files, shall we? I've had the tech department print what we'll need." He slapped the files on the desk. "Anything our staff found encrypted has been decoded. It should prove for interesting reading."

***

As the morning progressed, besides the odd break when Carlo refueled their cups with espresso, the men barely spoke.

Bryan had been leaning forward, his elbows propped up on the desk with his chair leaning on its front two legs, while the rear legs were raised slightly in the air. When he leaned back, the rear legs hit the floor with a large thump. "Son of a—" he exclaimed. "How could we have missed this?"

Startled by the outburst, Carlo looked up from the sheaves of paperwork he'd been perusing and asked, "What you got there?"

"A name. Our first real lead into who is behind the Dark Hands of Anubis."

Carlo got up from behind his desk, pulled his chair around and placed it beside that of Bryan's and sat down. "Show me what you've found."

"The Holtz family runs the Dark Hands of Anubis. Jazzie listed Reinhard Holtz, Sr. as the head of the organization. Your staff did an excellent job decoding what Jazzie had painstakingly encrypted."

Carlo allowed himself a brief smile, then said, "Thanks."

Bryan reached for his laptop. "I've heard of the Holtz family. Weren't they in the news recently about their family ties to the former Nazi regime?" He tapped into the search engine and said, "I remember now ... here's what I found."

Bryan read the news article aloud. "The uber rich Holtz family took part in activities or profited from the Nazi regime. They had ties to Nazism through contracts, slave labor and the appropriation of stolen goods. And they weren't the exception. More than a dozen European billionaires and their families benefited in a comparable way."

"And they are richer than ever today," commented Carlo.

"Some big brand names that we use every day were tied to families that flourished during the Nazi era." Bryan wiped at his red rimmed eyes.

"Like Holtz Enterprises. Jazzie's files indicate that their legitimately run businesses, while incredibly profitable, are fronts for their real goals: world influence and domination."

"And they use Dark Hands of Anubis to accomplish their more nefarious goals," said Carlo.

"Exactly."

"Unbelievable how the rich get richer by any means possible."

"Not to mention secret organizations like Dark Hands have global influence on government policy and public sentiment by manipulating the truth using social media. People are gullible and believe in anything they read without doing their fact-checking. These groups carry such weight, but are unaccountable. They are masters at surveillance and use their money to corrupt governments from within."

"With the mass of information out there, it's hard to discern what's real and what's not."

Carlo rifled through his own pile of papers. "Looks like she kept incriminating evidence on the Bianchis, too."

"Enough to cancel off any further deal-making with the Bianchis?" asked Bryan.

"One can hope. Old man Bianchi is gravely ill. No one here wants to see that bastard receive any special consideration."

"Well, it's up to Alessandro, his son, to make an application for his father, based on compassionate grounds. Then the parole board can decide."

"Still, the information we got from Alessandro was helpful, since it led us to the BC compound. That will play in the Bianchis' favor."

"True."

"Back to the Dark Hands. What are your next moves?" asked Carlo.

"I have an idea. Here's what I'm thinking ..."

Thirty-Seven
The Dark Web

LATER THAT AFTERNOON, Emma, Laura, Bryan and David gathered at the office of Jackson, Grant & Harris Investigations.

"Let's head to the boardroom," suggested Bryan. "I have interesting news to report."

Noticing their young intern, Trevor McAllister, was hovering at the door, David nudged the door closed with his foot. A flash of disappointment crossed the young lawyer's face before he spun around and headed back to the front desk.

Emma was the first to speak, after Bryan had described what he'd learned about the Holtz family's connection to the Dark Hands of Anubis. "So, how do we get to them?" she asked. "It seems they run legitimate businesses, and although Jazzie provided compelling information, how do we locate them?"

David's eyes brightened. "Through the Dark Web."

"Exactly," smiled Bryan. "Jazzie left a back door open."

"That must have been deliberate," he said.

"Indeed," said Bryan.

"She's still helping us, even from the grave," said Emma. The previous year, Emma had been kidnapped and taken to the Maldives. During the final confrontation, while Emma was held at knife point by Enrico Bianchi, Jazzie had tipped the scales and attacked Enrico. In the process, she had been killed, but had saved Emma's life.

"But what pretense will you use to contact them?" asked Laura, her brows knitting together with worry.

"I've already worked it out with Carlo. David will use the back door on Jazzie's laptop to contact Dark Hands, under the pretense he's looking to adopt a child."

Emma's mouth opened in surprise. "That's a brilliant idea."

"But what about passwords? Did she provide those?" asked Emma.

"No, but Emma, it's time you contacted Jazzie."

"That's a terrible idea!" exclaimed Laura.

"Mom, you worry too much. I've got this."

***

Emma made herself comfortable in Anna's Room on the zafu, her meditation pillow, which had been a gift from Anna. She had hand-woven it from natural fibers and its borders were an ornate design of elephants. She placed a notebook and pen close by, in case there was anything she might need to jot down.

Seated in the lotus position, she rested her hands on her knees with the palms facing up, in a symbol of openness and being ready to receive. She concentrated on her breath, using pranayama – yogic breathing exercises to calm and prepare herself.

Once in her meditative state, she telegraphed to Spirit Anna that she needed her. Soon, she felt her mentor's comforting presence.

Spirit Anna, I am so happy you're here.

I will always be here but not always present.

Confusion crossed over Emma's face. *I don't understand.*

In time, you will, but I am needed in other times and places.

You are leaving me? A tear rolled down Emma's cheek.

That is a matter of perspective, came the cryptic reply. *You seek to speak with Jazzie?*

Yes, we need passwords to reach the Dark Hands.

Be careful, my little one.

Always.

Moments later, the room cooled down, and she sensed Anna was withdrawing.

Anna?

No, it's me, silly. It's Jazzie, came the reply. *Any honey for my tea?*

Jazzie ... it's really you! Still with that sense of humor intact. Jazzie was alluding to the honey Emma served with her herbal teas. It was a clever way to reassure Emma that she really was communicating with Jazzie's spirit.

Yep. About those passwords ... hope you gotta good memory.

The website *www.Adopt-a-Kid-Hassle-Free.onion,* followed by a stream of digits, displayed on the movie screen of Emma's mind, scrolled by, then repeated three more times. The temperature returned to normal, Emma opened her eyes and reached for her notebook.

***

The next morning, David and Bryan were ushered into the New Elgan Police Services by Staff Inspector Carlo Carducci.

After pleasantries were exchanged over espressos, Carlo said, "Ready to get started?"

David squared his shoulders and replied, "As ready as I'll ever be."

"Excellent. Let me call Arnie in. He's got Jazzie's computer set up and ready to go." He punched the intercom button on his desk phone and said, "Arnie, you can come in now."

Arnie tapped at the door, entered Carlo's office and handed the laptop to David.

"Got the password codes?" he asked.

"Got 'em," said David.

Bryan's voice was strained, "And there's no way they can trace that it's us contacting them?"

"No. Tor protects a user's anonymity by bouncing their communications around a distributed network of servers called Tor nodes," said Arnie.

"And what about Tor's legality?" asked Bryan, clearing his throat.

"Although it's not illegal to use a Tor browser, the anonymity and access to the dark web, which exists within the deep web, is commonly used by criminals," replied Arnie. "And people like me, who work for law enforcement or the intelligence community."

"Can they tell what sites I'm visiting?" asked David.

"No, they can't easily see that."

"What about tracing the real IP address here at the station?"

"No, they can't see our real IP address." Arnie leaned against Carlo's desk; his arms folded in front of him. "Using Tor, also known as The Onion Router, users can access unindexed web content anonymously."

"Well, that's somewhat reassuring," said David. "Let's do it, then." He turned on the computer and opened the Tor browser.

David navigated to the website *www.Adopt-a-Kid-Hassle-Free.onion*. Immediately, a web form popped up. "It's asking me to fill out this online form. They're asking for a name."

"No need to fill that out since you already have login credentials."

"Please reassure me. You're certain they won't know who we are?"

"Jazzie had created a username to match these login credentials. They will think they know who you are, but they'll be wrong, and they won't know your location."

"Here goes, then," said David, hitting the submit button.

The site was austere and ordinary

"Not much into web design, are they?" commented David.

"That's deliberate. All Tor sites use the bare minimum of resources. It's a slow browser so you want the website to work. It doesn't need to look pretty. It would only slow down the website's performance.

A rudimentary chat window opened.

<State your business.

<<Looking for a kid to adopt.

<Age and gender?

<<Two. A boy.

<Describe your specifications.

David looked up from the screen. "This is cold. It's like ordering a kitchen appliance."

He keyed in his answer.

<<Blond, blue-eyed. Slim build. Germanic descent. Athletic. High IQ.

<Two is too young to determine IQ. The Stanford-Binet Intelligence Scale and predictive algorithms can determine potential IQ based on genetic history but are not a guarantee.

<<And if the child does not meet expectations?

<A full or partial refund for merchandise will be given, depending on usage.

"What the f—!" exploded David. "Usage?"

Bryan rested his hand on David's shoulder. "You're doing great, son. Keep on going."

<<Do you have inventory?

<Yes. Check back in forty-eight hours. 23:00 UTC time.
A message flashed across the screen. CHAT ENDED.

Thirty-Eight

Now We Wait

WHEN DAVID AND BRYAN returned to the offices, David burst through the doors, unable to contain his excitement and said, "We've made progress!"

Trevor looked up from the legal documents and asked, "What progress?"

"Oh, sorry, Trev, it's a case we're working on. Unrelated to your caseload."

Trevor looked away, hiding the expression of annoyance at the offhand dismissal of his question.

Hearing the excitement, Emma exited her office and said, "Shall I put some coffee on?"

"Yes, please. Let's meet in the boardroom in five."

Once Laura, Emma, Bryan and David were gathered around the boardroom table, they listened intently to the breakthrough David and Bryan had made at the New Elgan Police Services that morning.

"I can't believe you're going to try and infiltrate a child adoption ring," Laura shuddered at the news David related.

Bryan put his arms around her. "We've got to stop them."

"So, 23:00 UTC time is exactly what time?" asked Emma, reaching for her phone to google her question.

"I already checked, Emma. It's 6 pm."

"So, now we wait," said Laura.

***

Ever since Trevor had installed the bugs, spying on the team was much easier. No one at the firm had questioned why he wore earbuds, assuming he liked to listen to music while he worked.

While listening to the team's plans in the board room, Trevor unconsciously scratched his cheek and drew blood. The acne he'd had as a teenager had returned with a vengeance. The new wound joined the many other craters on his ravaged skin. His physician had said it was stress-related and had asked Trevor if he liked his new job. Trevor said he liked the work but found it challenging. There was no point elaborating.

When the investigative team had moved on to other matters, he slipped the encrypted cell into his pocket and walked over to the boardroom and knocked on the door. "Hey, guys, heading to the rest room. I'll be back shortly."

"No problem. Take your time," said Emma. "I'll cover the front desk for you."

A fresh wave of guilt came over Trevor as he headed to the restroom. Upon entering the washroom, he caught a glimpse of himself in the mirror and winced. *Geez. I've got to stop.* He applied some of the benzoyl peroxide gel on his acne, then entered a washroom stall, pulled down the seat cover and sat down.

He hit speed dial and waited for the encrypted call to connect. He and the mysterious stranger shared the same encryption key so that confidentiality was assured.

"Report," said the man, his voice hard and cold.

175

"The BC compound was successfully evacuated. The inventory should have arrived at the new location by now," said Trevor, his voice filled with apprehension. "But we had a problem..."

"Explain."

"One of the residents, and three children, managed to elude the elimination team."

"Let me guess. Samantha and those kids she took under her wing."

"Yes, sir. They've been questioned by the MacKenzie police. She doesn't know where the cargo was headed, though, so we should be safe."

"And the incinerator should take care of any evidence."

There was a lengthy pause, unnerving Trevor. *Why does he do that?* A moment before Trevor was about to ask if Reinhard was still on the line, the silence was broken.

"Did David Harris and his father-in-law, or the MacKenzie police, discover anything of note?"

"Nothing we know of, sir. The sanitation team was thorough."

"Excellent. Anything more to report?"

"David and Emma came back from BC early," said Trevor. He cleared his throat. "I heard back from the taxi driver who brought them from the airport to the hospital. The team wasn't successful in eliminating Bryan Grant. He's expected to make a full recovery. Any further instructions, sir?"

"Hold off on the hit, for now. And Dr. Sperling?"

"Was in hiding," said Trevor. "Probably ran out of drink. Lately, he's been seen in several local bars in Kelowna."

"Send a team to silence the good doctor."

"What about Harris and Grant?"

"For now, keep an eye on them."

"Yes, sir."

"What else have you found out?

"The twins are asking questions. So is Megan, Maggie's younger sister."

"Bring them in. Fly them to our new compound in Central America. Time to start up again. Oh, and find a local doctor. Someone more reliable than that idiot Sperling who won't ask so many questions."

"Anything else, sir?"

"Yes, one more thing. I'd like you to track down Evan and his daughter Simone."

Trevor's hands shook as he accessed his TOR account and contacted the killer-for-hire to hunt down Dr. Sperling, a team to kidnap Megan Stacey and Maggie Stacey's twin girls, Sandra and Cheryl, and another to locate Simone, the child Maggie and Evan had together.

Thirty-Nine

Simone and A Restless Soul

EMMA SAT UP with a start, pulling away the sheets that had covered both her and David. David mumbled in his sleep "Where're the sheets?" Before she even had time to answer, he rolled over and fell asleep again.

She checked the time on her iPad and was surprised to see that it was still early: eleven at night. She had the sensation that she had been sleeping for hours.

The communication that had awakened her and seared through her mind like a branding iron was clear: Maggie needed to talk. Grabbing her silk dressing gown and slippers, she crept out of the room, careful not to awaken David a second time.

The urgency of Maggie's message compelled Emma to head for Anna's Room. *Hang on, Maggie,* she telegraphed to the restless spirit. *I'll be right with you.* She settled on her meditation mat and opened her mind to Maggie.

Now, Maggie, how can I help? she asked.

Simone and the other two children. Do you have news?

Yes, we have some news. Samantha and three other children were rescued at the BC compound.

My children? The air vibrated with palpable excitement.

Oh, no, Maggie. I'm sorry. Three other kids.

Not mine, then. Maggie's apparition shook with grief. *Samantha, she tricked us. Evan ...*

178

Emma sent soothing thoughts to Maggie. *I know. But I have good news. She helped Evan and Simone escape.*

My little girl. She still lives. Objects in the room began to levitate and slowly rotate around Emma.

Calm down, Maggie. Yes, we believe she and Evan are still alive. We are currently searching for them both.

And what of my other two?

Cheryl and Sandra are safe. They met Megan.

Oh. Objects bounced up and down in the air, as if dancing a jaunty jig.

Emma' eyes widened in alarm when a precious Asian vase nearly collided with an antique bust of Shakespeare. *Please, Maggie, put the objects down.*

What of my other two? Charlie and Tammy?

Emma conjured up warm comforting thoughts and wrapped them around Maggie. *Please, Maggie, put my things down.* Although Maggie had lowered the items back to their original positions, the atmosphere remained infused with eager anticipation.

I need you to pay attention, Emma telegraphed.

All right.

Charlie and Tammy died with their adoptive parents in a house fire. We told you this before.

Noooo! The temperature in the room plummeted, and gusts of energy and swirling lights emanated from Maggie and swirled around Emma.

Maggie, stop it! Emma's protests did little to lessen the commotion Maggie was producing. In desperation, Emma called out to Spirit Anna. *Anna! I need you!*

As quickly as the disturbance occurred, it stopped. Spirit Anna stepped forward in full form and wrapped white healing energy around Maggie.

The aura coming from Maggie lightened as she responded to Anna's love. In her mind, she could hear Anna's reassurances to Maggie. *Emma and her team are doing everything they can to find Simone and Evan.*

When you are ready to go into the Light, you will be with Charlie and Tammy. They are waiting for you on the other side.

An image of a blond and pretty young girl in her preteens flooded Emma's mind. The resemblance to Megan and Maggie and the twin sisters was remarkable. In her mind, she heard Spirit Anna's voice. *This is Simone.* Then, after a pause, Anna continued. *Maggie, all will be well. Trust and have faith.*

Maggie's apparition faded at the edges until she had disappeared from Emma's sight and her mind.

She reached for the water bottle she'd placed by her mat. She drank greedily, easing her parched throat and parched lips. "Thank you, Spirit Anna," she said aloud, her voice quiet and tentative.

"How do we help Maggie move on to the next phase in the spirit world? She needs closure and I fear she will remain a restless soul until she's sure her kids are safe," said Emma, continuing to speak out loud.

Yes, the best way to help Maggie is to find her children.

"Thank you, Anna, for your help and guidance."

You do know I will be withdrawing?

"But why?" asked Emma."

I will be moving on to a higher dimension. My last assignment will be to help Maggie to finally adjust and move on from here to the Spirit World.

"But Anna, I still need you."

You will need to work with the Spirit Guides who are assigned to you. This will be your spiritual team for as long as you remain in human form.

Emma blinked at the tears gathering at the corners of her eyes.

Trust in this, my sweet girl. Your abilities will grow. In time, you will see the higher wisdom in this.

"But how do I find my guides?"

They have always been with you. Whenever you've had an inkling of something you should or shouldn't do, those were your guides working with you. It could show as a sign which could be in the form of an image or an animal or a bird. Be open and receptive.

"Anna, please don't—"

If ever you truly need me, I will be there, but it is time for me to help restless souls move forward with their spiritual development.

"Anna, I understand," said Emma, her voice cracking with emotion. "And thank you."

As Anna's presence faded, one last message entered Emma's mind. *Call Mona.*

She glanced at the French clock that held a place of honor on the mantle above the fireplace and noted that the ornate hands showed it was a little after twelve in the morning. *It's still early enough to try and get a good night's rest,* she thought.

Forty

Feeling Lost Without Anna

AFTER CRAWLING BACK to bed, and slipping between the sheets, Emma tried to fall asleep while reading a book on her iPad about meditating. Slumber would not come to her, though and for the umpteenth time she saw that the numbers on the digital clock had hardly progressed. *2:15. Too late to take something to help me sleep and too early to get up.*

Lately, her meditations had failed to calm her. The more frustrated she became, the less she was able to relax and be open to connecting with her spirit guides. *May as well try, anyway.*

She slid the covers off, careful not to disturb David yet again, and grabbed some comfortable yoga clothing from their ensuite closet. As she opened the bedroom door, soft light from the hallway filtered through, illuminating David's peaceful face as he slept. *Ironic,* she thought. *A couple of years ago, it was David who could never get a good night's sleep. Now, it's me.*

She padded back to Anna's room and settled on her mat to begin her pranayama breathing practice. She sat up tall, extending her spine to make room for her lungs to expand. Then she closed her eyes, and slowed her breathing, careful to breathe in and out through her nose. She extended the inhale and exhale to five counts each and felt the tension melt. As her stress and anxiety drifted away, her attention and focus increased.

She visualized a white light pulsing throughout her body, extending from the base of her spine all the way to the top of her head, and soon a healing energy enveloped her entire body. During this calm state, she set her intention to connect with her spirit guides.

She visualized who her guides might be. Remembering Anna's teachings from when she was still in human form, she recalled that each person had at least three guides; a main guide, a guardian angel, and a gatekeeper.

These guides were normally advanced souls whom she may have known in a previous life, or in this current one.

As calm as her meditative state made her, she was unable to identify who they might be. She had read that it takes time to develop this connectivity with one's soul guides and that she must be patient.

A firm resolve came over her. In the morning, she'd contact Mona Findlay, as both Spirit Anna and her mother had suggested, and make an appointment to see her. Perhaps guidance from Mona on this plane of existence might help her connect with her spiritual guides.

A sense of purpose filled her being and she now knew that she could sleep. Worried her wakefulness would disturb David, should she return to bed again, she unfolded one of the quilts Anna had made, settled herself on the couch, and arranged the quilt on top of her. Her last thought before drifting off to sleep was that she would definitely contact Mona in the morning for help.

***

Bright sunshine streamed through the windows onto the area where Emma slept. Slightly disoriented for a moment or two until her eyes adjusted to the light, she didn't at first see David sitting in the chair.

He wore an expression that transmitted both love and concern. "A rough night, honey?" he asked, handing her a cup of coffee.

"Oh, java," she said, taking a grateful sip. "I needed that. Thanks."

"No problem." David's eyes narrowed in anxiety. "You've got me worried. You were up several times last night."

"David, I am so sorry. I thought I hadn't awakened you."

"It's not that. I fell back to sleep each time, but I noticed you weren't in bed beside me, that's all." David took a sip of his own coffee. "So, what's going on with you?"

"It was an eventful night, but ultimately, I did finally get some shut-eye."

"Care to share with your best friend?"

"Yes, of course. First, Maggie contacted me. It was quite a wild ride. She was very restless. I couldn't control her."

"She didn't take over your body, did she?" David's posture straightened, telegraphing his alarm.

"No, nothing like last time." She shuddered. "It was more an interrogation. And she seemed to have forgotten that two of her kids had already passed on. When I reminded her of this, she got agitated. She levitated objects around the room." Emma shook her head in astonishment. "I can't quite believe it. It was like something out of an Exorcist movie."

"How did you handle it?"

"I asked for Spirit Anna's help. She sorted things out. Explained her two kids who'd passed were waiting for her on the other side."

Tears sprang into her eyes. "Oh, David, I'm losing Anna. She's moving on. She says she's been called to a new purpose helping souls move on to the spirit world."

"She's been hinting about this for a while. This can't be a surprise, anymore."

"No, I guess not," said Emma wiping at the moisture collecting at the corners of her eyes.

"But there's more, isn't there?"

"Yeah," she whispered.

"When you came back to bed, you read on your iPad for a while. Then you got up again."

"Yes, but I thought you were asleep."

"Em, I'm always aware of you, as if some unseen thread binds us together."

"You're right, I did get up again."

"So, what happened next?"

"I tried to contact my Spirit Guides, like Anna instructed me."

"And?"

"The meditation I had was better than I've had in some time. I was at peace, and I realized two things. One, that my guides have always been with me and two, that I need assistance in expanding my connection with them."

"Didn't your mom say you should be contacting Mona Findlay?"

Emma nodded. "Yes. And that's what I plan on doing today."

Forty-One

Emma Seeks Mona's Help

"THANKS FOR SEEING ME on such short notice," said Emma.

"I'm glad you reached out to me," said Mona. "Your mom said you might be contacting me."

Mona was a slender brunette in her mid-thirties with vivacious eyes that took in everything at once. Her tiny waist was encircled by a belt that matched the pretty, knee-length, floral-patterned dress she wore. Her dark hair had been twisted up in a graceful chignon.

A scent of earth, forest pine and a sweet citrusy smell wafted through the air. "It smells beautiful in here. Frankincense?"

"Yes, that's right. It's meant to help calm the mind and soul."

"It's lovely."

"So, let's talk a bit. I understand that you wish to be more in tune with your spirit guides."

"Yes. Do you remember Anna Tungsten?"

"Of course." A shadow crossed Mona's face. "She was killed the year before last."

"Yes, but she's been working with me and our team to help solve cold cases." Emma gave Mona a tired smile. "But Anna is moving on. She has been called to do spiritual work helping lost souls make their transition to the next realm. She says I need to be in tune with my own guides." Emma gazed downward. "I guess I have been relying too heavily on her, instead of developing my own intuition."

"But now it's time for Anna to cut the apron strings, so to speak," said Mona.

"That's a great way of putting it."

"Clearly, you have heightened abilities; otherwise you wouldn't have been able to work with Spirit Anna."

"I guess so. Anna told me during my training that there are at least three guides with whom I should be working."

Mona nodded and said, "A main guide, a guardian angel, and a gatekeeper. And there can be more than three, but never less than three, all depending on what is going on in your life."

"So, what does each guide do?" asked Emma, leaning forward eagerly.

"The main guide cares about your soul's evolution and helps you face the lessons we must learn, whether in our corporal bodies or in spirit form. What we learn or don't learn helps us get closer or further away from self-realization, or enlightenment.

"By learning to overcome the sense of self or ego, ultimately, we will reunite with the universal intelligence, or what some people refer to as the God-consciousness. When we attain this we are all connected, so what happens to one of us, happens to the whole."

"There was something odd David said this morning," said Emma. "He said he's always aware of me, as if we were connected physically."

"Interesting. David, without realizing it, is tapping into his connection with you. Imagine how this would be if we were tapped into all conscious beings."

"The harmony and synchronicity would be divine."

"Divine is exactly the right word," said Mona, smiling.

"And what about the guardian angel?"

"As the name suggests, your guardian angel will protect you whenever possible."

"Like when you have a feeling you shouldn't go out that day, and then later read on the news about a traffic accident you might have been in, if you hadn't listened to your inner self?"

"Exactly like that."

"Nobody would ever get hurt if they listened to their intuition, their guardian angel. But people do get hurt, killed even."

"But there is still free will. When a person's karmic responsibilities are completed for this lifetime, or if they succumb to reckless behavior, or have a lack of desire to listen to their instincts, their life can be cut short."

"I see. And what about the gatekeeper?"

"The gatekeeper's role is to protect you and shield you from any unwanted spirits."

"Like preventing a spirit from taking over during a séance?" asked Emma.

"Definitely. You can ask your gatekeeper for help at any time, especially when you are undertaking any mediumship or spiritual work."

"Oh, I haven't been doing that at all." Emma gave an embarrassed laugh. "I've had my body taken over by a very trouble spirit named Maggie. We're working on a missing persons case – *her case.*"

"This is where your gatekeeper will help you. Any situation that makes you scared or uncomfortable – ask your gatekeeper for help."

"That might have already happened without my knowing it. My mom told Maggie it was unacceptable and for her to withdraw. And she did."

"Excellent instincts on your mom's part. Your gatekeeper would have helped make that command a reality."

"So where are these spirits positioned?"

"Excellent question. Your gatekeeper stands to your left, the guardian angel stands behind you and your main guide stands to your right. They form a trinity of sorts."

"But there can be more?"

"Yes, they can come and go. For example, Spirit Anna served as your guide for a while, but she is withdrawing for her own work and also, because you are ready to work more closely with your key guides."

"So, how do I get started? I've not been able to relax lately, and I know that is key to being more receptive."

Mona said, "Absolutely. Can I prepare some tea for you? I have an herbal garden out back. All my herbs promote psychic abilities."

"I grow herbs, too. I am intrigued. What blend are you making?"

"No blend, for the moment. I will be serving you mugwort."

"What are its benefits?"

"Mugwort has been used in many cultures for centuries. It is believed that it activates the pineal gland, associated with the dream state and spiritual experiences."

"I see. Something to help enhance my abilities."

"Yes, that's right. Before you leave today, I will give you two more herbs to take home. One is yarrow and the other is damiana."

"I've heard of mugwort and yarrow before, but what's damiana?"

"It is typically found in Central and South America; however, the seeds or leaves can be purchased in Canada. I grow it in pots during the winter, but during the summer I let it grow in well-drained soil."

"So, what are the overall benefits of these herbs?" asked Emma, intrigued.

"Yarrow is believed to help enhance the ability to tap into one's psychic skills while damiana has powerful calming properties. When a person is less anxious and more relaxed, they become more open to intuitive or psychic insights."

"Wow, this is amazing."

"It is fascinating. I've studied herbology for years."

"I am eager to learn from you," said Emma, her voice tinged with excitement.

"Excellent. I'll brew a pot of the mugwort now."

Forty-Two

Dr. Sperling Meets His End

AARON SPERLING GLANCED furtively around the airport lounge at the Vancouver International Airport, waiting to board his flight to Toronto. He was confident he had covered his tracks.

When he'd received the encrypted order to evacuate the BC compound, he had followed the instructions precisely, feeling no remorse when several of the residents were executed by the eradication team. He was confident the incinerators would perform flawlessly and erase evidence, as they had in Ontario ten years earlier.

Yes, he'd followed the orders exactly, except for one thing – he had no intention of starting up a third operation in Nicaragua. It wasn't that the work sickened him. To the contrary, he'd taken great satisfaction in his job and its monetary benefits, more than he would have ever earned as a physician in Ontario, his earnings dictated and capped according to the rules of OHIP, the Ontario Health Insurance Plan. He had even enjoyed the odd perk with a young captive now and again. But at nearly sixty years of age, he wanted a change of pace. He wanted to retire.

When the last helicopter left the compound with its cargo of eligible young breeders and children ready for adoption, he'd driven his Range Rover to the local supermarket in MacKenzie, purchased food and a case of Jack Daniels.

Once ensconced in his motel room, he feigned drunkenness. He doused his face and arms, and clothing in booze and played the harmless, annoying drunk. Casual observers would not have given him a second glance, and if anyone from the Dark Hands of Anubis was watching him, they would report back that he was on a bender. In reality, Aaron was making plans for his escape under an identity he'd cultivated for two decades.

From Toronto, he had a connecting flight to Curaçao. He fingered the fake passport: *Jake Sanders*. He'd been funneling money into a bank account under that name for the last twenty years.

He'd chosen Curaçao because the banks were open to foreigners, both residents and non-residents of the island. All he'd had to do at the time was pass the standard 'know-your-customer' and 'anti-money laundering' verification checks, which he did with flying colors.

Sixteen years ago, he had purchased a villa on the outskirts of Willemstad. The home could accommodate six people and had air conditioning, which he seldom used, since the trade winds were prevalent most of the time. Whenever he felt overheated, he'd dip himself into the pool and then lay on the lounge chair and let the breezes caress his body.

The villa was elevated sufficiently so that the tiled roof tops of the houses below did not impede his view of the ocean. On clear days, he could see the waves crashing against the shore. On quiet days, he could even hear those waves.

He closed his eyes and visualized already being on the island, listening to the tropical birdsong. Troupials, a predominantly orange tropical bird that looked a little bit like Baltimore Orioles, mockingbirds, yellow finches, yellow orioles and house sparrows were frequent visitors to the seed and sugar water left out for them. Even while away, he had strict instructions for the housekeeping staff to keep the feeders replenished.

Aaron sighed with relief when business class, the first to board the aircraft, was called. *Almost there*, he thought. *Soon, I'll be in paradise.*

REVENGE IS NOT ENOUGH

***

The hacker working for the Dark Hands of Anubis reported back. "Sir, it's as you suspected: he's travelling under the name of Jake Sanders and has a WestJet flight destined for Curaçao. He'll be boarding in a few minutes."

"That stupid man really thought we didn't know his plans," said his boss.

"Instructions, sir?"

"Arrange for a greeting party at his villa. Make it a welcome to die for." The laugh was harsh and grating and struck a chord of fear in the hacker.

"Yes, sir. I'll make the arrangements."

***

The flight, a little over five hours, was uneventful. In business class, while sipping on wine and a delicious onboard meal, Aaron relaxed, allowing the tension he had been feeling the last several days to ease. Periodically, he read on his tablet or closed his eyes, allowing the hum of the plane to lull him into a light sleep.

The flight attendant nudged Aaron's arm gently. "Mr. Sanders, can you please adjust your seat to the upright position. We'll be landing soon."

He eyed the pretty attendant and asked her, "Heading back to Toronto after this?"

"No, I'm staying here for a few nights. I have some time off and thought I'd enjoy some sun."

"Really? Have a place to stay?"

Aaron imagined the young woman naked and under his control.

"I got a room booked, but I'm open to suggestions." She scribbled her name and number on a napkin. "Call me for drinks and then we'll see." She gave him a wink and moved on.

Noting her name, he said, "I will definitely call you." He took her hand and lightly stroked it with his thumb. "I'm Jake. I look forward to getting to know you better."

The flight attendant flushed slightly at the flirtation and pulled her hand back. "Tot ziens," she said in Dutch. "See you later."

Further down the aisle, he could hear her friendly voice, tinged with a light Dutch accent, repeat periodically, "Bags stowed in front, please. Straighten your seat. We'll be landing shortly."

Under the name Jake Sanders, he'd completed the mandatory online Digital Immigration Card earlier. In tandem with the automatic Border Security Kiosks Curaçao used at the airport, which allowed low-risk travelers to enter the country easily, he passed through immigration without difficulty. He bypassed the baggage area since he'd travelled light with one carry-on bag. Everything he needed was already at the villa. The agents barely gave him a glance as he passed through Customs.

As he exited the airport and was greeted by the warm winds and tropical air, a feeling of joy overtook him. *I did it!* he thought. *I'm ready to start my best life.*

***

The taxi dropped off Aaron at the front door and sped away, anxious to get to his next fare. Aaron sighed with relief. *I'm here. Finally.* He dropped his bag, went to the bar and poured himself a cognac, then padded through the rear walkout to enjoy the ocean view.

Feeling lonely, he pulled out his cell and called the pretty flight attendant. "Feel like that drink, yet?" he asked playfully.

"Jake. It's great to hear from you," she said, her husky voice infused with the promise of more. "Sure thing. Text me your address. See you in about an hour?"

"Looking forward to it," said Aaron.

He went back to the bar and poured another stiff one, then returned to the chaise lounge. He was so intent on the view, and the indulgence of his drink, that he did not notice the intruder lurking in the shadows of the cabana.

The pinprick was so slight, it could have been an insect. Aaron raised his hand to touch the skin, but noticed his arm was sluggish and slow to respond. *Am I having a stroke?* he wondered.

"No, it's not a stroke," reassured the assassin, as if reading Aaron's thoughts. "Greetings, from the Dark Hands of Anubis."

Recognition that these were his last moments of life flashed through Aaron's eyes before his hand relaxed, the half-finished glass of cognac slipping from his slack fingers and shattering on the Corallina tile below.

***

An hour later, the flight attendant's cab dropped her off in front of Jake's villa, which was shrouded in darkness.

She frowned and asked, "Can you wait a moment?"

The cabby nodded. "*Zeker,*" he replied in Dutch. "Sure. I'll keep the meter running."

"*Dankje.* Thanks." She pushed the gate open and called out, "Jake?"

She walked around the villa to the back and saw an arm draped over the side of a lounge chair. "Jake?" she repeated.

Alarmed by the stillness, she crept closer and touched Jake's arm. The slight push dislodged the body, and it fell sideways off the chair. Her eyes widened in fright, her senses overloaded by the sight, her feet rooted to the ground.

Her momentary paralysis was interrupted by impatient honking. *The cabby!* she thought. She backed away and ran to the taxi. "There's a body in there!" she shouted. "Call 911!"

Forty-Three

Remember Last Year in the Maldives?

EMMA AND DAVID sat across from each other at the dinner table. "David, this is so delicious," said Emma. "You've been spoiling me so much, lately." She tucked into the butternut squash and portobello-stuffed ravioli.

"Anything for you, Em," said David. "Since I've met you, I have begun to appreciate vegetarian options."

"And of course, chocolate," Emma grinned.

"That, too," he said smiling. "So, tell me how things went with Mona, today. Is she going to be able to help you?"

"She already has," said Emma, putting her fork down. "She's an amazing person! Besides being a powerful psychic, she's an herbalist and also volunteers at a wildlife rescue in Beeton, Ontario."

"Let me guess, Procyon Wildlife?"

"Yep, the one and the same. I'd love to do that kind of work one of these days. Their work rescuing and rehabilitating injured and orphaned wildlife in distress is truly inspiring."

"Em, but what about your meeting today?"

"Sorry, I got carried away," said Emma, with a wry smile. "You know what? Let's go sit in the living room. I have a lot to tell you."

"Fine," said David, piling up their used dinner plates. "I'll take care of them later."

They picked up their wine glasses and once settled on the couch, Emma continued. "We went over the types of spirit guides that help us. There are three main ones: the main guide, the guardian angel and the gatekeeper. We all have spirit guides." She stared over David's shoulder. "Even you do, David."

"What? Are they there?" Startled, he turned to look behind him.

Emma giggled with delight.

"Em, stop teasing me."

"Seriously, though, they are all there. But depending on how intuitive and receptive we are, we are not always aware of them."

Her face grew solemn. "Remember last year in the Maldives, when Jazzie kidnapped me in the hotel elevator? She'd tricked me into thinking you had texted me to come downstairs. My intuition was screaming at me to stay in the hotel room, but I overrode what my guardian angel was telling me to do."

"So, any closer on how to get in touch with them more directly?" asked David. "Maybe this is something I should be striving for, too."

"At today's session she gave me mugwort tea."

"Really? Sounds like some concoction straight out of a magical world featuring a young wizard," he teased.

"David, be serious. I'm trying to tell you." She playfully punched his arm.

"And what is it supposed to do?"

"It stimulates the pineal gland to enhance spiritual experiences."

"And?"

"There's more work to be done, but I have met my guides. Mona explained that guides are often souls we have known in previous lives."

"So, who are they?"

"My main guide is Salma. She's a guide that has been with me during several incarnations. She is helping me with my soul's evolution. My guardian angel is Pieter—my grandfather on my mother's side."

"And the gatekeeper?"

"That's Frederick. He's a scary one. Very fierce. He prevents any spirits from trying to harm me. If ever I feel afraid or threatened, I am to call on his help."

"Could he have prevented Maggie from taking over your body?"

"Yes, if I'd had the wisdom to ask him. I thought Anna and Mom finally expelled Maggie, but it was Frederick that saved me."

"Now that you are aware of this, what's next?" asked David. "Do you feel safer? More in control?"

"Yes, I do. I can continue my spiritual work with more confidence."

"Em, this is terrific news." David slid closer to Emma on the couch and encircled his arms around her.

"I do feel better. Less scared. Also, Mona gave me two more herbs to make tea with. One is yarrow and the other is damiana."

"And what do those do?"

"I am to use the yarrow during my meditations. It is supposed to enhance my psychic abilities." She leaned her head against David's chest.

"I should be getting better sleeps, too, with the other herb, damiana. It has calming properties, which will reduce my stress and make me more open to my intuition." She giggled and nestled closer to David. "It also has another side effect."

"What's that?"

"It's an aphrodisiac."

"Hmm ... I like the sound of that," said David, nibbling her ear. "Maybe you should make us both a pot."

"Shall we wash the dishes later?" asked Emma, her eyes sparkling.

Forty-Four

Megan and the Twins Go Missing!

The following morning, David rolled over on his side and was pleased to see Emma still sleeping. For the first time in months, she looked calm and peaceful.

He headed to the kitchen, prepared breakfast in bed for them both and then carried the tray with their morning coffees and oatmeal apple muffins to the bedroom. He wafted Emma's cup near her face and waited for her to open her eyes.

"Mmm ... that smells so good," she stretched her hand out and took the coffee. "Thanks, you're so sweet to me."

"I was thinking ... it's Saturday. What about taking a day off?"

"I'd love to, but I made plans to meet Megan and their nieces, Sandra and Cheryl, at Café Mokka."

"How are they getting along?"

"Fantastic. The three of them have really hit it off. You'd never know they'd met only recently." Emma placed her coffee mug on the night table, slipped out of bed and headed to the bathroom.

"How long are they staying with Megan?"

"Not sure," she called out. "Sandra has her own place downtown but there's talk the twins might move in with Megan permanently. Having found each other, those two have become inseparable. They're even dressing alike. And this is on the QT: they're working on some musical compositions together." She gave a sweet smile. "They're so happy to have family in their lives."

"Have they met Megan's father, yet?"

"Not yet, but soon, I think."

Emma glanced at her watch and said, "I should get ready. I have an idea. How about we go for a drive this afternoon in the MGB? I should be back by noon, and I could pack a picnic."

"I love that idea," said David.

"How do you plan to spend your morning?"

"I'm due for a good solid workout. I'll work on finding Evan and Simone, and then, of course, there's Dr. Sperling, too. Another loose end to investigate."

"Maybe I should cancel with Megan and the girls. Stay here and help you. We can go for coffee another time."

"No, you go ahead. We'll take the afternoon off like you suggested and go for that drive. Enjoy your time with Megan and the twins. Say hi to everyone for me."

"Will do," replied Emma, reassured. "Thanks, David. Love you."

"Love you right back."

***

David was so engrossed in his work that his mind didn't register the ringing. After a moment, it stopped ringing and then started again. *Damn,* he thought. *Probably an annoying telemarketer.* When he reached for his phone, first a flash of guilt, then worry, coursed through his mind. *Emma? Something must be wrong.*

"Hi, Em. What's up?"

"Oh, David, Megan and the twins are missing." She stifled a sob. "Megan missed their shift yesterday at Café Mokka. And they're not answering their cell. It's not like them. Their boss is worried and so am I."

"What time were you supposed to meet?"

"Ten-thirty and it's almost eleven now. I'm driving to Megan's house now."

"I'll meet you at their place. Please wait for me before you go in."

"I'll wait, but hurry."

"On my way." David scooped up the keys for the Kia EVS and rushed out of the house.

Once on the road, he said, "Siri, call Bryan Grant."

Before his father-in-law could respond, David said, "Hey Bryan, we've got a situation. Megan, Stacey, and their two nieces, Sandra and Cheryl, are missing. Meet me at Megan's house."

***

When David arrived at Megan's house, Bryan had already arrived. He had a protective arm draped over Emma's shoulder. Her face was pale and tear-streaked. She broke free of Bryan's embrace and rushed over to David.

"Thank God you're here. I'm afraid something terrible has happened." Her fingers trembled as she rummaged through her purse. "Here are Megan's spare keys. I forgot to give them back to Megan after their last holiday. I was watering their plants." She gulped while a fresh wave of tears began. "Will you go in first? I'm afraid of what we might find ..."

Bryan stepped forward, "David and I will check things out. Please wait here, Emma."

A few minutes later, both men came back out. "No one is here, Em," said David, his voice filled with compassion. "How about trying Megan's dad? Maybe Megan took the twins there?"

Emma looked off into the distance, her head tilted to the side. "The Dark Hands of Anubis have them," she said tonelessly, her eyes filling with fresh tears.

Forty-Five
Evan and Simone

EVAN FITZPATRICK WALKED his daughter, Simone, to and from school every day. After her tenth birthday, and self-conscious in front of her peers, she wouldn't hold his hand on the daily walk anymore. She refused to walk beside him and would often run ahead. How he missed that soft small hand in his, but he knew this was all part of his little girl growing up.

"Daddy," she'd objected, "all the other kids get to walk to school by themselves."

"Simone, honey," he'd said, "You're not all the other kids ... you are my kid, and I need to keep you safe."

Evan had done his best to buffer Simone from the danger that they faced each day, never knowing if this would be the day that the Dark Hands of Anubis would discover them.

Simone was three years of age when they escaped the compound in BC, and even after seven years, he looked over his shoulder every day, fearful his daughter would be snatched from him. He realized her memories of the days living in the cult-like community were fading, as they should be, but *he* would never forget.

The compromise the father and daughter had finally reached was that he would walk twenty feet behind her, close enough if something were to happen, but far enough away to give Simone the independence she craved.

"No running off," he'd admonished her. "I need to be able to see you at all times."

"Yes, Daddy," she'd said, a mischievous glint in her eyes betraying that she would do that very thing if she could get away with it.

"Simone! This is serious."

When she saw the fierce look in her father's eyes, she backtracked and said, "Daddy, I get it. The compound. You know I don't really remember much about it."

"And that's a good thing, honey, but we still need to be careful of our surroundings."

"Sorry, Daddy. I didn't mean any harm. I'm not a baby anymore." She thrust out her lower lip, pouting, making her appear the little girl she still was.

"I know that, sweetheart."

He tussled her naturally blond-white hair.

"Daddy!" she protested. "Don't mess with my hair!"

Evan smiled. *You'll always be my baby. Even when you're fifty*, he thought.

***

That little argument had been several months ago, and they had both fallen into the routine where Evan would keep a vigilant eye on Simone, while still giving her room to be with her schoolmates as they walked to school. Freedom to let her be a kid without living in fear. He was strong enough to handle the fear for them both.

When the bell rang indicating the school day was over, he waited the way he always did until he could see his daughter's wavy blond hair caught in the sunshine.

Simone burst out of the school, surrounded by her schoolmates. She looked up to see her dad, and gave a small wave and a big smile, before going back to the animated conversation with her friends.

Not all the kids had cell phones, but Evan insisted Simone carry one for safety reasons. "You call me anytime you need me," he'd told her.

Simone was the envy of the kids whose parents had not yet given them cell phones and today they were giggling as they took turns having selfies taken with his daughter.

She's as pretty and vivacious as her mother was, Evan thought, a pang of sorrow piercing his heart, the way it always did whenever he thought of his Maggie.

When Simone looked up, he pointed at his watch. "Time to go."

She nodded, laughed with her friends for a few more moments, said her goodbyes, and without breaking her stride, walked straight past her dad as if he wasn't there.

Still pretending to be independent, Evan thought. *She'll be a handful when she's a teenager.*

It happened so quickly Evan had no time to react. A late model, dark-colored sedan came to an abrupt halt beside Simone. One of the rear doors opened immediately and a man who'd been standing near a light standard grabbed her around her slender waist and threw her into the back of the vehicle, then jumped in beside her.

Seconds later, before Evan could fully comprehend the nightmarish scene that was unfolding, he collapsed to the pavement. A searing pain pummeled the back of his head, then there was nothing.

Forty-Six

Where's My Daughter?

EMMA ROSE FROM her meditation. It had been a fruitful session with her three guides providing her help.

She closed the door to Anna's Room and walked to the kitchen. She wore a somber expression. "David, besides Megan and the twins, Simone is gone, too."

"Unfortunately, I have news reinforcing that," he replied, placing his cell on the table. His expression was grave. "I was able to finally track down Simone and her father Evan. They've been living in New Elgan all this time, under the last name Fitzpatrick."

"But, David, that sounds promising."

"It should have been. Bryan was going to check with Carlo at the New Elgan Police Services to see if there was any background information we could get on the Fitzpatricks." He rubbed the back of his neck, trying to ease the tension. "Instead, he learned that Simone was taken—"

"—by men in a dark-colored sedan," stammered Emma, finishing David's sentence. "That's what I saw in the vision my guides showed me."

"There were plenty of eyewitnesses, too," continued David. "Simone was snatched right in front of her father while he was walking her home from school. Before he could react, he was struck on the back of the head."

"Oh, no, this is terrible. The poor man."

"He's at the hospital. It's serious. Bleeding on the brain. Before they sedated him, he kept asking, "Where's my daughter?""

"How awful."

"No kidding. He and his daughter have successfully eluded the Dark Hands of Anubis for seven years."

"Is he conscious?" asked Emma, tilting her head.

"Emma, I don't know, I'm waiting to hear from Bryan and Carlo. They hope to talk with Evan."

She shook her head, and said, "Sorry, David, I was asking my guides." She stared at the side, seeing but not seeing.

"I see. Thank you," she finally said. "My guides say Evan will make it, but right now, the doctors have put him into an induced coma. He may need surgery. The swelling on the brain is significant." She pulled unruly auburn curls away from her face and gathered her hair into a loose bun.

"Looks like Bryan and Carlo will have to visit later, when Evan comes to," said David.

Forty-Seven

The Dream

ON THE DRIVE TO the compound, Megan was surprised that they hadn't been blindfolded. The images of palm trees and beaches were replaced by roads deeply carved by the past rainy season.

The compound was at a high altitude and was ten degrees cooler than at sea level. Pleasant breezes ruffled Megan's hair, but that is where the pleasantries stopped.

After having been thrown into the enclosure, they had injected Megan with something. Slowly coming to, she assessed the situation. Their attention was drawn to a green light which flashed intermittently, and was surprised to see an ankle bracelet encircled their left ankle. Megan's body ached from the beating and prayed their captors did not know about their non-binary identity.

The door to the enclosure was wedged open with a rock. Daylight knifed through the open doorway, its beam piercing through the shadows of the hut.

A surge of fear pulsed through Megan at the sight of their two seventeen-year-old nieces who were also outfitted with house arrest ankle bracelets. The two sisters, still unconscious, were propped up against the wall of the hut. Even sleeping, they clutched each other protectively, their faces touching.

A little girl had wedged herself in between the twins. The child stared at Megan dully. Her dirty face showed streaks of white where rivulets of tears had earlier serpentined down her cheeks.

Megan's heart ached with sorrow at the sight of the ankle bracelet surrounding the little girl's slender ankle. They cleared their throat and asked, "Are you Simone?"

The child nodded and whispered, "I want my Daddy."

"I know, honey." Megan swallowed at the lump forming in her throat and spoke in a gentle tone. "The girls are my nieces, Sandra and Cheryl."

"They were really nice to me. A bad man gave them a needle and now they won't wake up."

Megan squinted against the light and was relieved to see the girls' chests gently rising and falling. *The sedative must have been powerful.*

"We should let them sleep. Why don't you come here and visit me for a bit?"

"Sure," said Simone. She scuttled over to Megan.

Megan pulled the child onto their lap, and said, "You can call me Aunt Megan."

The soft little body relaxed almost immediately.

"Would you like me to sing a nursery rhyme?' asked Megan.

Simone nodded and nestled against Megan's chest, her breathing growing soft as she listened to the song. Relieved when little Simone had fallen asleep, Megan wondered, *What could they possibly want with the four of us?*

Barely aware of the hard-packed earth they sat upon, Megan cleared their thoughts the way Emma had taught them. Despite their troubling situation, they felt a stirring of hope when their mind grazed that of Emma's.

They perceived that Emma was in an altered sleep but was certain they could reach her through the dream world. Their eyes widened in relief when they sensed Emma respond. Megan telegraphed mental images to Emma of their journey to the compound, and of the compound itself, in the hopes she'd understand her location.

***

Emma awoke with a start and gently nudged at the sleeping form beside her. "David, I know where they are!"

David was awake in an instant. "A dream? A vision?"

"No, telepathy. Megan reached out." She shook her head in disbelief. "She's in Nicaragua. Maggie's kids, too."

"Even Simone, the ten-year-old?"

"Yes, Simone as well. That's what Megan is showing me."

"Who took them?"

Emma's expression clouded with fear. "The Dark Hands of Anubis."

"Tell Megan we're on our way."

Emma sat up straight, leaned back against the pillows, closed her eyes and slowed her breathing. Sending out feelers, her mind searched for Megan and found them. *I hear you, Megan. We are coming for you.*

Emma! Thank God. You found us. Please hurry.

Forty-Eight
What's The Plan?

"I'M NOT SURPRISED the Dark Hands of Anubis has a connection to the human-trafficking business in Nicaragua," said Bryan. "The criminal groups in that country are notorious for exploiting women and children."

"This is worse than we feared," said Emma.

"This goes far beyond the sex trade," continued Bryan. "Forced labor is also prevalent, especially within the agriculture, construction, mining and domestic service industries."

Emma pulled out her iPad and searched further. "It says here people are exploited within Nicaragua, in nearby Costa Rica, Panama and the United States."

"I think we should all go," said Laura. "Make it look like a family vacation."

"Really?" asked David. "In Nicaragua? Although it is not as dangerous as it used to be, it wouldn't be my first choice for where to take a holiday. I prefer the safer Costa Rica."

"People do vacation there, though," said Laura. "The volcanoes and lakes are a big draw for tourists. I hear the country is stunning for its natural beauty."

"The country is poor with a lot of petty crime. They are the second poorest country in the world, next to Haiti," added Emma.

The four debated further. "What would our premise be for visiting?" asked Emma. "I checked the Government of Canada Travel Advisory website, and they suggest exercising extreme caution. The government is very unstable." She shuddered. "The site says people should reconsider travel to Nicaragua due to arbitrary enforcement of laws, the risk of wrongful detention, and limited availability to healthcare."

"Laura's idea to pose as tourists could work," said Bryan with reluctance.

"It's settled, then. We are all going," said Laura.

"Laura, honey, it could be too dangerous," Bryan finally said. "We need Emma to help us hone in on the location. We won't be traveling to the typical tourist destinations. Besides, we need you to stay behind and monitor the situation from here."

"I don't like this," said Laura. "I should be there with you to help."

"Mom," Emma said. "I think you should stay. I have a feeling you'll be of more help here than there."

"The least I can do is make the travel arrangements."

"There are no direct flights to Managua." She sighed with frustration. "Either one or two stops. I can book you a direct flight from Toronto to Liberia, Costa Rica." Laura looked up from her keyboard and continued, "From there you can either drive, take a shuttle or a puddle jumper to Agusto Cesar Sandino International Airport."

"Probably less conspicuous if we rent a car and drive to Managua," said Bryan.

"How long a drive is it?" asked Emma.

"From Liberia to Managua, three hours and sixteen minutes," said Laura. "You may have a lengthy wait at the border crossing from Costa Rica to Nicaragua."

"We won't need to rent a car," said David. "Let me call my friend, Owen. He'll loan us his four by four."

"That'll be great," said Bryan. "Less conspicuous, too, by not using a rental vehicle."

"And from there, where to?" asked Laura.

"It'll be up to me," Emma's face was white. "I'm the homing pigeon."

Laura touched her daughter's hand. "Honey, have faith in your instincts and abilities. We trust you."

"So, when do we head out?" asked Emma.

"Tomorrow morning," replied Laura. "I've booked the three of you on a direct flight for Liberia first thing. You'll need to be at Toronto Pearson International Airport by 6 am."

"Lucky our passports are up to date. Mom, do we need a visa?"

"No, Nicaragua does not require Canadians to get a visa."

"There is one lead that needs to be followed up," said David, his expression worried. "Tomorrow night, Bryan and I were supposed to meet up with Carlo using the Tor account to try and infiltrate the child adoption ring."

"Good point," said Bryan. "I'll give Carlo a call. We need to fill him in on our next moves, and in case things go sideways, I'll give him the number sequence for our satphone." He wiped his fingers across his forehead. "Carlo will have to handle the adoption ring lead on his own."

"I hope this lead pans out," said Laura. "The whole concept of this baby ring and abduction case leaves me awake at night."

"It is very upsetting," said David. "But our scheme should work."

"Unless they've seen through us. Then the gig's up," said Emma, a shadow crossing her face.

"I sure hope not," said Bryan.

***

In the other room, Trevor picked up the encrypted phone hidden in his desk and made the call.

"They're on their way to Nicaragua," he said, filling in Reinhard Holtz, the man who had transformed him from a person who once held a strong moral compass to one that was corrupt.

"You're kidding!" he said, his derisive laughter was chilling. "Emma Jackson is going to locate me by instinct. I'd like to see her try!"

"She apparently does have some psychic abilities. She helped track down the Bianchis in the Maldives last year using the paranormal," Trevor reminded him.

"And what's your impression of her?"

"Mine?" stammered Trevor.

"Yes, you dimwit. Your impression."

"She has this way of looking at you, but through you, as if she can read your thoughts." The younger man sighed. "She's beautiful and smart, but she makes me uncomfortable."

"Intriguing." The man let the silence lag, knowing that it unnerved people and kept them off balance.

"Sir?" Trevor's voice quavered.

"Get some men to Liberia airport. Have them wait for them. For now, they are to follow them."

"Yes, sir. And if they get too close?"

"We'll have our men ready. I must admit, I am intrigued. I'd like to see if she really can find us using her psychic abilities. If so, her talents won't be wasted under my employ."

Forty-Nine

Reinhard Holtz

REINHARD HOLTZ CARESSED the image on the screen that Trevor had messaged him. He admired Emma's auburn hair and green eyes that even in the photo blazed with energy and passion. It had been some time since he'd bedded a worthy woman. Perhaps she'd be the mother to his children.

Reinhard was second in command for the Dark Hands of Anubis and great grandson of the founder of the organization, whose roots were established during the Nazi era. Of Aryan birth, his skin was fair, and he took care to wear 60 plus sunscreen protection to maintain his clear and smooth complexion. He was tall and angular with sharp features. Even though he exercised obsessively, his efforts did not result in extra muscle and at thirty-three years of age, his musculature was still slender, almost adolescent like in appearance. That was, until one saw his face. Although handsome, the cruel eyes and mouth were etched into a straight-line which radiated disapproval and conveyed superiority, a concept instilled into him while sitting on his great grandfather's knee.

He eased back in his chair and gazed through the large window of his spacious corner office, which occupied the western wing of his luxury villa.

Unlike the compounds in Ontario and BC, he had built an extravagant villa for his private use. Nestled on the mountainside, with a high elevation of seven hundred meters above sea level, it was positioned so that the compound below, which was still under construction, could not be seen.

The sleek, contemporary design of the villa embraced the horizon and offered breathtaking views. Each room was bathed in natural light, with removable glass walls that provided a seamless transition between indoor and outdoor living. That option, however, was never used, since Reinhard's delicate Germanic skin was highly allergic to the tropical bugs that abounded.

Although unaccustomed to the hot Central American sun and heat, he found the views of the Maribios mountain range, located in western Nicaragua, breathtaking. Lake Nicaragua, together with Lake Managua to the northwest, were both originally part of an ocean bay that became inland lakes. From his high vantage point, he could see the Tipitapa River winding from Lake Nicaragua along a meandering path he knew would connect eventually with Lake Managua.

Supplies were obtained by the nearby cities of León and Chinandega; however, he never made the trek to those cities. He had a complement of people to do that for him, ranging from cleaners, landscapers, pool attendants, maintenance staff and a personal concierge.

Satisfied there was nothing more he could do for the moment, he pressed the intercom and told the pretty, young maid he'd like a bath drawn and for her to join him.

He exited his office and walked to the bedroom.

Fifty
The Haunting

REINHARD PUSHED AWAY the memory of the sun-dappled forest. *Maggie,* he thought with regret. *It could have been so different.*

She had been his first, but she had defied him. Taunted him and challenged his manhood. *That bitch deserved everything that she got. Death was not even good enough.*

But he was never able to forget her. After a few months of holding her in the Ontario compound, he'd visited Maggie. She was more beautiful than ever, and her terror of him was so exciting. He offered her a second chance. Unbelievably, she refused, but he took her anyway. Each parting thrust he made within her was a point being made that she was powerless to refuse him. *Maggie,* he thought again. *If you had let me love you.*

He had a hard time admitting that he was worried about David Harris and his investigators. They were getting too close. He comforted himself with the knowledge that he had a stringent security team that would protect him at all costs. For now, it would be easiest to let Emma, that strange but beautiful psychic, lead David's team to his lair.

He distracted himself by thinking about Megan, Maggie's younger sister, who incited the same desire to dominate and control that he'd experienced with Maggie. Megan, older now than Maggie was at the time, was a welcome diversion from his obsessive thoughts about Emma, that green-eyed beauty. *Maybe tomorrow he would have Megan brought to his quarters. She would be a delightful diversion until Emma was under his power.*

He flung the silk sheets off his sweaty body and slid open the glass doors to the private balcony. He stood there naked, enjoying how the mountain breeze caressed and soothed his body, blowing the moisture away. He held out his hands, remarking on how the moonlight made his skin look like alabaster. Pure and white. Virtuous. *Righteous.*

Parts of the mountainous landscape were cast in deep shadows where the white orb's light didn't reach, while other areas were illuminated with ethereal grayscale shades ranging from bone white to gray to black. The palm trees in the garden danced in the wind, their graceful fronds swaying, as if in ecstasy.

He craved nighttime and the shrouded safety it offered; a respite from the sunlight which hurt his eyes and his skin. He walked over to the hammock and slid in, and although he meant to rest for a while, the wind cradled him into a troubled sleep.

***

When Emma had learned through the dream state and from Megan's direct message via telepathy where her family was being held, Maggie had been standing by, a quiet sentinel, eager to act.

After Emma had conferred with her spirit guides that this was indeed the case, Maggie now understood where Megan and her children had been taken. *To the mountains of Nicaragua.*

It took one intense moment of thought, and there she was.

Her heart soared when she saw Cheryl, Sandra and little Simone huddled up against Megan, taking comfort from them and drawing from their strength.

Megan's beautiful. She thought in wonder.

She hovered over her three children, planting otherworldly kisses on the forehead of each child. All stirred in their sleep with soft smiles. *I will do everything I can to protect you,* she thought. She kissed her fingertips and placed her fingers gently on Megan's lips. *My dear, strong Megan.*

Maggie sensed Reinhard was close by. Her energy, which had lit up in swirls of joyous white light when she was near her family, spiraled into darker colors which rotated in angry spirals. Her soul engorged with rage: her sister, twin daughters and baby Simone abused by Reinhard Holtz, and years earlier, her other two children murdered in the house fire that also killed their adoptive parents.

To her astonishment, she now floated over the sleeping man in the hammock. *Reinhard!* She began to pelt him with malevolent thoughts, like sharpened knives, and watched with satisfaction how he kicked and squirmed like an insect pinned down by a thoughtless and cruel taxidermist.

She invaded his mind and tortured his soul with images of the scene in the forest where he'd raped her. But now, he was the one being pursued and she was the aggressor. Reinhard's agonized screams permeated through the woods she had conjured up in his mind. For him, this was as real as any reality could ever be.

Her enjoyment was so profound, she did not at first feel the presence near her and although she wished it not to be so, her power over Reinhard weakened.

Maggie! Stop it! What you are doing is wrong! said Spirit Anna.

It's my revenge. Maggie telegraphed back. *Leave me be.*

This is not the way justice will be served. It must be resolved by those still alive.

Stop managing me! Angry dark shades of energy swirled about her.

I worry about your soul's evolution.

I don't care. Leave me! Maggie's rage intensified and her power returned. *I will kill kim.*

I cannot allow that, said Spirit Anna. *This is not the way it's done.* She sent a stream of energy that engulfed Maggie in a lasso of white light, which neutralized Maggie's negative force.

No! Maggie screamed.

I am sorry, but this must stop now.

Maggie's grief was inconsolable. *Why did you stop me? He deserves to die! Child, soon you will understand.*

Spirit Anna wrapped loving energy around Maggie, attempting to comfort her. *This will soon be over and you will get the answers you need,* she telegraphed to Maggie.

Not enough. I need revenge.

Soon, you will learn that revenge is not enough. Revenge and justice will temporarily satisfy your soul but not assuage it. Maggie, you need to move on to the next level. It is crucial for your soul's development. Otherwise, you will be stuck in limbo forever.

I need to be near my children, she protested.

Maggie, they, too, will leave their worldly restraints after their life cycle has been completed. If they move on and you don't, then you will have no one.

I will wait for them ... then follow.

Possibly, but then your soul will not be evolving and may not be able to return to Source.

Maggie broke away from the Spirit Anna's spiritual embrace, shattering the warm illumination into jagged crystals of fractured light. Spirit Anna looked with compassion at the troubled soul. *She's not ready,* she telegraphed to her own guide.

***

The morning sun rose in all its blazing glory, searing Reinhard's eyelids with the most vivid nightmare he'd ever had. Maggie had been pursuing him and was about to kill him. *With a knife?* He was not sure. His arms and legs were sore, and at first, he could not move them. It was as if he was skewered to the hammock.

After some effort, part of which was his desire to avoid the daylight intensifying as the sun rose higher above the horizon, he swung his legs over, rolled out of the hammock and hurried back inside, to the protection of the villa.

Fifty-One

We're Being Followed

"HOW ARE YOU DOING?" asked David, who was at the wheel of the 4 x 4. "Any more impressions of where we should be headed?"

Emma, sitting beside him, said, "I think we're getting close. Maybe five or ten minutes more." They had passed through Managua a little less than two hours ago and were north of Leon. "We have to turn off highway NIC-12A soon and head up the mountainside toward the volcanoes."

"Driving's a bit tricky," said David, avoiding a pothole. "Let me know when I need to make that turn."

"Sure thing." Emma tapped on her cell phone. "It's a touristy area. There are over twenty guide companies providing tours of the volcanoes."

"You'd think they'd be hiding somewhere more obscure," said Bryan, frowning.

"Maybe it's like hiding in plain sight," said Emma. "I am sure this is where we should be headed." She frowned. "I'm getting a reading to head to a location between Volcán San Cristóbal and Volcán Casitas."

"Are these volcanos still active?" asked David.

Emma tapped on her Google map and expanded the information on the two volcanoes. "Well, Cristóbal is the most active one in Nicaragua, and in 1998, Casitas buried a village in a landslide."

"You take us to the nicest places," said David.

Bryan, who had positioned himself in the middle of the back seat so he could still see the road, said, "I hate to interrupt the banter. Someone has been following us."

David nodded and said, "I saw them a few miles back, but wasn't sure."

Emma began to turn her head to look. "Don't look back, Emma. Best they don't realize we've noticed them," said Bryan.

"I will see if I can get any impressions from them," said Emma. Her expression grew grave. "They've been sent by the Dark Hands of Anubis." Her eyes creased with concern. "For some reason ... they are very interested in me."

David turned his eyes away from the road temporarily and threw Emma a worried look. She shook her head slightly and lightly touched his hand resting on the steering wheel. "It doesn't make any sense."

David glanced at the rearview mirror. "They're gone. I don't see them," he said.

"For now," said Emma, shuddering.

Bryan's cell vibrated. "It's a text from Laura." The furrow of lines in his forehead deepened as he relayed Laura's message: "The pens were missing from the stationary cabinet. Laura was about to tap on Trevor's door to see if he might have a spare pen when she overheard him talking. She peeked in and saw him on a different cell than he normally uses."

"And?" asked Emma.

"It says here in her text that Trevor was talking with someone about our plans to rescue Megan and the girls." Bryan's voice was grave. "Laura heard him tell whoever was on the line that we're in Nicaragua."

David cleared his throat, "He must have been tracking us."

"Trevor?" Emma's hand flew to her mouth like a startled dove. "Using our phones?"

"Yeah, I think so." Bryan gave a heavy sigh. "Pull over, David. We'll have to dispose of our phones. Hand me your cells." Bryan pulled out the SIM cards, got out of the SUV and crushed them under the heal of his boot. Then he threw the three cells in different directions into the rainforest.

"At least we still have David's encrypted satellite phone," said Emma.

"For emergencies," said David.

"And this is one of them," said Bryan, his expression grim with worry. "David, can you hand me the satellite phone, please? We need to call Laura."

Bryan keyed in the number for Laura's cell and said, "Hi, Laura, are you still by yourself?"

"Yes, Bryan. My door is closed."

"We've discarded our phones, based on your suspicions that they have been traced."

"Where are you?"

"Getting near the compound, according to Emma's intuition."

"Anything I can do to help?" asked Laura.

"Yes. It's urgent you leave the office right now. Go see Carlo at the New Elgan Police Service. Tell him about your suspicions concerning Trevor."

"I'm putting on my coat right now. Bryan ... I'm worried."

"Me, too."

"Be careful."

"We will. And another thing – call Harold Kruger. Ask for one of his security guards to escort you home from the station and to stay with you."

"I'll call now to arrange it," said Laura.

"Good. I love you," said Bryan. He disconnected the phone.

"Oh, my God," whispered Emma. "Is Mom in danger?"

David cleared his throat, "We're all in danger."

***

Reinhard Holtz savored the rush of adrenaline when he read Trevor's text: *David and the investigative team are headed your way.*

Maybe there is some truth to this woman's psychic gifts, thought Reinhard.

He sent a message to his men following the group. *Time to grab them. Create a distraction.* He was looking forward to meeting the enigmatic Emma.

Fifty-Two

Carlo Carducci

CARLO'S NORMALLY SMOOTH olive skin was puckered in a frown, which joined his eyebrows together.

"Come on in, Laura," he said. Noting her frazzled appearance, he asked, "I was making an espresso. Would you like one?"

"Please."

Carlo prepared the coffees, handed one to Laura and then settled in behind his desk with the other.

"This is good," said Laura, taking a sip.

"Now, tell me what this is all about."

"We've had a spy amongst us at the office," said Laura.

"Who, pray tell?" asked Carlo, perplexed.

"Trevor McAllister."

"Really?" he said, surprised. "I knew his dad. Are you sure?"

"Yes, unfortunately. I overheard Trevor telling someone on the phone about Bryan, David and Emma's plans."

"This is serious."

Laura nodded and said, "I've warned the team." She picked up the tiny espresso cup and took another sip. Her fingers wobbled as she replaced the cup back in its saucer. "Bryan removed the SIM cards and destroyed the phones. They'll be using the encrypted satellite phone instead."

"Hopefully, they'll be able to elude the Dark Hands of Anubis, now that they can't be geolocated by them," said Carlo.

"Maybe ... but I think Emma has got the team so close that it might be easy for the Dark Hands to find them anyway."

"Trevor was not aware of the encrypted satellite phone?"

"I doubt it. I don't know for sure, of course. Anything's possible."

"I do have the number for the satellite phone," said Carlo. "Even though the communications can be encrypted, the technology that enables their global connectivity also means people using the network could determine the phone's location with the right tools."

"Oh," said Laura, crestfallen. "Does that mean Dark Hands could find them?"

"As long as they don't have the number, no, they can't. But we could. Think of it this way: our department might be able to track them, too."

"This is better news than I expected," she said.

"I don't want to alarm you, Laura, but you might be in danger, too."

"That's what Bryan said. He told me to come to you immediately, and then afterward, Harold Kruger's security team will protect me."

"Good move on Bryan's part." Carlo drained his coffee cup and said, "Time to bring in Trevor for a little chat."

"It's after five. He's probably left the office by now."

"Do you have his home address?"

"Yes, actually. I have his contact information on my iPhone." Laura read the details out to Carlo, while he jotted them down on his notepad.

"Anything else you can think of, call me," said Carlo.

"Thanks," said Laura.

"For what?"

"For taking this seriously."

"I knew Anna quite well."

"Oh, you did?" asked Laura, surprised.

"She showed me, and a lot of the guys here, that we can't discount the paranormal. Before her untimely death last year, she helped lead us to clues that solved a lot of missing persons cases. "I've got faith in your Emma and her abilities, but we need to do our part to keep them safe."

Laura stood up and reached out to shake Carlo's hand. "Thanks again."

He cradled her hand in both of his. "Try not to worry too much. Go home and get some rest. I'll be in touch if I get any breaking news, and you do the same."

***

Carlo's frown returned. He hoped the comforting words he'd given Laura Grant were not hollow and that Bryan and the rest of the team would come out of this alive. He picked up his desk phone and contacted Dispatch. "Send some officers over to pick up Trevor McAllister at 55 Maple Lane."

He leaned back in his chair, checked his watch and contemplated his next moves. With still five hours before he'd be logging into the Tor account and contacting the shadowy figures behind the website, there was time to initiate one more move.

His own sixth sense, if you could call it that, was compelling him to start tracking the satellite signal immediately. Knowing this would take time, he reached out to a friendly judge within the judicial court system, to gain proper authorization.

***

At five minutes to eleven at night, Carlo said, "Arnie, thanks for staying late."

"No problem," said Arnie from tech support. He opened the Tor browser, then navigated to the website, *www.Adopt-a-Kid-Hassle-Free.onion,* and logged in. "Here's hoping this works."

Seconds later the chat window opened.

<Welcome back.

<<Any news for me?

<Good news.

<<We have a baby boy. Twenty-two months old. All parameters requested are available.

Carlo and Arnie looked at each other, shocked at the clinical approach.

"Like David said before, this really is cold. *Parameters?*" asked Arnie.

<<Excellent. When can we take possession?

<We?

<<My wife and I.

<Money first.

<<How much?

<4 Bitcoin. Sending Bitcoin wallet address now.

"Holy shit!" said Arnie, "That's about $340,000 US dollars. Almost $500,000 Canadian."

The long string of characters containing both letters and numbers for the Bitcoin wallet flashed across the screen.

<<Got it.

<Payment due in advance of delivery. Pick up details of the merchandise to follow, once payment is received.

<<Will send payment in the am.

<Check back tomorrow, 23:00 UTC time, for payment confirmation.

A message flashed across the screen. CHAT ENDED.

Fifty-Three

The Traffic Jam

THE HERD OF CATTLE clogged the road completely. David reluctantly came to a stop and threw his hands up in the air in frustration. Like in so many rural Latin American countries, time stood still.

He muttered, "It could be 1824, 1924 or 2024." His eyes searched the area for the herder but he saw no one.

"I have a bad feeling about this," said Emma. "Can we turn around?"

"Easier said than done," said David. "It'll be difficult. Not enough room."

The road was indeed narrow, with dense bush on one side and steep drops on the other, without the security guard rails would have provided.

"This would be a perfect place for Reinhard's men to ambush us," said Bryan, gazing at the thick tropical forest on each side. "I wonder where the cattle herder is."

"Dunno. There should be one close by. We'll have to wait it out," said David. Noticing the temperature gauge, he commented, "Starting to overheat." He shut off the vehicle's engine.

The bull made a lazy pass around the truck, the rest of the herd following him. After the last cow had passed, David said, "Finally."

He turned the Suzuki back on and put the engine into first gear. They'd only traveled a few hundred feet when Emma cried out in shock. "Oh, my God! Look!"

Before his mind had time to register the blood-splattered man lying at the edge of the road, an armed vehicle pulled out from a hidden laneway in the rainforest. The vehicle parked on an angle, blocking the Suzuki.

The driver remained in the army truck while three Hispanic men spilled out of the vehicle: two trained rifles at them while the other, a burly man with a pockmarked face, carried a baseball bat.

Clutching the satphone in both hands, Emma pointed it through the open window and confirmed there was a SAT signal. Her fingers rapidly tapped, *We've been ambushed. Surrounded by armed men. Send help.* She hit the send button, prayed the technology would get the message to her mom and cranked the window closed.

Noticing the pockmarked man approaching her side of the vehicle, she screamed, "David! Lock the doors!"

"Already done!" yelled David. "Did you get the message out?" He revved the engine with the intention of eluding their attackers by backing away from the blocked army vehicle. His effort was short-lived, when a volley of rounds disintegrated the tires.

"Yes, I think so—" Emma screamed in terror. Her reply was cut short by the impact of the baseball bat against the passenger side window, followed by a shower of glass that cascaded over her, stinging and pelting her bare arms.

"Emma, hide the phone!" said Bryan.

She nodded and tossed it behind the seat, seconds before the man with the baseball bat dragged her through the demolished window's opening. She shrieked as her bare legs connected with the rough shards of glass jutting from the windowsill.

David launched himself out of the driver's door, ran to the passenger side of the vehicle and tackled Emma's attacker, giving her time to break loose. "Emma!" screamed David. "Run!"

Emma ran toward the thick rainforest cover, unaware of her bloodied legs. She stopped short when a rifle shot cracked through the air and one of the attackers shouted, *"Alto!"* She looked over her shoulder, then turned around. The two men with assault rifles were pointing their guns at Bryan and David.

The third man sauntered up to Emma, leering. He grabbed her forcibly by the wrist and hauled her, kicking and screaming, to their armed vehicle. One of her frantic kicks connected with his shin. Her efforts were rewarded with a backhand to the face.

"Puta!" he said. *Bitch.*

Emma gasped, then slumped over and was thrown into the back of the army truck.

Bryan shouted, "Hey, don't you hurt her." He struggled against the ironlike muscles that had seized him and was rewarded with a punch to the stomach with the butt end of a rifle. Winded, Bryan stopped resisting, his world narrowing to one immediate and desperate task: working on trying to get back his breath.

Distracted momentarily, David's attacker sniggered at his fellow ruffians' actions, giving David a split second to act. He whirled around and threw a punch at his assailant, unaware there was a fourth man approaching from the rear. The sharp pain at the back of his head caused instant nausea and disorientation. His vision grew dim, and soon he joined Emma in the land of the unconscious.

Fifty-Four

Our Worst Fears Have Materialized

LAURA WIPED AT the moisture collecting at the corners of her green eyes, dulled by grief and worry. Her hands shook as she punched in the number for the New Elgan Police Service and sighed with relief when Carlo answered. "Staff Inspector Carducci speaking."

"Thanks for taking my call, Carlo."

"Of course. So, what's going on?"

"I got a text from Emma saying they were being attacked. I tried calling back but haven't been able to get in touch with them." She tried to swallowed the constriction forming in her throat. "They must have been captured."

"Laura, where are you?"

"At home."

"Can you come down to the station?"

"Sure, but I'm not up to driving."

"Ask one of the security men to drive you down."

"Leaving now."

Twenty minutes later, Laura burst into Carlo's office. He had an espresso waiting for her and said, "Here, drink this."

"Thanks."

"So, our worst fears have materialized." Carlo sat back in his chair, the espresso sitting unnoticed on his desk.

"Yes."

He picked up his desk phone and dialed out. "Can you give me a status report on Bryan Grant's satellite phone?" His eyebrows were knitted together with worry. "I see." He placed the phone back in its cradle.

"Any news?"

"The signal is still transmitting but has stopped moving."

"How long ago?"

"Half an hour ago. Assuming they still have the satphone with them, either they're at their destination or—"

"—or their phone's been left behind." Laura put her hand on her mouth, her eyes wide with fear. "Would they have turned off the satellite phone?"

"Not likely. Their best bet would be to hide the phone so that it could keep transmitting their most recent location."

"If that's the case, how long would the battery last?" she asked, her lips compressed together with worry.

"Most satellite phones are designed to last as long as thirty hours in standby mode."

"And since it's still transmitting, but not moving, they must have hidden it somewhere before their capture?" asked Laura, her expression lightening.

"Possibly."

"So, what's your next move?" asked Laura.

"I will need to get in touch with the local authorities for help with this."

"How?"

"We go through INTERPOL. We can't go in without authorization." He gave her a reassuring smile. "This is how it works. The New Elgan Police Service contacts the Royal Canadian Mounted Police."

"The RCMP?"

"Yes, the RCMP is Canada's National Central Bureau (NCB) for INTERPOL. They then request for help through INTERPOL's secure communications network."

"What about Nicaragua? Are they members of INTERPOL, too?" asked Laura, overwhelmed by the depth of bureaucracy needed to initiate the rescue mission.

"Yes, their national police force is a member of INTERPOL, too. Like Canada's RCMP, the National Nicaraguan Police Force serves as Nicaragua's NCB for INTERPOL.

"Each country's NCB is responsible for coordinating and managing all international police cooperation within their own country."

"Sounds complicated. What about cross-border crimes, such as kidnapping?" asked Laura.

"That, too. Their scope includes working with INTERPOL on cross-border crime investigations."

"Like abductions?"

"Exactly."

***

Emma raised her bound hands and wiped blood from the corner of her mouth. Her arms and legs stung from multiple abrasions but her worry for David and Bryan superseded any pain she felt.

She was in a hot, windowless, small shack. She grimaced as she pulled against the ropes tied around her wrists. Too tight. She wiggled her fingers to keep them from growing numb.

Her senses told her that David and Bryan were still alive. Mental images of them bound and secured in a similar shack were like photographs etched on the retinas of her eyes.

She sat in the lotus position, deepened her breathing, and expanded her thoughts. She found Megan and their nieces in the adjoining shack. Close together, at least.

Next, she reached out to her mother, who shared some of the psychic abilities Emma had. They had often played a game of telepathy, and Emma, the more powerful of the two, would often be able to broadcast her thoughts to her Mom. *Here's hoping that works today,* thought Emma. *Mom, can you sense me?* She released a breath she didn't realize she'd been holding when her mother's reply filled her mind.

Yes, dear, where are—

Emma was pulled roughly to her feet, the connection with her mother severed.

***

Laura stood up abruptly, knocking over the chair, her expression a mixture of fear, relief and awe. "Emma contacted me via telepathy. She's never done that before."

"And?" asked Carlo, excited.

"I don't know ... our connection was interrupted."

"Laura, why don't you stay in town tonight? That way, you can come back to the station more easily."

"I suppose I could stay at David and Emma's," she said, frowning. "But there's Snuggles."

"Snuggles?"

"Our ginger cat. He doesn't like to be left alone." Laura straightened her shoulders. "All the same, I think I'll go home. Harold's security men will keep an eye on me."

"As you wish. I will call you if we have any news."

"Thank you, Carlo. This means a lot to me," said Laura.

"You are most welcome. We'll do what we can to get your family back home."

Laura stood up to leave when Carlo's desk phone rang.

His expression grew dark. "I see. Hang on a sec." He placed the call on hold, and said, "Laura, can you wait a minute? There's been a development."

Laura pulled off her light spring jacket, hung it over the back of her chair, and sat back down, her intelligent jade green eyes puzzled.

Carlo resumed the call and said, "Start from the beginning." After the call had concluded, he gently replaced the phone in its cradle. "That was one of my officers."

Laura watched him warily, telegraphing that she feared the worst. "What's happened?"

"It's Trevor. He's been found dead."

"What?" Laura's hand flew to her mouth, like a frantic bird trapped indoors, desperate for freedom outside. "It looks like suicide. A hanging. But considering everything that's happened..."

"It wasn't suicide at all, was it?" Laura's eyes were wide with terror. "You think Dark Hands of Anubis got to him first. Before he could talk."

"Yes, I do." Carlo gave a heavy sigh. "We'll know more once the forensics team goes over the scene. I'm heading down there now to supervise."

"So anything we could have learned from Trevor has died with him," said Laura.

"Possibly." Carlo hesitated. "Laura, please reassure me: you do have that security detail, right?"

"Yes, they're waiting for me downstairs."

"Excellent. I will be in touch."

Fifty-Five

Introductions are in Order

WHEN EMMA WAS LED out of the shack by her captors, she blinked, as she adjusted to the bright outdoors. She was in the center of a small village with tiny Adobe shacks covered with tin roofs.

A tall, fair-skinned man with honey-colored hair, wearing a wide-brimmed safari hat, addressed her. "How delightful to meet you." He squinted at the relentless, hot and harsh Nicaraguan sunlight.

A waft of the sunscreen he was wearing drifted over to her, making her gag at the cloying coconut smell. He was clearly uncomfortable in the sun, more used to the coolness of the building he had left than the tropical heat to which he was now exposed.

"Who are you?" Emma stammered, as she looked up into ice blue eyes.

"Really, shouldn't you already know?" A flash of disapproval raced across the man's face. "Aren't you supposed to be psychic?" He gave a cruel laugh.

"Well, I—"

"What's my name?" he demanded. He pulled a hunting knife from his belt and pressed the tip against the thumb of his left hand. A delicate bubble of red rose bloomed upward, then collapsed into itself and dripped lazily to the ground, "Yes, it's sharp enough."

The name flashed before her eyes. "You're Reinhard Holtz. One of the leaders of the Dark Hands of Anubis."

"Very good. But can you prove you really are psychic?"

Emma looked at him with resentment, then turned her head away in disgust.

Reinhard grabbed her chin and forced her to look at him. Emma nearly fainted at his touch, as a wash of terrifying images infused her mind. She recalled her vision of the girl with the blond hair running and taunting her pursuer. *Oh my God, he's the one that raped Maggie in the forest the day she went missing.* The realization left her reeling with terror and revulsion.

"Look at me!" Reinhard commanded.

"I can't—you're sick," Emma said, nausea threatening to dislodge the bile.

"Get one of the girls. The older one. Megan, her friend," said Reinhard. "This is going to be fun."

Two men returned a few minutes later, dragging Megan by the arms. Although Megan's feet were bare, they tried to hamper their progress by digging into the hard packed soil with their heels. The men eyed each other, shrugged, and lifted the struggling prisoner up, Megan's legs now cycling useless cartwheels in the air. Emma was shocked at her friend's appearance but reassured by her fierceness. Despite their clothing in tatters, their hair matted and dirty, the look in Megan's eyes was strong and defiant.

They threw them in front of Reinhard.

"Megan," cried out Emma. "Are you hurt?"

"Nothing broken." Megan licked at dry and cracked lips and said, "They've got Maggie's twins and her youngest."

Emma nodded, "I know."

"Enough idle chat," said Reinhard. "I'd like to find out exactly how you knew to find us."

"You wouldn't understand." Emma's eyes had narrowed to slits, as she spat out her answer.

"That's where you're wrong."

With a serpentine movement, he pulled Megan up by the scruff of the collar and held the hunting knife to their throat. "We are going to play a game. I am going to test your psychic abilities."

"If you get the answer wrong, I will slice off her right ear lobe."

"You mean their right ear lobe," said Emma with defiance.

"Their? I only see one little woman here."

Megan shook her head, her eyes pleading for Emma to stop. "My friend is non-binary. They identify with both genders."

"What nonsense is this generation being taught in North America?"

"Tolerance, understanding—nothing you could appreciate."

"Why, Emma, you have hurt my feelings." The anger emanated from him in pulses, like a heat wave. "I'm a sensitive man." His look became pensive. "Well, maybe I'll cut somewhere less noticeable." Megan flinched as he took the knife and slid off the buttons of their shirt. "Looks female to me."

"Stop!" said Emma. "Ask your questions."

"Good. That's better." His smile was arctic. "First question: how did you know about coming here? To the volcanoes of Nicaragua?"

Emma choked back the fear, "You wouldn't understand."

"So you've already said." He pressed the knife against Megan's throat. "Start talking."

Fifty-Six

Emma

━━━━━━━━━━━━━━━━━━━━

SHE RAISED HER GREEN EYES to Reinhard in defiance. "You're nothing more than a rapist. You're sick. Get away from Megan," she growled.

"You certainly are feisty." Reinhard's smile did not reach his eyes. "Tell me how you *really* found me. I want the truth."

Emma was terrified by the knife Reinhard held at Megan's throat. Her mind weighed how best to answer this question. Although much of finding the final location had been based on her communications with her Spirit Guides, more of it had to do with the solid detective work done by David, Bryan, her mother, and the invaluable assistance from Staff Inspector Carlo Carducci.

"I'm a psychic. *Maggie* asked me to find you."

"That's preposterous."

Emma could sense his false bravado and pushed on. "No, it isn't. Maggie is Megan's sister. Surely you see the resemblance." She glared at him. "And those girls you have in the shack, those are Maggie's daughters. But you already know this."

Reinhard released Megan and kicked them in the stomach. He twisted his body around, spun back, then kicked Emma in the abdomen. The momentum knocked her to the ground, the hard-packed earth grazing her left cheek. She peered up through her tangle of auburn hair, eyes defiant. She refused to give him the satisfaction of her tears.

With one hand, he grabbed a fistful of her hair and with the other grasped her chin, forcing her to look at him again. Shock registered when Reinhard's touch sent images bolting through Emma's mind. His inner psyche caused her more distress than the pain radiating in her cheek bone. She grimaced, steeling herself against his evil and recoiled in surprise as she probed his subconscious. *Maggie. You're afraid of her!* Her eyes widened in surprise. "She's haunting you!"

"You don't know what you're talking about." His terror was palpable and so strong Emma could taste the bitterness in her own mouth. The fear transformed to barely suppressed rage. "Guards, bring her to the villa." His look was cold. "We will talk further there."

"Yes, sir. And the other prisoner?"

"Throw her back in with the younger females." He turned to go, then said, "Bring them food and water."

***

The guards grabbed Megan by the armpits, ready to drag them back to the shack. Megan shook them off and said, "Let go of me. I'm coming."

Taking careful note of their surroundings before entering the shack, Megan noticed a similar structure at the end of the row. *Is anybody in that one?* they wondered, feet faltering.

"*Andale!*" said the guard, giving Megan a rough push forward. *Keep moving.*

One final shove and Megan was back in their prison. The guard reattached the shackle around Megan's ankle and pushed them against the wall, his maleness evident through his clothing.

"*Dejarla*," said the second guard. "Leave her. The boss doesn't want the goods molested." Disappointed, the first guard leered at Megan, then released them and left. Megan's legs gave out and they slid to the ground.

Eyes readjusting to the dimly lit shack, Megan noted with relief that Sandra and Cheryl were awake, and that the three girls were still together.

Simone's tear-streaked face broke open with relief. "Aunt Megan, you're back." The little girl ran over to them and wrapped her thin arms around Megan. "I'm so scared. Hungry, too."

"It's normal to be scared, but I need you to be brave." Megan looked up at the twins, who were staring at them in wide-eyed fear. "How are you two holding up?"

"Feeling groggy," said Cheryl.

"They drugged us," added Sandra, rubbing at her eyes.

"What is this place?" asked Cheryl. Megan surveyed their three nieces. *How much to tell them without causing panic?*

***

Maggie had drifted closer to her family. She noticed that Spirit Anna was once more by her side. *Are you going to help me stop this or not?* Maggie demanded.

Yes, all in good time, Spirit Anna said. *But the humans need to play their part first, then we as guides can help.*

***

Emma stumbled over the rough terrain leading up the mountainside to the white villa, unable to secure her footing adequately. Each time, the guard gave a cruel tug of the rope that was leashed to her bound hands. *Vamos*, he said. *Let's go.* His cruel mouth was a red slash against a pock-marked face that had been ravaged by his youth's hormones and poor diet.

"I'm coming," she said, her anger forming an acidic knot in her stomach. "*¿Adonde vamos?*" She asked where they were going in her high school Spanish.

"*¡Cállate!*" Shut up! He gave a vicious tug on the rope, which caused Emma to fall forward. Without her hands free to break her fall, she edged her body sideways so that her face would not take the full impact. Her left cheek dug into loose pebbles and she stifled a small cry of pain. She was jerked back to her feet and they resumed the steep climb to the villa.

As she and her captor crested the last steep incline, she saw Reinhard waiting at the summit, standing beside his Jeep.

He approached Emma and made a tsk-tsk sound while he grabbed her face and examined the abrasions on her cheek. "That won't do," he said to the guard. "This is unacceptable."

Emma flinched when he touched the fresh cuts, the oils of his fingers stinging her skin.

He gave her a stern look and asked, "Are you going to behave?"

Emma nodded, knowing that her best option for avoiding further injury and staying alive was to cooperate.

"I can't hear you. Answer me," Reinhard demanded.

"Yes," she replied with a soft voice, her lips and throat dry from the hot Nicaraguan sun and the exertion from the climb.

"Good. I don't want to damage that pretty face," he said. "But I will if you don't behave." He untied the ropes, letting them fall to the ground. "Follow me, and we'll get you cleaned up."

Emma didn't know what was worse: the cruelty or the kindness he feigned now.

She followed him toward the entrance of a cave. *What now?* she thought. Momentarily blinded from the departure of bright sunshine to the interior of the dimly lit cavern, she blinked her eyes, desperately trying to take in her surroundings.

The cave had been enlarged into a rectangular shaped hallway, which led to two stainless-steel elevators illuminated by overhead LED lights. A panel displaying an electronic keyless entry system with a buzzer mounted between the two sets of doors.

The elevator on the right was smaller, like those one would normally see in most hotels. However, the one on the left was much larger and functioned as a service elevator.

"What is this place?" she asked, still blinking.

"Home," said Reinhard. "And now, your home, too."

My home? she wondered. *He's crazy!*

Reinhard pushed the buzzer and said, "Maria, we have a new visitor." Seconds later, the service elevator opened, and a young Hispanic woman exited.

"Take her to the guest suite. Run her a bath and lay out some fresh clothes for her."

"Sí, señor," said the woman quietly. "Come with me." She took Emma's arm and guided her into the elevator.

Reinhard gazed at Emma thoughtfully, and said, "We'll talk later."

"About what?" she said, snapping.

"A proposal."

As the doors slid closed, she stared at him in confusion, her stomach twisting more, pangs of fear and hunger competing for her attention.

***

246

Emma was led by the housemaid into the spacious guest room. The queen-sized bed sat on a raised platform. Mosquito screen netting gracefully surrounded the bed and a slight breeze from the open window billowed the delicate folds.

The views of the mountainside were breathtaking. Any other time, she would have appreciated the stunning vista, but now, her heart was aching with worry about Bryan and David. And for her friend Megan, and the girls. *What was to become of all of them?*

Having been beaten and then dragged up the mountainside, she was too exhausted to use her psychic powers to reach out for help.

The maid motioned Emma toward the steaming bath, which was at the opposite end of the room. Using *le*, the polite and respectful word for *you*, she asked, *"¿Puede ayudarle?"* Can I help you?

Emma nodded and let the young Hispanic woman help her undress. Sitting on the edge of the bath ledge, she raised her arms and winced when the torn top was removed.

The maid's brown eyes were filled with compassion as she tenderly removed Emma's soiled clothing. Emma pointed at her ankle bracelet.

"No, es possible."

Not knowing much about ankle bracelet technology, she assumed from this reply that the unit was waterproof.

Noticing a yellowish bruise on the woman's arm, Emma asked, "¿Qué pasó? ¿Reinhard?"

"Sí." Although her eyes were kind, they were also impartial, as if to suggest that to offer more would be dangerous.

"¿Cómo se llama?" What's your name?

"Maria."

"Mucho gusto. Me llamo Emma." Nice to meet you. I'm Emma.

"Lo sé." I know.

Once Emma was naked, Maria guided her into the steaming water and began to bathe her. Although her touch was gentle, Emma flinched. Then she surrendered at the words, "*Calmerse.*" Calm yourself. The sweet scent of exotic floral fragrances mixed with aloe vera soothed her abrasions. She choked back her panic and thought, *Relax. Regroup. Open your mind*.

Maria helped her out of the bath, wrapped her in a soft, silk kimono and guided her to the plush chair in front of the vanity table.

"Oh, no," said Emma, alarmed when she looked at her reflection in the mirror. The nasty cuts on the left side of her face were red and swollen. She raised trembling fingers to touch the wounds, but Maria stopped her. She opened one of the glass jars sitting on the table, and let Emma smell it. The scent of coconut oil, calendula, frankincense, lavender, oregano, and tea tree oil wafted enticingly. Emma was familiar with this blend and knew that the salve held anti-bacterial healing properties. She closed her eyes in appreciation of Maria's gentle fingers as they applied the ointment. Once done, Maria said, "*Descansarse ahora.*" Rest now.

Although Emma was determined to remain awake, once nestled under the soft covers with the light winds caressing her skin, she began to relax. Before she fell into a dreamless sleep, her last thought was *David*.

Fifty-Seven

Bryan and David

DAVID STRUGGLED IN and out of consciousness. He was aware of the coarse hemp rope cutting into his bound wrists and of the hard earth beneath him. In his dream state, he sensed a presence niggling at the edges of his mind.

It's me, David.

Em? Where are you?

Close by, my love.

Are you hurt?

No.

Thank God.

Remember: no matter what, I love you.

Em? Don't go—

Don't worry, we will find each other. No matter what.

Reassured by Emma's promise he drifted down into a deeper level of blackness.

***

Bryan woke to a dagger of sunlight that pierced through the cracked boards of the dimly lit shack.

His rotator cuff ached from lying on his right side, the old injury complaining at the uncomfortable position in which he found himself. In front of him, his hands were so tightly bound that his fingers were numb. He tried to regain some circulation by wiggling them. His ankles were also bound, but with duct tape, and they had no sensation whatsoever.

He winced at the throbbing pain in his shoulder and maneuvered himself until he was upright, then leaned against the rough boards. Except for the blinding shaft of light, the rest of the shack remained in darkness. A body lay prone on the dirt floor about twenty feet away.

"David," said Bryan, his voice cracked from lack of use. "Wake up, son."

David made a soft moan, moved slightly, then was still once more. Bryan slid his bottom, inch by inch, across the floor until he reached David. Even in the dim light, Bryan noted with alarm a dark stain beneath the younger man's head. Blood had soaked into the soil.

Bryan raised his bound hands as best he could, cradled his forearms under David's head to support him, then shimmied his legs until they were positioned beneath David. He then rocked back and forth until David's head and shoulders were on his lap.

He pulled his bound hands back and with the limited range of his fingers, touched the back of David's head, to try and assess the extent of the injury. He sighed with relief that there was no fresh blood. *How hard did they hit him?* Bryan wondered.

Bryan spoke in urgent tones, trying to revive David. Eventually, David's eyes fluttered open, unfocussed at first, then in recognition.

"Bryan, what the hell happened?"

He tried to sit up, then moaned and leaned back against Bryan's legs.

"Don't try to get up. We were ambushed. Then attacked. You've taken a hard blow to the head."

"How long was I out?"

"Hard to tell. Half a day, maybe longer."

"Emma? Where is she?" David said, his voice filled with worry. He pulled his athletic frame to an upright position.

"Don't know."

David creased his eyebrows together. "Wait a minute. She contacted me while I was dreaming. Said she'd find me."

"In the meantime," said Bryan. "Let's work on untying each other. My hands are really numb. Can you try and loosen the knots?"

David flexed his hands, moving his fingers nimbly. "Okay. Can you shift toward me a bit more?"

Bryan turned so that he and David were sitting opposite each other, their bodies parallel. Both men's bound hands were within reach.

David started pulling at the hemp rope, patiently working at the knots. "It's too dark in here. If we move in tandem, we should be able to shift to that shaft of light."

"Good thinking," said Bryan.

Sweat beaded on both men's foreheads as they maneuvered their way toward the back of the shack, where the welcome beam of light shone.

"Almost there," grunted David.

"Thank God," said Bryan. "My rotator cuff is killing me." Bryan had injured it years ago when wrestling a fugitive to the ground. The arrest had been successful, but the damaged shoulder was a constant reminder whenever he overexerted himself.

"Let's rest a bit. I'm still lightheaded," replied David. "Parched, too."

"The amenities are lacking."

"I see you've not lost your sense of humour."

After their brief break, David said, "Let's get this done."

Their hands finally positioned so that David could see the knots properly, he began to work on them. By the time, David had loosened

Bryan's bonds, his fingernails were bloody and cracked. But Bryan was free.

Bryan shook off the last remnants of the rope and said, "My turn." He massaged his hands and moved his fingers to gain back circulation, then began working on the restraints around David's wrists.

Once both men's hands were free, Bryan gestured toward their bound legs and said, "The duct tape will be a challenge."

"Got an idea for that," said David. "Saw this on a YouTube video." He stood up, took the rope that had previously bound him and used it as a seesaw to loosen the duct tape where it gaped slightly at the top between his legs.

Bryan, seeing what David was doing, also began working at his bindings in the same way.

Within minutes, the two men were free of their restraints.

"Now what?" asked David.

"Let's look around, see what we can use to defend ourselves." Bryan began a methodical search of the shack. "Not much here."

"What about those loose boards?" David nodded toward the daylight shining through. "Might be able to pry them apart, use them as a weapon."

"It's risky. We don't know where the guards are stationed. They might hear us."

"What if we waited till nightfall?" suggested David.

"That might be safer."

"While I was unconscious, did they ever come in to check on us?"

"No."

"So that means they are leaving us here to rot—"

"—or they are due to come back any time," said Bryan, completing David's thought.

"We have two choices. One, we pretend we are still bound and one of us ambushes them when they come in or—"

"—or two, we loosen those boards and escape."

"I'm in favor of the second option. To get out of here."

"Agreed."

Fifty-Eight

Where's Emma?

"DAMN, IT'S HOT in here," said David, his vocal cords arid and straining from thirst.

"I hear you," said Bryan. "I can handle the hunger, but thirst ..."

"They've got to come for us, eventually."

"I agree," said Bryan. "But when?"

David eyed the light emanating through the vertical slat in the shack's wall. "What time do you figure it is?"

"Dunno, but the light's not as intense as earlier. Maybe close to four in the afternoon?"

"I've been looking at that broken slat all afternoon," said David, gazing at the jagged edge of wood. "Do you think we could start?"

"Not yet," said Bryan, softly. "We agreed to wait till after dark."

"Yeah, I know," David grunted. "It's tough waiting."

"Nightfall should come in about two hours. Nicaragua is close enough to the equator that the length of day and night doesn't vary much throughout the year and are approximately equal in length."

"It gets very dark in the mountains. I suggest we make note of the exact position of that slat," suggested David.

"But we'd have to be quiet about it."

David pulled off his shirt and knotted the sleeve around the splinter of wood, so they would be able to feel their way to the crevice, now their sole hope of escape.

"Bryan, I think you should lie back down where you were when they brought us in. Let me place the ropes around your hands as if you were still bound. Then, if someone does come in, before nightfall, we could still try and ambush them. I'll position myself near the door, in case that scenario pans out."

"Good. I like this Plan B," Bryan said, his expression more optimistic than before. "Let's get some rest. Come nighttime, we have a lot of work to do."

The men exchanged looks of mutual respect; the kind of understanding that is forged by having worked closely together in other challenging situations, such as the one in which they found themselves now.

***

"Hey, Bryan," whispered David. "How are you doing there?"

The older man gave a grunt, and said, "I was having a nice dream about a juicy steak till you awakened me. Is it time?"

"Yeah, I think we should give it a shot now."

"Man, it's dark in here," commented Bryan.

"Sure is." David walked in a clockwise direction along the inside circumference of the structure, his hand gliding along the wall, groping for his shirt. "Damn ..." he muttered under his breath, when he stumbled against some loose rocks on the earthen floor.

"What happened, son?" asked Bryan quietly.

"Yeah, I'm fine. I tripped. Too bloody dark."

Several seconds later, David heaved a sigh of relief. "Found it." He eased his fingers around the sharp edge of the wood and pulled and was rewarded with a satisfying crack. Both men held their breath.

"Do you think anyone heard that?" asked Bryan, his voice filled with tension.

"Not sure, let's wait a bit and see if there's any response." After five painful minutes of waiting, David resumed the task. He wrapped his shirt around the loosened shard and used it as a lever to pull it toward him. This time the crack was muffled by the cloth.

"There's a moon tonight," said David.

"We'll have to be careful, but the light could be to our advantage, as well."

David gave a small grunt in agreement and continued to work for ten more minutes. "I'm done. The space is wide enough for us to leave," he said. He unknotted the shirt, noting the rips and tears in the material, and put it back on. "That was my favorite shirt."

"What are we waiting for, then?" asked Bryan, still holding the rope that had previously bound him. "This might come in handy."

David gave a curt nod and said, "Time to find Emma."

The moonlight shone on both their faces, their steadfast looks of determination mirrored in each other's eyes; resolute and firm. Accustomed to the dim interior of the hut, the bright moon made it easy for Bryan and David to adjust to their surroundings. They moved away from the clearing, taking shelter in the nearby dense brush.

From there, they could see that adjacent to their shack were two other similar structures. A soft murmur of female voices was coming from the one furthest to the right. The one in the middle was silent, its door yawning open on its hinges.

"Do you think Emma is in there?" mouthed David, nodding to the shack on the right.

"Maybe."

"Let's check it out." David moved forward, anxious to discover if Emma was there, but Bryan pulled him back, the older man's hand like iron, clasping David's upper arm.

Bryan shook his head. "No, son. Wait."

"But I don't see any guards."

"They could be on patrol."

"Let's hang around a bit before we move in. See if there's a pattern," suggested Bryan.

"I guess you're right," said David, his tone reluctant.

After another five minutes, David said, "I can't take this anymore. I'm going in." About to get up, he stopped when the sound of animated voices drifted over. A single guard escorted two Hispanic women, who were carrying plates piled with food. They entered the clearing. The guard was flirting with the younger of the two women and not paying attention to his surroundings.

"If some of that food was meant for us—"

"They'll soon discover we've escaped," said David, completing Bryan's thought.

"Now's our chance," said Bryan. "You're younger. Go take him out. I'll take care of the women."

David bolted from his position and raced toward the guard, taking him down with a football tackle. Before the guard could register what was happening, David sat on him, pinning him to the ground and pulling his arms behind his back.

Meanwhile, Bryan raced toward the women. One was about to scream, but when she saw Bryan's unthreatening position: arms open, face soft and kind, she hesitated. He spoke softly and said, "*Tranquila.*" Stay Calm.

"Claro," said the older of the two women, her features drawn, signs of abuse clearly evident on her scarred face. The younger one, still pretty and vivacious, had eyes that spoke of hope. In perfect but heavily accented English, she asked, "Señor, you are here to rescue us?"

"Bryan, a little help here," said David, interrupting the exchange. "Hand me the rope."

"Here you go." He tossed the rope to David.

With his knee, David ground the man's face into the earth, then hogtied his hands behind his back while Bryan held their captive's squirming legs down. Still sitting on the man's back, David tugged roughly at the sleeve of his own shirt until it tore away. He lifted the man's head slightly and before the subdued guard could utter a scream, he stuffed the cloth into his mouth. He patted down the subdued man and discovered both a hunting knife and a 9mm pistol.

"This will come in handy," he said to Bryan.

"Definitely." Sensing he was being watched, Bryan looked over his shoulder, nudged David with his elbow and said, "Look who's here."

Megan stood at the threshold of the shack.

"Bryan!" Megan's eyes were huge with surprise. "You're here!"

"Thank God," Bryan said. "Are you hurt?"

"No, just scared and hungry." Two teenage girls and a little girl joined her from the recesses of the hut.

"Is everyone accounted for?" he asked, his voice grim with worry.

"All accounted for, except—" Megan choked back a sob.

"Where's Emma?" interrupted David.

Fifty-Nine

A Bird in a Gilded Cage

TOWARD DUSK, EMMA AWOKE and stretched her arms out, reaching for David. Her hand met an empty spot. "David? Where are you?" she called out, then stopped herself, remembering. Her eyes took in the strange surroundings, the memories of the last twenty-four hours flooding back. *Oh, God.*

The doors to the walk-in closet were open, displaying an assortment of clothing ranging from summer dresses made from flowing fabrics, romantic silky tops and flattering Palazzo pants, loose and comfortable for hot weather. On another shelf were a series of sandals of different styles, clearly meant to complement the beautiful outfits. Since her own clothes had been taken away by the maid and not returned, Emma decided to don one of the lovely garments.

Mom would have a field day with these fabrics, she thought sadly, as she fingered the delicate materials. She chose a white pantsuit with matching low heels and quickly dressed. She walked up to the full-length mirror, her sorrow temporarily forgotten as she inspected the image of the green-eyed, auburn-haired young woman. She stepped closer and noted with relief that the abrasions on her cheek were already fading. The healing salve had worked its magic overnight. Thankfully, the cuts on her arms and legs were hidden by the flowing material of the outfit.

A light tap on her door was followed by the entrance of a maid, different than the one who had helped her the night before. She eyed the pretty young maid, wondering where her caregiver might be.

"*¿Donde esta Maria?*" she asked. Where's Maria?

The maid's body grew rigid with fear and shook her head. "No sé." I don't know.

The woman kept her gaze averted, set the tray of food on a small table and left the room.

Emma's stomach leapt at the assortment of food: roasted chicken with plantains, *curtido,* a chopped cabbage salad and the side dish of Central America, *gallo pinto,* which was rice, beans and a fried egg. And *Pinolillo,* a sweet cornmeal and cacao-based drink, made of ground, toasted corn and a small amount of cacao. The fragrant beverage made her mouth water.

Being a vegetarian, Emma recoiled at the thought of eating the chicken and ignored the fragrant roasted meat. *Maybe later, if I have to,* she thought.

She hoped Megan and the three girls would be given food, too. She pushed away the momentary guilt, knowing the food would give her nourishment and strength and tucked into the plantains, the salad, beans and rice and the egg. Partway through her meal, she took a sip of the Pinolillo and gagged. *Bitter.* She saw the maid had thoughtfully left several packets of *azucar,* which she gratefully poured into the offending drink. *Too much sugar,* she thought, *but what the heck? I can use the energy boost.*

Once satiated, Emma walked to the arch leading from the beautifully appointed suite to the balcony. The drop from her balcony was significant. Even with her athletic abilities, there was no way she would be able to scale down the side of the villa, let alone navigate the steep precipice. On this side of the mountain, it was a sheer drop to the rocks below. *A real fortress,* she thought.

Next, she examined every corner of the room for opportunities. Nothing viable. Not even something to fashion into a weapon. *Not much I can do with soap and shampoo,* she thought bitterly.

Looking out at the stunning vista, she compared herself to a bird in a gilded cage with no way to escape. *At least not yet,* she reminded herself. *Have faith.*

She pulled one of the cushions off the love seat, placed it in front of the open window and sat down. Opening her mind, she summoned her guides and was soon aware of their reassuring presence. *Please tell me help is on the way,* she asked of her Guardian Angel. *Yes* was the immediate and comforting reply.

Images of David and Bryan escaping the shack, subduing the guard and releasing Megan, the twins and little Simone cascaded through her mind. More impressions came of her mother seeking help from Carlo at the police department.

Reassured by this positive news, Emma drew herself into a deeper meditative state, with the goal of finding a way out of her predicament.

***

David kept his voice calm, all the while fighting the panic that roiled in his stomach, as if he was a lifeboat tossed about in the sea. "Where's Emma?" he repeated.

"Earlier today, Reinhard took her," said Megan.

"He told the guard to take her up to the villa."

"Where is that?" asked Bryan.

"Close by, I think," said Megan. "They went up through that path," said Megan pointing. "Reinhard was very interested in her psychic abilities. He kept grilling her on how she found his location." Megan frowned. "I got the feeling he already knew she was an empath."

David met Bryan's gaze and said, "Trevor?"

"Without a doubt," was the older man's reply.

David turned to the two women who were hovering in the background, arms wrapped around each other, eyes wide with fear. Grateful for the Spanish he'd learned while in Costa Rica the previous year, David asked, "How long a climb is it to the villa?"

The older woman went into a detailed description of how far the climb was and even volunteered how the entrance to the villa was hewn from a cave that had been extended into a tunnel. A large shaft had been bored vertically to accommodate one passenger elevator and another elevator large enough to work as a staff and service elevator.

The first level of the staff elevator opened directly to the servants' quarters. The second level contained a modern commercial kitchen with laundry facilities. The third floor of the villa comprised a spacious area with multiple suites, which was accessible by staff whenever their services were required, using a digital master key.

"Do you know where they are keeping Emma?" Her expression was blank for a moment until David gave her Emma's description.

"Claro, María sabe más," she said. *Sure, but Maria knows more.*

The older woman nudged the younger one forward. She raised her eyes shyly and said in sing-song but impeccable English, "The pretty girl with red hair and green eyes. She's in the guest suite. I took care of her earlier today."

"How do I find her suite?"

"She's in the suite overlooking the mountains."

"You mentioned we need a master key." "Sí," she said, hesitating a moment. "You will help us escape?"

"Yes, of course," said David. "Then, here," she said, her expression resolute and determined. "You'll need this. This is my keycard for the private suites."

Following Maria's detailed explanation, David thanked the women and then asked, "*¿Pueden esperarnos aquí?*" Can you wait for us here?

"Sí," they chorused.

"Megan, you and the girls should stay here, too."

"No choice," said Megan, pointing to the ankle bracelets the three younger girls wore. "We'd alert them if we moved out of range."

David glanced at the food the Nicaraguan women had brought. "You and the girls should eat."

"So should you and Bryan," said Megan. "There's enough for all of us to share. It'll be quite the climb, and your bodies need fuel to keep going."

"Megan's right," said Bryan.

David picked at the plate of food Megan held out, grabbing the *plantanos*, plantain, which would be quick to eat.

Bryan took a few spoonfuls of the gallo pinto, the beans and rice dish, then pushed the plate away. "I'm more thirsty than hungry," he said. "*Tengo sed.*" One of the women stepped forward and handed him a canteen. Bryan took a long drink, then said, "*Gracias.*" Returning the canteen to the woman, she shook her head and pushed the water bottle back to Bryan. "*Guárdala.*"

"She says for us to keep it," said David. "Ready to go?"

"As ready as I'll ever be."

The older Hispanic woman smiled at them both and said "*Vaya con Dios.*" Go with God.

Sixty

A Proposal

AT THE SOUND of a light tap on her door, Emma arose from her meditation, annoyance registering on her face when she realized her visitor was Reinhard. "Oh, it's you," she said.

"Emma, I trust you have rested," he said smiling at her as if she was a treasured guest who had not been brought here by force. "Did you enjoy the food?"

At first, unsure of how to reply to this monster who now played the role of a gracious host, she decided to match his mask of civility with her own. "Yes, thank you."

Reinhard gestured to the loveseat, a question mark in his eyes.

"Oh, sorry," said Emma, retrieving the cushion from the floor. "I was meditating."

She brushed past Reinhard and replaced the cushion on the couch.

He sat down and motioned for her to sit beside him, then draped his arm along the back edge of the seat.

Every fiber in Emma's body recoiled from the nearness of him, but until she understood his endgame, she thought it better to comply. She forced her body to relax and called on Frederick, her GateKeeper Spirit Guide, to keep her safe.

"I can get you a proper cushion, if you wish," he said, his lips curving into a smile.

Emma was baffled by this overt politeness. "That would be nice, but I am sure I won't be staying long enough for you to bother." Fearing she'd offended him, she returned his smile, "I wouldn't want to put you to any trouble."

"It would be no trouble whatsoever, Emma. What's this special cushion called?"

"It's a Zafu cushion. It elevates your hips and aligns your spine, when sitting in the lotus or half-lotus position."

"Excellent. I will have one ordered in. Special delivery."

"Well, thanks, I guess," said Emma. *What's his game?* She tilted her head as an insightful message came to her from Pieter, her Guardian Angel. *Stay polite. Keep him engaged.*

Reinhard cleared his throat. "I'm afraid I must apologize. My hospitality up until now has been deplorable. Allow me to make it up to you. I will be happy to get you your Zafu."

"Reinhard, why am I here and not with the others?" Emma could no longer contain her curiosity.

"I have a proposal."

"A what?" stammered Emma.

"Your psychic gifts are extraordinary. Stay here. Develop them. Help my operation grow. And maybe in time—"

"Yes?" Emma asked, intuiting what he was about to say, but hoping she was wrong.

"Become my wife. Join me as the Dark Hands of Anubis continues its long lineage of uber children. Together, you and I and our progeny can own the world."

"I don't want to own the world!" she protested, "And I'm already married! Happily." She swallowed back the gorge rising in her throat, her recent meal ready to make a reappearance. "I can't!"

"That won't be a problem for much longer. You will be a widow soon." Reinhard gently took her fingers in his hand, raised them to his lips and kissed them. His eyes were hard like blue ice, but his smile remained engaging. "You don't need to answer right away." He dropped her hand abruptly and said, "You have till tomorrow morning."

He rose from the loveseat and without another word, he exited her suite, leaving her to wonder how she could best deal with this psychopath.

Sixty-One

Look, if Things Go Badly

CARLO'S EXPRESSION WAS STERN. "I advise against it. It's too dangerous."

Laura's jaw was set with determination. "Every person I love is in Nicaragua: Emma, David, my husband Bryan. I can't stand by. My daughter ... she needs me."

"Bryan would have my hide if you came into harm's way."

"That's not for him to decide."

Carlo looked at her thoughtfully. "There is one way. You can accompany me to Nicaragua, but you will wait at a safe house until the operation is over."

Laura was about to protest but then stopped. "You're right," she conceded. "You'll bring them to me the moment they're freed?"

"Yes, that's the plan," said Carlo. "Remember, this is an INTERPOL joint task force between the RCMP and the NCB. We're invited as guests, but the operation is really run by INTERPOL."

"I have been meaning to ask you about the child adoption ring," said Laura. "With so much happening, I forgot it was a lead that you, Bryan and David were working on. Did anything come of it?"

"Yes, actually. We made successful contact with the ring, which we believe is run by the Dark Hands of Anubis."

He gazed at Laura, weighing how much to tell her. "We've made the transfer in bitcoin in exchange for the purchase of a two-year-old Aryan boy."

Laura's hands flew to her mouth. "Oh, no, how horrible. Selling children for profit." She looked at him in surprise. "Where did you get the funds?"

"From a private donor."

"That's generous of them," said Laura.

"Indeed. We are to make contact again later tonight, at which time we'll be sent delivery instructions." He smoothed back his thick mane of hair. "We're working with the RCMP and INTERPOL on this one, too."

"Do you think—?"

Carlo cut her off, anticipating her question. "It's possible, Laura, that the delivery coordinates we get from the adoption website on the Tor dark web browser will be one and the same."

"God, I hope so," said Laura.

***

The white orb in the night sky illuminated David and Bryan's path, helping them avoid the twisted roots that meandered over the rough terrain.

"This is quite the climb," said Bryan. At nearly sixty-five years of age, he was tired from the heat and although he'd had water, he remained dehydrated. Those factors, coupled with overexertion, had taken their toll. "I need to rest for a bit."

"Let's take five," said David. "Look, there's a tree stump over there. Sit down." He unstrapped the canteen from his shoulder. "Drink some more."

Bryan looked at the younger man with fondness. "Thanks. I'm not in the best shape anymore, but a small break should do the trick."

"How long do you figure we've been walking?" asked David.

"Maybe fifteen minutes."

"We should be there soon, according to the two women."

"Why did he separate Emma from the rest of them, I wonder," said Bryan.

"I suspect it has to do with her psychic capabilities. I'm worried sick." David massaged the back of his neck, trying to ease the knot of tension that was developing. "Ready to get going?"

"Yes, I'm ready," replied Bryan.

Several hundred yards later, the path opened into a large open area that had been bulldozed flat. Perched at the top of a rock cliff was a white villa, which shimmered and glowed in the moon's rays.

"Look," said David. "There's the opening at the base, where the servants enter. "Let's head there." David quickened his pace, making it somewhat of a challenge for Bryan to keep up, but by then a second wave of adrenalin had kicked in, giving him the impetus to keep up with the much younger man.

David pressed himself against the roughly hewn rock and waited for Bryan to join him.

"They don't seem too worried about security here," commented Bryan. "It's like a fortress."

"The Hispanic women said that the elevator was to the immediate right of the tunnel entrance," said David, creeping toward the entrance. "I think you should wait here. I will go in alone."

"Son, are you sure?"

"Look, if things go badly—"

"David—," objected Bryan.

"—if Emma and I don't make it out, you need to get Megan and the girls and the two Nicaraguan women to safety."

"How long do I wait for you here?"

"Maximum thirty minutes. Then head back down to the others."

"I don't like splitting up like this," said Bryan, reluctantly. "Son, be careful."

"Always." The moonlight showed the resolve in David's face. "You keep the gun." He handed the 9mm pistol to Bryan. "I'll keep the knife. Better for use in close quarters."

Noting the older man's creased and anxious face, David said, "Dad, it's gonna be fine. It has to be." He grasped Bryan by the forearm, then pulled him into a bear hug.

Bryan's voice caught in his throat, the emotion so strong, he was at a loss for words.

***

Megan looked at Maria with deepening concern. "Are you sure you want to do this, Maria?"

"Sí, I must do this. Señor Reinhard is a very bad man. He kidnaps women and children and sells them. Men, too, for hard labor." Maria's voice faltered. "I also was kidnapped and taken here to be a maid and also used for—"

"Entiendo. I understand." Megan placed a comforting hand on Maria's. "We'd come with you, except..." She pointed at the ankle monitors.

Maria shook her head, "I know the trail and will find help. It is best I go alone." She glanced at tear-streaked Simone, who was clutching Megan's arm. "The young one would be too frightened in the jungle."

The two twins, Cheryl and Sandra, looked at Megan and said, "She's right. Besides, David and Bryan said we should wait here. Remember, Reinhard and his men may be monitoring our ankle bracelets. We really do need to stay here, so that we don't cause any suspicion."

The older Nicaraguan woman approached Maria and kissed her on the cheek and murmured, in a soft and caring tone, *"Cuídate, querida."* Take care, dear.

Maria nodded, and within seconds disappeared into the dense brush.

Sixty-Two

A Grisly Discovery

CARLO AND INSPECTORE MATEO LÓPEZ stopped in the clearing. The inspector was the officer in charge of the task force to rescue Emma, David, Bryan, Megan and their nieces. He worked for his country's branch of INTERPOL's National Central Bureau (NCB), and reported directly to the Comisionado, or Commissioner, on ongoing cases. He had been specifically assigned by the Commissioner to head the investigation into the disappearance of Bryan's team.

Higher-ranking officers, like Mateo, who worked with Interpol were generally quite proficient in English. Since Carlo's Spanish was rudimentary, he was grateful that Mateo spoke English fluently. He had complimented Mateo on his excellent English and asked him where he'd learned it.

"My mother was an American who fell in love with my dad when she visited Nicaragua. After I was born, she insisted I learn English. Before she passed away, she tutored many more kids. Whenever I was ready to give up, she'd remind me, 'You will have many more job opportunities in life if you also speak English'." Mateo's eyes lit up. "I have the career I have today because of her."

In his mid-forties, he had dark brown eyes and like so many Nicaraguans, was a family-oriented man. He was warm and kind when he first greeted Carlo. Carlo had taken to the man immediately, appreciating his friendly and open demeanor. He was grateful that the RCMP had contacted the

Nicaraguan branch of INTERPOL, and better yet, that the NCB were open to him being present, even if not as an acting officer, at least as an observer.

As members of the national police force, Policía Nacional de Nicaragua, Mateo and his fellow highly-trained officers were combing the area. Two canine officers worked in tandem, their dogs ready to please their masters in the search for leads.

"The GPS signal for the satphone was last shown as coming from that direction," said Mateo, advancing toward the edge of the road. He aimed the powerful flashlight down.

"Do you think we'll find it?" asked Carlo, joining the officer.

"Hopefully. It might be lost in the dense brush."

Carlo surveyed the rough terrain, moving his own flashlight back and forth, then stopping. "Wait a minute. What's that over there?" he asked.

He pointed to an area of brush about two hundred feet down the steep incline, where the vegetation looked disturbed.

Grabbing a pair of binoculars, Mateo said, "I see a vehicle down there."

"That's rough terrain. How are we going to get down there?" asked Carlo. A feeling of dread washed over him. "Do you think anyone is down there?"

"Impossible to know without getting closer." He spoke on his radio. "We've found something. Have the dogs brought here."

The canine officers appeared a couple of minutes later, their dogs whining and eager to be off-leash. Once released, they both charged down the mountainside, aiming straight for the vehicle. Frantic and urgent barking erupted within seconds.

After a rapid exchange in Spanish with the canine officers, which Carlo struggled to follow, Mateo said, "The dogs have been trained to issue different types of barks, depending on the nature of what they've found."

He gave Carlo a grim look. "Based on the type of whines the dogs are making, their handlers say the dogs may have found a body."

Carlo nodded, his look equally severe, and asked, "So how do we get down there?"

"Our men are experts in navigating this terrain and a couple of our officers do mountain climbing as a recreational sport. Luckily, they are on the team tonight." He picked up his radio, his Spanish rapid-fire. "We are going to need two officers to rappel down to what appears to be a crash site."

Carlo paced along the side of the road, anxiously waiting for news of what the two mountaineers had found.

After what seemed like an interminable amount of time, the Nicaraguan lead officer's radio came to life. "*Claro.*" Understood. He turned to Carlo. "The men have made a grisly discovery. They've found a body in the vehicle."

"And?" Carlo held his breath, hoping it was not Bryan or one of his team members.

"It's not one of your friends. An old *gaucho*. A cattle herder. Looks like his death was quick. A gunshot to the back of the head."

"The poor man."

"I'll have my men ask around if anyone has gone missing, but some of these cattle herders lead solitary lives and up in the mountains here, people may not realize a family member has gone missing until weeks later."

Carlo shook his head, perplexed. "But why would he be in the vehicle?"

"Hard to know. What's that expression you North Americans use? Wrong place at the wrong time? That would be my best guess."

"Did the men find anything else?"

"Yes, the satphone and a knapsack. They're bringing the body and those items up now."

Sixty-Three

I Knew You Would Come

THE ELEVATORS WERE straight ahead, exactly as Maria had described. She had explained that the security guards monitored the live-feed cameras twenty-four seven but seldom left their posts. To avoid the motion detector and cameras, she told David he would need to stay as close to the roughly hewn walls of the hallway as possible.

He heaved a sigh of relief when he reached the elevators, then tapped the keycard Maria had given him against the panel for the service elevator.

After a tense few seconds, the service elevator doors glided open noiselessly and David entered. He pressed the button for the third floor, his heart beating hard while the car ascended to the top floor. He slipped out of the elevator, not knowing what challenges he might encounter.

The moon shone through the archway, helping him see his surroundings clearly. Surveying the opulent space, he noticed the corridor was wide with two arched doors on each side. Shadows played with the intricate carvings of toucans: their figures creating the illusion that they shimmered and moved.

An expansive window at the end of the hall showed one of the most incredible vistas he had ever seen. The clouds swirled by at eye level, floating like soft willowy wisps in the midnight air. *Like being on top of the world,* he thought. He shook himself from his reverie. *Time to find Emma.*

He placed his hand on the first paneled door, wondering how to best locate Emma. Silence was paramount, since he must not risk disturbing

Reinhard. He walked to the next door and detected a soft and familiar vibration coming from within; on a subliminal level, he could feel, more than hear, the word *Om* being chanted. His body vibrated with joy, their energies flowing and syncing as one. *Emma! He'd found her.*

He tapped lightly at the door, hoping the soft sound would not awaken anyone else. The chant stopped, leaving him bereft. *Pull yourself together*, he admonished himself.

The electronic door lock flashed red, indicating the door was closed. *Not surprising,* thought David. He fished out the master digital keycard that Maria had given him, tapped it against the reader and was relieved to see the light flash from red to green.

He looked right and left, ensuring no one had seen him, then slipped inside. A shaft of moonlight fell across Emma's silhouette. She was sitting in the lotus position at the window, facing toward the breathtaking mountain view.

Nighttime had leached away all color, casting the world in subtle shades of grey, white and black. As if kissed by the moon, her hair cascaded around her shoulders, giving the wavy tresses a serpentine look, as if drawn in Indian ink. She turned toward him and rose, the moonlight capturing her expression of relief and joy.

"Emma," he said softly. "I'm here."

"Yes, my love, you are," she said.

He rushed toward her and pulled her into his arms. "I've been so worried."

"I knew you would come," she said, her body relaxing into his. She pulled away from him, giving him a serious look. "It's not safe. We should go."

David looked at her bare feet, "Get your shoes on." He frowned, pointing at her left ankle which was enclosed by the ankle bracelet. "What do we do about that?"

"Nothing we can do about it but run," she said, grabbing a pair of sandals with low heels. "Let's go!"

***

Reinhard tossed and turned; his sleep disturbed. He was back in the sun-dappled forest, running after Maggie, desperate to claim her. Her long hair flowed in the light like gold.

"Maggie," he cried out in his dream. "Stop running."

The girl stopped, stumbled, righted herself and continued running. "Maggie!" he shouted. "Stop!"

She turned around, her beautiful face transformed into a mask of hatred and anger. Recoiled by the ferocity of the look, the intense hate, he faltered. "Forgive me," he said. Her revulsion penetrated him to the core, immobilizing him. He attempted to step forward, but his feet were rooted to the earth.

Maggie gave a hollow laugh, so unlike her musical laughter when she was alive, and walked back toward him. "You're mine, now." She carried a knife in her hand and raised it high over her head, and with an arcing motion aimed for his chest.

That final moment of terror and anguish was too much, and with a gasp, Reinhard awakened, a searing pain radiating in his lungs. He eased back on the sweat-soaked pillow and gasped, trying to regulate his erratic breath.

Fighting to regain control of his traumatized soul and body, he gradually became aware of an insistent chiming. Hands shaking from the vivid nightmare, he picked up the tablet and saw a warning message flash across the screen: *Sensor Alert*. The alarm to Emma's suite had been triggered. Worse still, her anklet bracelet indicated she was on the run.

Fingers trembling, he expanded the screen which showed video of David Harris entering Emma's room, then minutes later the two of them fleeing toward the elevator.

How did he get away? he thought, *and more importantly, how did he get here?*

He threw on a pair of pants, then faltered, shocked to see an apparition.

It was Maggie. Was he still dreaming?

His vision blurred at the edges. "You're not real," he said, but his voice faltered, betraying his lack of conviction.

"You are very much mistaken. I am real," said the spirit, edging toward him. "You destroyed me." The light surrounding the apparition pulsed with ominous energy, dark and sinister.

"You're not real," Reinhard repeated. Mantra-like, he continued to say the words. "You're not real, you're not r—"

He stepped forward and was repelled by a wall of energy, which threw him backward. "You always were a bitch," he snarled. "You got everything you deserved."

He stepped forward again, and once more, his body was flung backward. This time, his head hit the side of the bedpost. Maggie floated over Reinhard's unconscious body, visualizing constricting his windpipe, imagining the delicate hyoid bone fracturing.

A soft voice entered her consciousness. *Maggie, this is not right. Stop.* It was Spirit Anna.

Maggie reluctantly relinquished the stranglehold on Reinhard's throat. *But he destroyed so much.*

That will be his Karma to deal with. Not yours.

A flash of understanding coursed through Maggie's soul as Spirit Anna gave Maggie insight into Reinhard's future. *He must follow his dark path until he comes full circle toward the light.*

I understand now.

Sixty-Four

Help is On Its Way

GASPING FOR BREATH after having run the lengthy corridor, David and Emma stumbled into the elevator. David punched furiously at the button to close the doors. When they finally began to slide shut, the two exchanged a relieved look.

Emma leaned up against the wall to give herself support and slipped on the opened-toed sandals. "These will work in a pinch, but they aren't the greatest."

She tilted her head to the side and her eyes took on a faraway look. She opened them and said, "That was Spirit Anna." She gave David a reassuring smile. "Reinhard was in pursuit but Maggie bought us some time by knocking him out."

"How?" asked David.

"Not sure. For now, he's temporarily incapacitated. But we need to move fast." She frowned and added, "Spirit Anna says it's a matter of time before he comes to and that we need to hurry."

Once they exited the elevator and entered the tunnel, David placed a restraining hand on Emma's arm. He pointed to the cameras and whispered, "Replicate my movements exactly."

She mouthed a silent yes and followed David out of the tunnel toward freedom. Emerging into the midnight air, Emma asked, "What's next?"

"We head back down. Bryan will be waiting for us at the huts."

She nodded, her eyes wide with worry. "No time to waste. Reinhard may be waking up soon."

***

A loud snap reverberated through the dense bush. The lead NCB officer held up his hand, indicating everyone to be quiet. *"¿Quién va ahí?"* Who goes there? The rustling in the bushes stopped. He motioned to one of his officers to investigate, who gave a slight nod, acknowledging the order.

Moments later, a young Nicaraguan woman was pulled, kicking and screaming, out of the bush. *"¡Suéltame!* Let go of me!"

"Let her go," said Mateo. She fell to the ground, shivering in the night air, exhaustion marked on her face,

"Bring her some water. Chica, what are you doing here?" asked Mateo, his voice fatherly and kind. While he spoke to her in soft tones, another officer placed a thermal blanket around the girl.

"¿Cómo te llamas?" What's your name?"

"My name's Maria. I ... I escaped from the Villa Blanca. There are others. They need your help!"

She stood up, her body swaying, and said, "Please, I must show you the way." Maria's eyes rolled up in her head, her body suddenly slack, as if boneless. Fortunately, a nearby officer reacted quickly, catching her before she collapsed. He gently lowered her to the ground, took off his jacket, rolled it up and positioned it under her head, then covered her again with the blanket.

"Any idea where this Villa Blanca is located?" asked Carlo.

Mateo turned to his men and asked if they knew anything about the White Villa.

One of the officers stepped forward and spoke in Spanish. Mateo inclined his head, then said, "Gracias," and turned to Carlo. "There's a rumor among the locals that a rich German has moved into the Villa Blanca. He brings people from outside and doesn't hire any locals. Some people say he brings in forced labor."

"So, that was where Bryan and the others must have been headed," said Carlo. "Their case in Ontario, where they discovered a child adoption and abduction ring, led them to Nicaragua."

Mateo frowned. "This is a huge problem in our country. Human trafficking, not solely for the sex trade, but for menial jobs. And these people are sold throughout Central America, even the United States."

"It's a horrible situation," said Carlo.

"Your friends," said Mateo. "That was a dangerous thing to do on their own – going after the Dark Hands of Anubis." He frowned and continued, "My men tell me that the locals call this man the *El Gringo Pálido,* on account of his pale skin. He does not like the sun."

"What's he doing here then?" laughed Carlo.

"No doubt building connections with the worst criminal elements in our society—the drug trade and human trafficking."

"So, how do we find this bastard?" asked Carlo. "Judging how quickly Maria found us, he must be close by."

"Agreed." Mateo called over one of his men and asked him to bring his laptop. The device was a rugged military unit that had a long battery life, could withstand extreme temperatures and could withstand being dropped. It could also operate police surveillance drones.

The men gathered around the technician and watched him manipulate the satellite imagery. The technician sighed in frustration and spoke in short staccato bursts to the inspector.

"What's going on?" asked Carlo.

"He's having trouble getting a clear image of the villa. The mountains are causing a visual barrier," answered Mateo.

"What about using the drone?" asked Carlo.

"That will be our next step," agreed Mateo. He instructed the technician to fly the drone to the area where they suspected the villa might be situated.

"Too bad Maria can't show us," said Carlo, looking at the sleeping girl.

"We weren't counting on her help to begin with," sighed Mateo. "However, if need be, we can awaken her. For now, let the *Chiquita* sleep."

The drone rose in the air, its green and red navigation lights flashing and the powerful strobe light exposing the rugged terrain as if it was day.

***

Reinhard came to, lightheaded and nauseated. He touched the back of his head, his fingers exploring the egg-sized lump that was forming. Disoriented at first, he wondered why he was on the floor and then remembered. *Emma and David were getting away!*

Adrenalin, induced by anger, pulsed through him. Grabbing his weapon of choice, a 9mm Heckler & Koch USP, he tucked it in his waistband and hurried out of his suite. Rushing toward the elevators, he thumbed out a frantic message to the security guards stationed on the first level. He pushed repeatedly for the elevator until the car finally ascended to his floor and opened.

Once on the main level, he shouted to the guards to join him. They piled into his Range Rover and careened down the road. *How long was I unconscious?* he wondered. *How far did they get?*

***

Emma tripped on the rough ground and landed on her rear. She yelped with pain, holding her left ankle. "Ridiculous sandals," she snarled, pulling each one off and hurling them into the bush. "Dumb to think I could walk, let alone run, in these things."

"Em," said David, worried. "Can you walk?"

"I sure as hell will," she said. "Our lives depend on it."

David's eyebrows rose in surprise at her profanity.

"Help me up?" she asked.

David stretched out his hand and grasped hers. Emma winced when she put weight on her ankle. "Oh, God, that hurts! And this stupid ankle bracelet doesn't help matters!"

"Em, are you sure you can do this?"

"I have to. Help support my weight on the left, please?" Her eyes filled with moisture from the pain, the moonlight glittering her tears into silver.

A set of headlamps from a fast-moving vehicle cast its light like a scepter across the severe landscape. "Em, they've almost caught up to us." He jumped into the ditch, pulling Emma with him. "Stay still. Hopefully, they didn't see us."

***

The drone descended slowly over the small clearing with the three shacks, transmitting the video images back to the men, who watched the screen intently. Detecting a slight movement, Carlo asked, "Can you bring it in closer?" Mateo nodded and asked the drone pilot to move in tighter.

"Look! There are people leaning against the middle shack!" said Carlo, unable to contain his excitement. A woman stepped out in the middle of the clearing, looked up and gave the thumbs up. "I think that's Megan!" said Carlo.

Mateo asked the drone pilot to zoom in even closer. Three young women, a child and an older Nicaraguan woman were huddled together, looking up at the drone. When the pilot panned out more, another man, ten feet away, was propped up against the second shack, bound and gagged.

"¡*Vamos!*" said Mateo, grinning. "Let's go get your friends."

"I don't see David and Emma," said Carlo, deflated.

Mateo slapped Carlo on the back. "What do you English like to say? Keep the faith!"

"You're right."

***

"Shit," whispered David. "They've stopped."

"What do we do?" asked Emma, her previous bravado having evaporated.

"How's your ankle?"

"Not great. It really hurts."

"I'm going to create a diversion. Lead them away from you."

"Oh, David, no," said Emma panicked. "Please don't leave me."

"Em, there's no choice. I'll be back for you. Keep out of sight."

"I don't like it," she said. "Please come back to me."

"Em, always."

"I love you."

"Me, too."

David burst out of their hiding spot and ran across the road. He could hear the shouts of an enraged Reinhard.

A pistol shot shattered the night. "Halt!" commanded Reinhard. David stopped and turned toward the man, the headlights of the vehicle blazing into David's face, blinding him.

"Where is she?" Reinhard snarled. "She's mine. You have no right to have a woman like that. You're not worthy."

David held himself in, refusing to take the bait and instead, answered, "By now, long gone. Reinforcements are on the way," he added, in the hopes this would goad Reinhard into doing something foolish.

"I don't believe you," he said, his voice petulant.

"What you believe doesn't matter and doesn't make the truth any less real," David retorted.

"I've no time for your silly games." The glacial expression on Reinhard's face hardened into a cold mask of hatred. "I should have killed you and Bryan immediately."

He aimed his pistol at David, ready to take the shot.

"What?" he screamed, as the first of the INTERPOL vehicles came racing toward both Reinhard and David. Instead of firing at David, he swiveled and aimed his gun at the approaching vehicle.

David reacted immediately, rushing back to where Emma was hiding.

"This is INTERPOL!" Mateo shouted through the megaphone. "Put the gun down!"

"Never!" answered Reinhard, emptying his pistol into the oncoming army truck, the bullets bouncing off the armored vehicle harmlessly.

Seconds later, bullets riddled his body. Reinhard's expression was one of astonishment, his illusion of invincibility shattered.

With Reinhard dead, his men quickly surrendered, having no stomach to continue a grievance in which they did not believe. They were mercenaries and had no interest in losing their lives.

David gently lifted Emma out of the ditch and carried her as if she was the most precious cargo in the world to the waiting jeep.

Bryan grinned and held out a satphone to Emma. "Someone wants to talk with you." She took the phone Bryan offered and said, "Mom?"

"Hi, sweetheart," said Laura, reining in the emotion she'd been keeping in check. "I'm so glad your safe."

"Where are you?"

"In a safe house, here in Nicaragua."

"I can't wait to see you," said Emma.

"Nor can I."

"And then, home?"

"Yes, as soon as everyone is checked over medically and deemed fit to travel, we will all be heading home."

Sixty-Five

Farewell

EMMA ENTERED ANNA'S ROOM, cradling the mug of mugwort tea. She set the steaming mug beside her, enjoying the fragrant aromas, reminiscent of lemon balm, mint and sage. She arranged herself on her meditation mat so that her legs were comfortable and her spine was aligned properly.

She took a sip of the floral and citrusy tea. *Delicious.* Now that I'm back home, I'll need to send a thank you note to Mona for having introduced me to this wonderful tea, and for her help and guidance.

She cleared her mind and summoned her Spirit Guides. Behind her, she sensed the comforting presence of her guardian angel, her gatekeeper remained vigilant to her left and the main guide stood to her right. Their soothing presence enfolded her in a spiritual blanket of safety and calm. She sent her thoughts of thanks and gratitude to them. *How did I live so long, not being aware of their reassuring presence?* she wondered.

A voice filtered into her mind. *Because, my dear, you were not ready.*

"Spirit Anna," said Emma out loud, her heart leaping with joy. "You're here!"

You have done very well, my child.

I did not expect to hear from you so soon. I thought—"

Time is a fluid thing. We have much to show you.

Emma's breathing softened as she entered a trance. Images of a young woman came before her, her long, golden-white hair blazing in the sunshine. *It was Maggie.* Her expression was soft and gentle. Her spirit was at peace.

I came here to thank you. Because of you and your family, my babies are safe. They have Megan. They have a home.

Maggie's image shimmered and pulsed with her soul's light. *I learned that revenge is not enough, but not in the way I believed. Spirit Anna has shown me this. I am ready to move on to the next world.* On each side, two swirls of lights, coalesced into the shapes of two children and behind them blazed even more energy, in multiple human forms.

"Charlie and Tammy?" asked Emma. These were the children who had died along with their parents in the house fire. "And your mother and grandparents, too."

Yes! My family is here to take me through the tunnel.

Spirit Anna hovered nearby. *Maggie, it's time now.*

Maggie's spirit form became more ethereal, its structure dissolving along the edges until she and the two smaller balls of light merged into one, then disappeared completely.

"Spirit Anna?"

Yes?

"I am beginning to understand. This is your work now."

Yes, my child.

Emma withdrew from her trance, her mood bittersweet because her time working with Spirit Anna was truly at an end, but also joyful, because of the successful efforts of the investigative team. Along with Spirit Anna's guidance, they had helped Maggie gain the peace she needed to move on to the next dimension.

Sixty-Six

Time for Some R & R

SOFT BREEZES FILTERED through the fresh green leaves of spring. The laughter was infectious and a welcome relief from their recent ordeal.

Mother and daughter were sitting together on the old-fashioned Victorian swing in Emma's luscious garden. "I'm so glad it all worked out," said Laura, taking her daughter's hands in hers and lightly brushing them with her lips. "I was so worried."

Constructed of wrought iron, the swing's graceful curves and delicate scrollwork evoked a gentler, nobler time, eschewing the do-it-yourself swings of today, made of flimsy aluminum or wood.

David had lovingly restored the ironwork, cleaning it first with an iron brush, then painting it with a bronze-colored rust-proof paint.

The seat was wide and could accommodate two people comfortably. Long ago, the cushions had faded, and their stuffing deteriorated. Laura's mother had cheerfully taken on the task of making new plush cushions, the pattern of the material featuring lovely English roses.

The scent of lily of the valley wafted over them. Emma closed her eyes and took in a deep breath. She leaned against the backrest of the swing and returned her mother's gentle smile. "It's good to be home."

David and Bryan were standing over the BBQ, deep in conversation about the merits of charcoal grills compared to propane.

"Nothing tastes better than charcoal-grilled food. Slow cooking, slow lazy days, takes me back to simpler times," said Bryan.

"Maybe so," said David, "but dinner takes so long to prepare! And I'm hungry now!"

"But that's the point of it," said Laura, laughing. "Taking the time ... being with family and friends."

"That reminds me," said Emma, jumping off the swing. "Our guests should be arriving soon. David, give me a hand bringing out the snacks?"

"Sure thing, Em," he replied. "Anything for food..."

"Really, David?" She placed her hands on her hips. "Food?"

"No, uh, I meant anything for you."

Emma laughed, "Come on, silly. I'm teasing you. Let's get you something to eat."

***

In the kitchen, David wrapped his arms around Emma and said, "I love you."

"'Cause I feed you?" She deftly scooped hummus onto one of her homemade tortilla crisps and said, "Open up."

"Em, these spreads are fantastic. My favorite is the red pepper spread, but I love the tapenade, too!" He ate several more of the appetizers Emma had prepared but when he reached for another, she playfully slapped his hand and said, "Save some for our guests."

Right on cue, the doorbell rang. "That'll be them now!" Emma said, her voice filled with enthusiasm. "Can you greet them, David?"

"On my way."

Emma could hear Megan's cheerful voice. "Cheryl and Sandra, come with me. The kitchen is where the magic happens at Em's house."

Megan eyed the assortment of appetizers Emma had prepared and made herself right at home. "Wow! Em, if you weren't so intent on solving

291

crimes, I'd beg you to partner up with me. We could start our own Mediterranean-style restaurant together."

Emma flushed with pleasure. "That's a major compliment coming from you." She passed a tray laden with goodies to Megan. "Can you take these out for me?"

"Before you head outside, Megan, anything to drink for you?" asked David.

"Sure, a glass of Chardonnay would be awesome."

"What about you two?" asked David, taking a step back in surprise. "Wow, I can't tell either of you apart."

"Neither can I, most of the time," said Megan, smiling.

Cheryl piped up, "Now that I know I have a sister – a twin sister – we're having a lot of fun doing things together—"

"—and it's a blast fooling people," Sandra said, finishing Cheryl's sentence.

"Like finishing each other's sentences," they both chimed in at the same time.

"Can we have beers?" asked Cheryl.

David shook his head and said, "No can do. You're seventeen. How about Heineken Zeros?"

"We weren't serious," giggled Sandra. "The near-beer will be great."

Emma's phone chimed. Glancing at it while placing bowls with potato chips on the outdoor patio table, she said, "That was Carlo. He's running late. He's picking up Evan and his daughter. They should be here in another ten minutes."

"I'm looking forward to meeting Evan," said Laura. She got up off the swing, gave Megan a hug, then settled herself at the patio table "It's great to see you, Megan," she added.

"It's good to see you, too, Mrs. Jackson, er, I mean Mrs. Grant."

"Now, now, Megan," Laura admonished, her lips uplifted in laughter. "You know you can call me Laura."

"I know," grinned Megan. "Old habits ..."

"How is everyone doing?" Laura asked.

"Better than when we were in Nicaragua. Those are days I'd like to forget." Megan gave an involuntary shudder.

"It was a terrifying time," replied Laura, placing her hand gently on Megan's. "Any word on how Evan and Simone are doing?"

"The hospital released Evan several days ago. He's expected to make a full recovery, but he hasn't been given the green light to drive yet," said Megan. "That's why Carlo is helping out."

"That's nice of Carlo," said Emma.

"And Simone – how is she doing?" Laura asked. "Being kidnapped must have been so traumatic."

"As you know, until her dad's release, Simone was staying with me. Time with her sisters has been good, but she couldn't wait to go home to be with her dad," said Megan, taking a sip of the white wine. "She has been doing surprisingly well. Cheryl and Sandra are also doing great. The group therapy sessions have been helping all of us."

Megan looked at their two nieces with fondness. They had taken over the swing and were sipping on their non-alcoholic drinks, pretending to be tipsy.

"Are they still estranged from their adoptive parents?" asked Emma.

Megan nodded. "For now, but who knows? They feel a great sense of betrayal. It's good they've found each other."

"It's good you've all found one another," said Laura.

"True," said Megan.

More laughter floated amongst the group. "I hear a party is happening here," said Carlo. "No one was answering the front door, so we decided to follow the voices here." He swung open the side gate to their backyard garden and was followed by Evan and Simone.

Bryan left his place at the grill and firmly gripped Carlo's hand, then pulled him into a bear hug. "It's good to see you. I'll never forget what you did for my family."

"Anything for a friend." He returned the grip, conveying the deep connection and respect the men held for each other—one of loyalty, trust, and a shared sense of achievement.

"Come on in," said Bryan.

"Let me introduce everyone," said Carlo. "This is Evan. And of course, all of you already know Simone."

The little girl had been holding her dad's hand tightly but at the sight of her two older sisters, she raced away and sandwiched herself between the two twins on the swing.

"Thanks for inviting me," said Evan. "It's a pleasure to meet you all. Thanks for bringing my Simone back to me. She's all I have to remind me of Maggie."

"You really loved her, didn't you?" asked Laura, her eyes watering.

"Yes," he said. "I really did."

Carlo separated from the main group and approached Bryan and David. "Not to break up the festivities, but I heard from Mateo at Interpol this morning."

"Anything of interest?" asked David, handing Carlo a beer.

"Thanks," said Carlo, clinking his beer bottle against David's, then Bryan's. "I learned a couple of interesting things. Dr. Sperling's body was found in a villa in Curaçao."

"Murdered?" asked Bryan.

'Yes, he was poisoned. It took the police a while to find out who he was, though."

"How come?" asked David, raising his eyebrows.

"He traveled under a false name but when the police dug further, they traced the dead man's identity back to Aaron Sperling," said Carlo.

"Fascinating. You said you have two pieces of news," said Bryan.

"I do." Carlo took a sip of beer and continued. "On the second level of the villa, there was another living area leading off from the kitchen. Dark Hands of Anubis hadn't fully set up shop, but there were three young women already living there. Young German girls, each about three months pregnant."

Emma, having noticed the men had moved off and appeared to be in serious conversation, joined them. Hearing the tail end of the conversation, she asked, "So, what about the women who disappeared from the BC compound scant hours before David and Bryan showed up?"

Carlo gave his head a sad shake. "Wherever they were taken, it wasn't to Nicaragua. The women may have been sold, the kids adopted out for a price or..."

"Dead?" Emma's hands flew to her mouth. "Our worst fears confirmed, then."

"Yes, sadly so. The British Columbia divisional headquarters for the RCMP found human remains."

"Any chance for DNA analysis of the remains?" asked David.

"Not likely. The extreme heat in the crematorium destroyed the DNA, making identification next to impossible."

"So, a dead end," said Emma, dejected.

"Not really," said David. "Megan, the twins and Simone were saved, not to mention myself, Bryan, and you, too, Emma."

"That's true," she said brightening. "Whatever happened to that adoption website on Tor?"

"The New Elgan Police Service handed over that part of the investigation to the RCMP branch of INTERPOL. No word yet." Carlo cleared his throat. "There is one more piece of interesting news I have for you."

"Oh?" asked Bryan.

"I got news last night that old man Bianchi passed away last week. Cancer finally got the bastard. Even with the high doses of morphine, it was a very painful end."

The group fell silent.

A shadow crossed over David's face. "It's for the best. I wish he'd rotted in prison a lot longer than he did." He gave a big sigh, shaking off the conflicting emotions. "He caused a lot of heartache."

"It's strange, though," said Bryan.

"What is?" asked David.

"What you went through, solving the murder of your previous self, led to what we do now."

"True. Now, we can help people in similar situations using the paranormal to solve cold cases," said Emma, gesturing toward the three giggling children on the swing. "Like how we helped Maggie. Look at them: her whole family has been reunited."

"It is a wonderful thing," said Laura, who had joined the conversation. She placed her hand on her daughter's cheek.

"Oh, no!" Emma gave a short yelp. "Guys, the BBQ!"

"Sorry, Emma," said Bryan. "Duty calls."

Byran grabbed a pair of oven mitts and lifted the lid of the BBQ. Fragrant wafts of smoke billowed up. "All good," he coughed. "Dinner will be ready soon."

"Let me grab some more wine," said David. "I have a great red from the Okanagan Valley."

"I hear it's nice there, this time of year," said Emma.

"You know the trouble about being in love with a psychic?" David asked the group.

"What?" asked several of the guests.

"You can seldom surprise her!"

David grabbed Emma around the waist and whispered in her ear, "Tickets are already booked. We leave tomorrow morning."

"Oh, I'd better go pack—"

"No need. For once, I'm one step ahead of you."

***

The End

Message from the Author

Dear Reader,

Thank you for reading my book. I highly value your opinion! Please consider leaving a review on Amazon.

Your feedback helps other readers discover this book. Visit the book's page on Amazon, and click "Write a customer review," and share your thoughts.

https://www.amazon.com/gp/product/B0FBFFH22W

or if you prefer, visit the QR link here and scan using your smartphone:

Your review makes a meaningful impact.

Thank you for your time and support!

Best regards,

Angela van Breemen

***

Also by Angela van Breemen

Past Life's Revenge:

A David Harris and Emma Jackson Mystery – Book One.
Available at:
https://www.amazon.com/Past-Lifes-Revenge-Paranormal-Suspense-ebo
ok/dp/B0DSTGSYJ3

About the author

Angela van Breemen is delighted to be releasing her second novel in the David Harris and Emma Jackson Mystery Series – Revenge is Not Enough. She is currently working on the third book in the series, Revenge Not Taken Lightly.

She is an avid writer of poetry, belongs to the Wordsmiths Writers' Group based out of New Tecumseth, Ontario, Canada and is a member of the Crime Writers of Canada and the South Simcoe Arts Council and the Writers Union of Canada.

Angela is a Soprano Soloist. A firm believer in giving back to the community, she often sings for different charitable organizations.

Music and poetry have been an integral part of her life, and in early 2024 she launched her debut album, In The Breeze. Celtic in nature, it includes three original pieces of music, based on her poetry.

Angela volunteers for Procyon Wildlife Rehabilitation and Education Centre, a group dedicated to the rescue, rehabilitation and safe release of orphaned and injured Ontario wildlife.

She lives in Loretto, Ontario with her husband Peter Thomas Pontsa, author of the Inspector William Fox Series.

You can connect with Angela on:

https://angelavanbreemen.ca

https://www.facebook.com/angela.vanbreemen.5

https://www.instagram.com/stories/angelapearl55/

https://x.com/breemenangela

https://wildsongbird.ca

Subscribe to her newsletter: https://angelavanbreemen.ca/contact-us

Preview of Revenge Not Taken Lightly: Book 3 of the David Harris and Emma Jackson Mystery Series

Chapter 1

THE MIDDLE-AGED COUPLE knelt on the stone floor of the chapel, as if in supplication. Their hands were tied behind their backs and another tether linked their bound hands together. Two additional cables had been looped around this tether and were looped through eyelets mounted on each side of the solid wooden pew behind them. This strange contraption was designed to keep them somewhat upright, although the weight of their bodies caused them to lean forward.

The woman's wavy grey hair cascaded forward like a waterfall obscuring her face, its tips brushing the floor in a swaying motion.

Regaining consciousness, the man moaned softly, rivulets of blood trickling down his chin and dripping onto the porous stones. The ancient sandstone absorbed the moisture, as if taking an unholy communion.

"Albert, how badly are you hurt?" asked the woman in a hoarse whisper. "Can you move?"

Terror caught in her throat at his reply. "I'm sorry, Alice ... it wasn't supposed to end this way."

"What do you mean?" she asked.

His head lolled, and his body tilted to one side, tugging at the bindings on Alice's wrists and almost toppling her. The ropes dug even tighter into her wrists at the tension caused by Albert's dead weight, but the bindings attached to the pew kept her sitting upright. Her panic escalated when she saw that her husband was no longer conscious. "Albert?"

The door to the chapel opened abruptly and a blast of cold air permeated the tiny sanctuary. Facing the altar, with her back to the entranceway, Alice tried to raise her head and turn to see who or what had entered, but the binds restricting her movement were too tight.

Aware of a presence but unsure of whom it might be, a mixture of terror and hope coursed through her. Terror won the battle of conflicting emotions, when her abductor spoke. "Don't trouble yourself on my account."

She could hear his ungainly shuffle as he walked past her and her husband, mounted the steps and then positioned himself behind the lectern. Morning light was beginning to glow through the stained-glass window, enveloping his white hair in an ethereal halo.

"Why are you doing this?" she asked, her voice hoarse from hours of screaming.

"Simple. Because I can. And because you owe me."

"What could I possibly owe you? I don't even know who you are," she said, raising her eyes to meet those of her captor's, then squinting at the light which stabbed at her retinas.

"Maybe not Mrs. Tang, but *he* does," he said, pointing at her husband's prostrate form.

"No, how can that be? Albert would never know anyone like you."

The man heaved a big sigh. "But there you are wrong, Alice. Soon to be dead wrong," he said, laughing at his macabre joke. "Ah, but shall I call you Alice?"

"No," she said, defiance overcoming her panic and fury. "You may not call me Alice."

"Pity. Death is such an intimate thing." His smile broadened, as if he was chatting at a dinner party about canapes. "I think I shall call you Alice, despite your objections."

He took the chalice from the altar, picked up an ornately engraved knife, which glinted gold in the candlelight, and approached Alice and Albert.

In that moment, Alice knew it was over. Her face, previously a mask of terror, transformed into one of peace and determination. "You won't get away with this. My daughter will make sure you pay for this."

"I already have," said the male from the shadows. "And it's your daughter who will be the one who will pay."

"No, please, not Thelma!" Her eyes widened with horror as the killer positioned himself behind Albert. He grabbed a fistful of Albert's thinning hair, lifted his head and sliced the knife across Albert's jugular. He placed the chalice underneath the stream of red, filling the cup to the brim. He carried the chalice to the altar and set it down with reverence.

"Pity your husband had so little stamina. No fun at all," he said, walking back toward Alice.

"Please don't—" The knife sliced through the air a second time.

***

Thelma Tang is innocent. Emma awoke wild-eyed, her heart pounding, confused at the strange words. She reached over for David, a wave of reassurance washing through her when she touched his warm and solid sleeping body.

"What is it?" he asked, murmuring softly in his sleep.

"I am not sure."

He sat up straight, awaking instantly. "I'm listening." He poured water into a crystal glass from its matching decanter. "Here, drink this."

"Thank you so much, David. I don't know what I'd do without you," she said, accepting the glass and taking a sip. She gazed at him gratefully.

"So, tell me about this vision. Or was it a dream?"

Emma shook her head and said, "I don't know. It was weird. This felt more like a direct communication."

"Strange," said David. "What do your guides say?"

Emma tilted her head to the side, the way she always did when she was listening to her spirit guides give her advice. "They say that this is bona fide information. That we need to talk with Bryan and Carlo at the police department."

David glanced at the antique clock on the armoire. "It's three in the morning."

"Too early to call then," said Emma. "I sure do miss working with Bryan every day."

"Me, too."

"I know, but after our last case, Bryan realized he wasn't ready to retire. He missed being on the job too much."

"Yep, he missed the badge, more than likely," said David, stifling a yawn.

"I have to admit, it's better for our team with him acting as a liaison officer at the New Elgan Police Service," said Emma. "Still, I miss him."

"Emma, you see him at your mom's place for dinner every Sunday night." David was referring to Laura, Emma's mom. Two years ago, in a double wedding ceremony on a beach in Costa Rica, her mom and Bryan had married, as well as Emma and David. "And we both talk to him at least once or twice a day."

"Yeah, I know," said Emma. "You're right."

David took a second glass and poured himself some water. "More?" he asked, waving the crystal decanter.

"No, I'm good."

"Besides, with my private investigator license, we make a more solid team, since as an officer, Bryan can access information we can't."

Emma grew quiet.

"What is it, honey?" David asked her.

"That name. Thelma Tang. It rings a bell, but I can't quite place it."

"Me, too. How about we take a look?" He grabbed his iPhone, which was resting on the nightstand, pressed down on the side button of the device and commanded, "Siri, provide me all the information you have on Thelma Tang."

Seconds later, Siri answered. Thelma Tang was a seventeen-year-old girl who was tried in an adult court for the murder of her parents Alice and Albert Tang. Although the murder weapon was never found, circumstantial evidence indicated she was the murderer. The most compelling evidence was that Ms. Tang had chatted on social media platforms about her desire to gut and kill her parents. From the moment the charges were laid, Ms. Tang maintained that she was innocent and pled not guilty. She claims that she was framed, that someone had hacked her social media account and that the killer is still at large. Sentenced in 2024 to life in prison with no chance of parole for 25 years, for the first-degree murders of her parents in 2020. Despite two subsequent appeals, Ms. Tang remains incarcerated in the Grand Valley Institution for Women, the single federal women's prison in Ontario.

"Wow, that poor family," said Emma, shuddering.

"No kidding. So, what do you think?" asked David. "Is this our next cold case?"

"Yeah, I think it might be." She pulled the blankets up under her chin, yawning. "It's still early. We should go back to sleep."

"Good plan," said David. He pulled Emma toward him, wrapped his body around her in a protective cocoon and nestled his face into her hair, breathing in the scent of lavender. "Let's get some shut eye. We'll talk with Bryan in the morning."

He waited for her reply but Emma had already nodded off, secure and safe in his arms. Her body's inhalations and exhalations were like a soft summer breeze.

***

Revenge Not Taken Lightly will be available in the fall of 2026.

Manufactured by Amazon.ca
Bolton, ON

51379418R00189